P9-DNQ-319

## “TARGET PE[illegible]

“Too easy . . .” Mr. K’s voice trailed off. Up to now the smell in the office from Mr. K was one of excitement and exertion. Now, suddenly, she smelled fear—

Angel looked up at the holo. What she saw there hurt her eyes. It resembled none of the previous graphics. It didn’t have a sane geometry. It looked solid, but it rotated in a manner that three dimensions couldn’t accommodate. The colors pulsed in a rhythm that made her want to shut her eyes.

And it looked like it was aware of her.

“What is—” Mr. K started to ask.

*Target is backtracking signal. Engaging defenses. PENETRATION OF BASE SEC—*

A wave of red shot out from the holo. Even as the hypersonic roller coaster began to reverse, the pulsing red signal overtook it. The holo was washed in a sheet of solid red.

The lights in the office died, the controls under the surface of the desk blinked out, and Mr. K jerked violently, snapping his helmet free of its cabling. He collapsed, unmoving, behind the desk. . . .

DAW Proudly Presents
These Hard-Hitting,
Action-Packed Science Fiction Novels
By S. Andrew Swann:

FORESTS OF THE NIGHT

EMPERORS OF THE TWILIGHT

SPECTERS OF THE DAWN

# SPECTERS OF THE DAWN

S. ANDREW SWANN

DAW BOOKS, INC.
DONALD A. WOLLHEIM, FOUNDER
375 Hudson Street, New York, NY 10014
ELIZABETH R. WOLLHEIM
SHEILA E. GILBERT
PUBLISHERS

Copyright © 1994 by Steven Swiniarski.

All Rights Reserved.

Cover art by Jim Burns.

DAW Book Collectors No. 959.

If you purchase this book without a cover you should be aware that this book may have been stolen property and reported as "unsold and destroyed" to the publisher. In such case neither the author nor the publisher has received any payment for this "stripped book."

First Printing, August 1994

1 2 3 4 5 6 7 8 9

DAW TRADEMARK REGISTERED
U.S. PAT. OFF. AND FOREIGN COUNTRIES
—MARCA REGISTRADA
HECHO EN U.S.A.

PRINTED IN THE U.S.A.

Dedicated to three remarkable women:

First—
Jane Butler, my agent, without whose unbounded enthusiasm my career wouldn't exist.

Second—
Sheila Gilbert, my editor, who had the temerity to buy this before it was written, and without whom this book wouldn't exist.

And most important—
Margret Ann, Peg, my mom, without whom I wouldn't exist, who infected me with this creative mania in the first place. (Placing the blame firmly where it belongs. At least I'm not too far gone. I could have been a poet.)

ACKNOWLEDGMENT

Thanks to the Cleveland SF Workshop.

# CHAPTER 1

It was a clean sweep for October—the fourth Monday in a row that Angelica Lorenzo y Lopez wanted to tell her boss to grease his head and go pearl diving for hemorrhoids. Her shift was a half hour into nirvana and they could have flushed the whole place for all she would care. *Ralph's Diner* was dead in the water. Half an hour waiting for Judy to show up to relieve her, and Angel hadn't waited on one effing table.

Her greaseball boss, Sanchez, was sitting in his little yellowing manager's office, peering through his little one-way mirror at his nickel-and-dime empire as if he was too lordly to cover for Judy. Angel thought of giving the finger to the mirror. She admired her self-control for not giving in to the temptation.

Judy was late every effing Monday and Sanchez gave no never mind every time Angel complained. Angel had decided that it must be one of two things—either Judy was going for joyrides in Santa's lap back in the manager's office, or it was because Angel was the only nonhuman who worked in the place.

Probably both.

A restaurant in the Mission District, of all places, and Angel was the only moreau serving tables. And Sanchez wondered why business sucked.

And boy, did business suck.

There were a total of *three,* count them, *three* whole people in the place. One was a regular, one of the street people who came in for coffee every afternoon. He was an old graying rodent with thinning fur and naked spotted-pink hands that shook as he drank his *one,* count it, *one* cup of coffee. In the back sat a small black-and-gray striped feline who was slowly shredding a bacon cheeseburger—a pink's food, but the cat didn't seem to mind. The cat's ribs showed under his fur, and Angel tagged him as a recent immigrant who'd probably never seen real human food.

Those two, and her. A rat, a cat, and a rabbit. For once, at a hundred and twenty centimeters—not counting ears—Angel was the biggest one in the room. *Ralph's* was so empty you could land a ballistic shuttle down the checkerboard linoleum aisle.

From the looks of things she didn't even have a reasonable expectation of getting a tip.

During Angel's third glance at the clock, Judy finally showed.

"About time, pinky," Angel said as Judy ran through the front door, out of the fog.

"Don't harass me today. I've had enough sh—"

Angel hopped down off the stool she'd been sitting on. She could hear Judy trying to quiet her labored breathing, and Angel's nose told her that the moisture on Judy's face was more sweat than condensing fog. Judy had rushed to get here more than forty-five minutes late.

Angel's heart bled. "I might miss the whole first quarter—"

"I'm sorry about your football game."

"Yeah, right." Angel stretched to remove her denim jacket from the coatrack.

"You'd want me to risk my life on those roads—" Judy started.

"Don't do me no favors, pinky." Angel stormed out the door without bothering to clock out.

Angel had little sympathy. The pink wench had a car, while the poor ol' morey rabbit had been doing without wheels since she'd sold her ancient prewar Toyota to cinch the money to move to this burg. Somehow, this poor old lepus pedestrian was always on time—

Except, of course, when some human woman goes and makes her late. Angel sighed as she pushed through the thickening fog on Howard Street. All those moreaus who weren't eating at *Ralph's* were probably at the game or at some bar that had a holo feed from the action. She, unfortunately, was due for the latter. Tickets for Earthquakes games were at a premium that she just couldn't afford.

Her destination was a little bar nestled in the newest part of the coast south of Market Street, *The Rabbit Hole.* Unfortunately, *Ralph's* wasn't on the coast. Angel had thought she'd have the time for a nice leisurely walk—she should have assumed that Judy would be late again and scouted a game cast that was closer by.

It was a rare bar that didn't charge a cover that rivaled the ticket prices. The NFL would have had a monopolistic conniption, but the NonHuman League didn't have much legal clout, and was probably grateful for the exposure.

She didn't have much of a choice if she was going to be in time for the game. She took a deep breath soggy with fog, and started running.

Small Angel was, but she was a genetically engineered rabbit whose great-grandparents had been designed for combat as part of the Peruvian infantry. The musculature on her thighs was half again as broad as her hips, and her feet were as long and as broad as her forearms. A few humans thought lepine moreaus were funny-looking or cute—but with rare exceptions, they were the fastest infantry ever to come out of the gene-labs.

She bolted down Howard at full speed, with barely three meters of visibility, telling herself that it wasn't the smartest thing to do.

Even as she thought it, a band of ratboys emerged in front of her. The fog sucked up sound and smell as well as light, so she had no time to stop when she realized they were there. She was leaping over their heads before they had time to realize she was bearing down on them. She retreated down a steep section of hillside, letting the fog soak up their curses.

She tried to pace herself so she hit the cross streets with the lights. She only had one close call with a remote driven van that freaked when she appeared in front of it. She left the Areoline van with its horn blaring, hazards going, and its collision avoidance program absolutely convinced it had hit something.

She made the trip in less than ten minutes. It was five to six when Angel got to *The Rabbit Hole,* to find it almost as empty as *Ralph's.* One table of moreaus, two feline, two canine, and a fox. That was it.

"Wha?"

The answer was on the holo behind the bar. Angel walked up, mesmerized. On the holo was the president of the United States. He was in the process of blaming the latest run of interspecies rioting on aliens from Alpha Centauri.

"Shit."

Angel climbed on to a seat in front of the bar and watched President Merideth do his schtick. It was a lost cause.

"Shit."

She'd been looking forward to the game all week. Frisco vs. Cleveland, and she wasn't even going to see so much as one down. She twitched her nose and said, "Ain't fair. Bet he'd wait till the end of the game if it was the N-effing-L."

She waved the bartender over. He was a moreau rabbit, but his fur was white as opposed to her spotted tan. She ordered a Corona and lime and closed her eyes. Yeah, she'd just missed a crowd of moreys. The scents of a dozen species still hung in the bar's air along with the perfume of a like number of beers that had christened the bar in the past hour. A rich, empty smell.

Angel chugged the Corona and ordered another.

Another boring weekend loomed on the horizon. Home with Lei, or more likely, alone. Lei always seemed to find things to do with her free time. Things that generally blew more capital than Angel could afford. Sure, Lei was willing to pay Angel's tab for an evening out—

But Angel was never comfortable with that. She'd stay home and probably vegetate in front of the comm watching the latest news reports of the fighting in New York and LA.

Around the fourth Corona the bartender's whiskers sat at a slightly condescending angle. "What can I do for you, Miss?"

"Refill me."

"Don't you think you've had enough?" It irritated Angel to notice that the bartender's voice held no trace of the slight lisp normal for a lepus. Almost sounded human.

"Ain't driving, and the game got zeroed." She pushed her glass at him. "Nothing better to do."

The bartender shrugged and bent over behind the bar.

Angel stepped up on the seat so she could lean over the bar and add, "Find a lime that doesn't taste like a used rubber."

The bartender shoved another Corona at her while, on the holo, Merideth began to invoke the names of the Joint Chiefs and several leading scientists.

Angel snorted and sipped her drink.

Preempted by aliens. Great. Angel was effing sick of aliens. She had hoped the media would have gotten over its alienitis over the course of the summer. Hell, everyone and their brother had been milking the story since January.

Still no end in sight.

So the CIA or the FBI or someone finds a bunch of white blubbery things nesting under the Nyogi tower in Manhattan. Even if the MannSatt news service had done a God-help-us live broadcast from an alien "lair" under the Nyogi tower two months before Bronx artillery zeroed the building. So what? Even if they come from another planet, it's better than letting the Japs run things, right? Look what happened to them.

But it kept coming, aliens, aliens, aliens. It couldn't be escaped even if you killed the comm, because that effing huge white-dome alien habitat they built over the ruins of Alcatraz was the most prominent thing on the Frisco skyline.

*So what are we going to do? Go to war with a planet a few light-years away?*

Talk about unreal.

Tabloid stuff, but it was tabloid stuff that was getting hard news coverage. After a half century of isolationism, it seemed that the U.S. had found a new evil empire. Leaks from the blessed U.S. government made the aliens look like some sort of interstellar covert action experts that were doing the kind of political destabilization games that the CIA used to excel at—or said it excelled at, anyway.

All supposed to keep anyone from getting off this rock.

"But why," she mumbled. "It's such a *lovely* planet."

Personally, Angel thought Merideth was just grabbing at anything that gave him even a remote hope of reelection. Or, failing that, of leaving office without becoming the most despised president since H. Ros—

Angel felt the hackles rise on the back of her neck, under the collar of her denim jacket. She looked up the bar and saw that the bartender was gone.

She smelled a pink smell.

"One furball left. Seems upset about something . . ." A human voice, behind her.

No, Angel thought to herself, don't turn around. The bartender was right, you've had too much to drink.

*Did everyone else just up and leave?*

"Wassa matter, something *wrong* with our President?" Another human spoke.

*The Rabbit Hole* was a morey hangout. Why'd pinks have to walk in and fuck with her? They didn't hassle the other moreys. She would've heard *that.*

She tried to ignore them. Perhaps they'd leave.

"Think he's bein' disrespectful." The first voice. How many were there? Angel should have been able to gain a rough estimate from their smell, but stale lime was flavoring everything.

And, damn it, they couldn't even get her gender right. Just because she didn't have globs of fat on her chest like a human woma—

"Talking to you!" said a third pink with the ugliest bass rumble excuse for a voice that Angel had ever heard. A hand grabbed her shoulder and spun her around on the bar stool. Her drink flew out of her hand, splashing on the legs of the nearest human.

Three young human males. Hispanic, black, and anglo. She was the only morey left in the bar.

The three closed in around her, a wall of jeans, leather,

and hairless flesh. Even the heads. They were all shaved totally bald, down to the eyebrows.

The baldness meant one of two things. Either they were some rabid prohumanists who'd taken the morey slang term *pink*—meaning hairlessness—to heart and depilatoried their whole bodies. Or they were Hare Krishnas.

They weren't chanting.

The anglo pink had his hand on her shoulder. He'd been the one she'd doused with Corona. The sleeves of his jacket were torn off, revealing one bicep tattooed with a flaming sword. The glass she'd been drinking from rested by one of his boots. He raised his foot and placed it on top of the glass. A second later there was the gunshot sound of the glass giving way.

He ground the pieces under his boot, smiled, and looked like he was about to enjoy a nice game of trash the rabbit. The black was shaking his shoulder. "Chuck the bunny, Earl. That's not what we're here—"

She told herself that these guys weren't a hard-core gang, or they'd have trashed the bar by now. The adrenaline was pumping, and she could feel the edge on her nerves driving her to do something. She held herself back, but her muscles were vibrating with the effort. She couldn't explode, not when she was drunk, and if she went along, she might get out of this with her hide intact.

Earl wasn't listening to his friend. "Look't he did to my jeans—"

The pronoun did it. *"I'm a* girl, *you shitheads!"*

Angel grabbed the seat of the bar stool, spun around, and planted a back-kick directly between Earl's legs.

That ugly bass voice gasped and was choked off with a breathless squeak. He lost his grip on her shoulder and fell to the ground, clutching his groin. Angel's kick was something of consequence.

Especially when she *meant* it.

The bar stool was still spinning, and time rubberbanded, slowing as it stretched.

"Earl, you fuckhead—" Angel heard the black say to the lump on the ground. She was slipping off the stool, into the gap she had made in the wall of humans, even as she heard the whistle of air toward her.

She ducked, but not in time, as something very hard slammed into the right side of her head.

She stumbled away from the bar stool, head thrumming, vision blurred. The fur on that side of her face was suddenly warm and tacky. She backpedaled, paralleling the bar, retreating toward the bathrooms.

The hispanic was twirling a chain in his right hand.

To hell with the nonhuman gun control laws. She was going to dig her automatic out of the underwear drawer and start carrying it again.

The hispanic swung the chain, but she managed to dodge it.

As she dove, blood got into her eye. Blinded, she ran—and slammed into a wall. The entire right side of her body went numb with the shock of the impact. She didn't start aching until she was assdown on the floor.

The hispanic laughed. Angel didn't feel fear or pain, just a stomach-churning embarrassment. Even after five Coronas she should be able to handle herself better.

The hispanic's laughter stopped so abruptly that she forced her eyes open, despite the blood gumming them shut.

She was on the floor next to the "men's" room. It gave her an oblique view of a black-furred arm sticking out the door. In the hand was an equally black Heckler and Koch 10-millimeter Valkyrie automatic.

Her gaze shifted to the three punks. Earl, the fuckhead anglo, was on the ground in a fetal position. The black was bent over him. The one with the chain was halfway to the door to the bathroom.

A calm voice with an almost liquid Brit accent echoed out of the bathroom. "Please drop the chain."

"We know you. Fucking hairball don't . . ."

"Scare you?" The owner of the arm stepped out of the bathroom. He had to be the handsomest vulpine Angel had ever seen.

"Chico," said the black, "I think Earl's dyin."

"Shut up with the names, man." Chico, the one with

the chain, was losing his bravado. He tried to face down the vulpine. "If cops catch you—"

The fox laughed. A soft sound, but deep. "They'd approve of you? Please, drop the chain and leave."

"Damn it, Chico, I'm calling an ambulance." The black ran out of the bar. In search of a public comm, Angel thought.

She looked at Earl.

Earl wasn't moving.

She looked at Chico.

"You can't fuck with this—" Chico wasn't moving either.

The fox cocked the automatic. "Please."

The sound of the gunshot was deafening. It was still echoing in Angel's sensitive ears when she heard the sound of metal hitting the ground.

The truncated section of Chico's chain was swinging about three centimeters short of his right hand. The rest of the chain lay on the floor.

"Fine, keep the chain," said the fox. "Just leave."

Chico bolted, nearly tripping over Earl. The fox kept his gun aimed at the doorway for a few seconds before he holstered it.

He wore a green suit that looked good on him—unlike most every other sort of pink-type clothing you could drape on a morey. The green brought out the luster of the red fur on his face and tail. She barely noticed that it was tailored to conceal a shoulder holster.

He held out a black-furred hand to Angel. She realized that she'd been on her ass all along. She grabbed his hand and frantically pulled herself to her feet.

"Please," he objected. "Be careful. Head wounds—"

"Bleed a hell of a lot," Angel snapped. She shook her head. "Sorry, I shouldn't be short with you."

"You can't help the way you were designed." His engineered vulpine mouth managed to form a rather nice smile. And Angel realized that her savior had just taken a cut back at her.

She rolled her eyes and walked over to Earl. The world was looking a lot less shaky. A combination of adrenaline and an engineered metabolism seemed to have cooked off most of the alcohol. She was somewhere between the tag end of a buzz and the start of a splitting migraine.

Earl was curled into a ball. It looked liked she had not only done a number on his balls, but had had a pretty bad influence on his pelvis and a few ribs as well. Earl'd coughed up his share of blood. Fortunately, Angel could still hear him breathing. She shook her head. "I didn't think I hit him that hard."

*Yeah, but look at him now—sailed two meters before he landed.*

She felt the fox's hand on her shoulder. "Are you going to wait for the ambulance to show up?"

From the way he said it, she knew he didn't intend to stick around. She didn't blame him. It was illegal for a morey to own a firearm, and considering what was happening in the rest of the country, it wouldn't be pleasant to have the cops catch you with one.

"Think his friends really called an ambulance?" she asked.

He shrugged. "There's a comm up on the corner. We can call one from there."

Angel nodded.

Behind them, on the bar's holo, President Merideth finished speaking with a plea to end interspecies violence. The broadcast rejoined the morey football game. Frisco-Cleveland, scoreless in the third quarter.

Angel ignored it.

They saw the ambulance land from across Mission Street. Its lights were barely visible descending through the fog—rotating flashers cutting slices out of the night air. For a few seconds, sirens and the foghorns off the bay fought a muffled battle for attention.

The ambulance led the cops by about twenty seconds. A crowd had gathered out in front of *The Rabbit Hole,* and Angel and her companion were half a block up the street. The cops didn't pay any mind to them or to any of the two or three dozen moreaus up and down Mission.

The two of them stood in the doorway of an old earthquake-relief building, a whitewashed cinder block cube that was wrapped in a cloak of graffiti, across the street from another relic of the '34 quake, an on-ramp for the old Embarcadero Freeway. The on-ramp rose into the fog, so the abrupt stop it made in midair wasn't visible. The end hung somewhere over Howard Street and anyone who drove on it now would eventually crash into the luxury condos that held sway on the new coast south of Market.

The ambulance took off, sirens blaring. Angel shook her head and winced when she started feeling the cut on her cheek again. She'd managed to wipe most of the blood off with a towel she stole from the bar, but she needed to get home and clean up.

The fox noticed her distress, and he handed her a handkerchief.

She pressed it against the side of her face. "Shit like this ain't supposed to go down here."

"It happens everywhere."

"This is San Francisco. We're supposed to dance hand in hand over golden hills with flowers behind our ears."

A soft laugh came from the fox. "Would you prefer LA? An incident like this down there and police would start a house-to-house—"

"And in New York the National Guard would call in an air strike. I'm still disappointed. I moved here to avoid this shit."

"Where'd you come from?"

"Cleveland."

"I'm sorry."

They stood there in silence for a few minutes, watching the phoenix-emblazoned cop cars disappear into the mist, one by one.

"Damn," Angel said. "I don't even know your name."

The fox turned his head toward her and smiled. "We've missed the formal introduction, haven't we? My name's Byron."

Byron held out his hand, still smiling. Most moreaus

Angel knew of didn't have much of a repertoire as far as facial expressions went. Angel's own smile amounted to a slight turning at the corners of the mouth, but Byron's muzzle crinkled, his eyes tilted, his cheeks pulled up and his ears turned outward slightly. He smiled with his entire face, and somehow it looked natural, not like a fox aping a human.

Somewhere there was a British gene-tech who was very proud of himself.

The smile was infectious and Angel mirrored it, even though it hurt her cheek. She took his hand. "Angel."

"Angel." He said it slowly, his voice lending her name an exotic tone. The smile grew a touch wider, as if she'd just provided him with the answer to a complicated problem as opposed to just her name.

"Lovely name," he said and Angel thought to herself that an English accent seemed to fit perfectly in a vulpine mouth.

And she'd always thought of her name as casting against type. "Where'd you learn to shoot like that?"

"Section 5, Ulster antiterrorist brigade. God save whatever's left of the monarchy." Byron shrugged. "U.S. citizen for fifteen years, but I can't shake the accent."

"What's wrong with your accent?"

"A vulpine accent is a few steps below Cockney. I'd lose it in a minute if I could."

Angel thought of the bartender who tried so hard to sound human. "Don't. I like it."

Byron shook his head.

"Trust these ears. You have a very sexy voice."

Byron smiled again. They were still holding hands and he brought his other hand up to trace the undamaged side of her face. "I would never argue with an angel."

He lowered his hand and looked down Mission. The cops had all left, and the sky was dark beyond the fuzzy light of the streetlamps. A late October chill rolled off of the water. Angel shivered slightly.

"Apparently," Byron said, "the crisis is over."

Angel nodded and let go of his hand.

"We really should do something about your face—"

"Fine, really."

"I have a first aid kit in my car."

Angel looked up at Byron's face and the look in his eyes made her wonder exactly what he was thinking, and if it was anything close to what she was thinking.

# CHAPTER 2

Angel knew something unusual was going on when Byron walked off toward the bay. Wordlessly, she followed him as they paralleled the water past the new Oakland Bay Bridge and into the forest of condos on the postquake coastline. Occasionally the fog would roll back far enough for Angel to see some of the coast-hugging "reef" out in the bay. Even though it was less obvious here than it was on the coastline between Market and Telegraph Hill, if you looked at the forms sticking out of the water, it was easy to imagine the fifty-sixty meters of wharf and landfill that had slid into the bay during the big one.

There was something perverse in having people pay a good hundred K to live right on the edge of the destruction in a shiny new luxury condo. If anything, it proved a direct relationship between wealth and stupidity. Angel could only make out the vaguest outlines of the first story of the building they approached—but from that glimpse Angel decided that the people living there had to be *very* stupid.

Byron led her to a secure parking garage adjacent to the building. His car was parked in one of the reserved parts of the garage. Money to service the parking had to run better than the rent on her apartment. The car fit the place.

Angel finally spoke. "A BMW?"

"A BMW 600e sedan," Byron responded. He pulled a small remote out of his pocket. He pressed a few buttons and the trunk popped open.

"I'm impressed." The sloping blue vehicle did everything to exude money and power short of grabbing her by the scruff of the neck and shaking her. She could be looking at a hundred grand, easy.

Angel finally noticed the cut of Byron's suit. A morey wearing a suit had to have money. But Byron's suit wasn't an altered human three-piece. The damn thing was tailored for a fox. That was nearly as impressive as the car.

Byron rummaged in the trunk and came out with a green case with a red cross on it. He handed it to her. "Let me give you a place to sit." He pressed a few more buttons on the remote and the passenger door opened behind her. The leather bucket seat rotated ninety degrees to face the open door.

Angel stared at it and didn't move.

"It isn't going to bite."

Angel shook her head. "Never seen a car that did that." Sitting, she sank five or six centimeters into the contoured seat. She wished she had furniture this nice at home.

The first aid case rested on her knees. Byron opened it. "First thing, let's clean that off." He withdrew a package of gauze and a bottle. "This may sting a little."

Byron opened the bottle and Angel got a sharp whiff of alcohol. He doused the gauze and rubbed the fur on her cheek. Her eyes watered and her wince must have been noticeable. Byron pulled away the gauze, which was now red with her blood.

Angel looked up at a slightly blurred fox. "What?"

"It looked like I was really hurting—"

"I'm fine."

"You're crying."

"I'm not crying!" she sniffed. "Just dress the thing."

Byron nodded and went back to cleaning off her wound. It hurt like hell. Angel tried to get her mind off of it. "So—" She grimaced as Byron applied fresh gauze. "—what you do for a living?"

He pulled a small razor out of the kit. "Overpaid delivery boy." Byron shaved the hair from around her wound. She felt a slight tug, and one of her whiskers fell in her lap. "Until I was laid off," Byron finished. From the sound, he didn't want to talk about it.

Angel sat, silent, as he finished binding up her face. When he was done, she was scared to look in the side-view mirror. But despite her fears, the dressing only formed a small rectangle on her right cheek.

She touched her cheek lightly. "At least the scars will be symmetrical."

He leaned over to peer into the small mirror. "I'm curious about that other one." He reached over her other shoulder and touched the reflection of her other cheek. On her left cheek was a scar that pulled up one corner of her mouth in a permanent smile.

"Long time ago. You don't want to hear."

"Maybe I do." His finger dropped from the mirror, but his arm remained draped over her shoulder.

Angel sighed. He really didn't want to hear this. "Ten years ago, a sleazy excuse for a ferret tried to rape me."

There was an uncomfortably long silence. Byron finally said, "I'm sorry."

"I told you."

"Perhaps I should take you home."

Did she screw up? Still had his arm around her shoulder—good, Angel thought. Let's just not tell him what *happened* to that ferret.

"I'd appreciate the ride."

Byron let go of her and walked around to the driver's side. "Where am I going?"

"The Mission District," Angel said, rehearsing in her mind how she was going to ask him up to her place. If he was paying any attention, he could probably smell what she was feeling. She certainly could—even over the stale lime from *The Rabbit Hole*—and the lust-smell was making her self-conscious.

Angel's building was near the center of the Mission District, in the heart of a swath of San Francisco's ubiquitous Victorians and pseudo-Victorians. Many of the houses Byron drove by had survived two major quakes—in fact, there were jokes that restoration work had done more damage in this part of the Mission District than any earthquake could.

Despite the historical context, Angel still thought of her place as an architectural assault. A bay window squatted over an entrance that tried to look like a Roman arch. Both were flanked by square towers that were topped by merlons, of all things. The whole thing sat on a brick foundation wrapped in wrought iron that was close enough to the tilted street that it gave the illusion of being canted at a dizzying angle. The street was so cockeyed this far west on 23rd that, while there were six steps to the door on the right, there were only two to the left.

Byron pulled to a stop between a beat-up off-blue Ford Jerboa and a hulking, heavily modified Plymouth Antaeus. He turned his wheels to the curb and said, "Nice place."

Angel glanced up and down 23rd, but he had parked right in front of her house. "You're talking about that house, there?"

Byron shrugged.

No accounting for taste. Give it time, Angel thought, eventually she'd be in love with anachronistic monstrosities like the rest of the city.

But she wasn't going to hold her breath.

"Come in for a drink?" She wished she'd come up with something less cliché-ridden for the time she spent thinking about it.

"My pleasure, Angel." It might have been her imagination, but Byron made her name sound like an endearment.

Angel led him upstairs to her flat, having forgotten totally about her roommate. And, having forgotten about Lei, of course Lei was there in the living room waiting for them.

Angel had barely opened the door before Lei bounced off the couch and said, "Early night. How are you—What the hell happened? Are you all right?"

Angel opened her mouth to say something.

"And who's this?" Lei finished without taking a breath.

Lei was a Vietnamese canine, but Angel had suspicions that she was really an odd-looking ferret with hyped reflexes. Lei was already shaking Byron's hand before Angel had managed to get a word out.

"Lei," Angel finally managed, stepping out of the way so Byron could enter the second-story apartment. "Byron.

Byron, Lei." Angel felt a little overwhelmed, being squeezed between a pair of two-meter-tall moreaus.

"Pleased, I'm sure." Byron said with a slightly amused smile plastered on his face.

"Sorry I'm back early," Angel said, "but things came up."

"Really no problem," Lei said, then whipped her head back to face Byron. "I can *imagine.*" Angel felt Lei's tail swat her on the ass.

*"Lei—"* Angel began.

"How did the game go?" Lei asked as she stopped pumping Byron's hand.

Angel stood there, for a second not getting Lei's question.

"Angel, the *game.*"

"I, uh—" For some reason Angel glanced at Byron. "Don't know."

"After all your—" Lei glanced at Byron herself. "Oh, yeah, things came up, didn't they?"

"Well, yes, you see—"

"Oh, my, look at that time." Lei didn't look anywhere near a clock. She reached past Angel to grab a purse hanging off the back of a chair. "It was nice meeting you, Byron." She pumped his hand again. "But I have to go. Things to see, people to do."

Lei turned and gave Angel a very broad wink before she slipped past Byron and out the door.

"Lei?" Angel sighed as she heard the door downstairs swing closed. "I hate that."

"Interesting person."

Angel closed the door as Byron walked in. She looked over the living room. Great, Lei'd been cleaning again. Byron was going to to think she was some anal neat freak. "Make yourself at home." Were clichés the only thing she could come up with? "I'm going to change into something more—" *Don't say comfortable!* "—clean."

"Please, take your time."

Angel walked into her bedroom and ripped off the blood-spattered shirt and looked at herself in the mirror. "You're still a little drunk," she whispered at her reflection as she manhandled her jeans off over her feet. "Got to be it."

She looked around for something to wear. Compared to the spotless living room, her room was a blast crater. Angel started by trying to find something that smelled clean, and ended up shoving a double armful of clothes into the closet.

She had to make an effort to avoid further cleaning. "Calm down, Angel," she whispered.

She looked at her reflection. She could just forgo the clothes. Clothing was a human quirk anyway. It was her place, right?

She grabbed a robe from the closet, a metallic-green thing that she'd bought in Chinatown. She almost walked out without ripping off the price tag. She tossed the tag under the bed.

"I really need a drink."

Angel walked past the living room and rummaged in the fridge. Coke, Budweiser, a lonely bulb of Ki-Rin, a bottle of white wine . . .

She grabbed the wine.

Angel walked out into the living room and Byron was leaning back on the couch, jacket and tie off, watching the comm. Angel walked up next to him and handed him a glass.

"The local game's blacked out, but I found the Denver game."

Angel looked up in time to see the Denver Mavericks' quarterback get destroyed in a sack that involved a fox, two tigers, and a canine. "*Yes!*" Angel said at the sight, almost spilling her wine. "You a fan?"

"Was there any other reason to be in that bar?" There was something odd in the way Byron said that. "The service is bloody rotten and I can't say much for the clientele. With one exception, of course." He toasted her with his glass. God, she loved that accent.

Angel killed the light and sat down next to Byron.

Byron continued, "Of course, I started watching *real* football—" The Mavericks were second and five, and Al Shaheid, the canine quarterback, sent an incomplete pass off into nowhere. Byron winced. "Didn't he see that? Rajhadien was wide open."

"What do you mean *real* football?" Third down and Shaheid was backpedaling with the ball. "Sack the bastard!"

"Soccer." Somehow, Shaheid slipped through a gap in the defense and ran for ten and a first down. "Yes!" Byron said with as much enthusiasm as Angel had shown in response to the sack. "But, as far as I know, the States is the only place they let moreaus play anything professionally."

"What's your team?" Angel asked, sliding into a comfortable nook under Byron's left arm.

"Denver—"

"You bastard! I'm tempted to throw you out right now." Byron's tail moved around behind her, and Angel reached down and idly began to stroke it.

Angel felt Byron's sharp nose nuzzle her ear. "I suppose you're Cleveland?" he whispered.

"Are you kidding? The worst team in the league?"

"How about the Warriors?" Byron asked as the Mavericks' opponents got a flag on the play. Someone had used their claws again. Trust the Bronx Warriors to do that at least once a game.

"I don't believe you." Angel slipped a hand into Byron's shirt, stroking the fur on his abdomen. "You're in the town with the best team in the league."

"Last year maybe."

Angel set down her drink and started undoing the buttons on his shirt. "Last year, this year, next year, every year—"

"That's why I'm not an Earthquakes fan." Byron set down his own drink. "They're all so full of themse—" One of the Mavericks' receivers had broken out and was running down the sidelines. "Go, go, go." Byron began quietly chanting, as Angel undid his pants.

Angel glanced back at the comm and saw the touchdown. They put up the score and it was Mavericks, 25 to zip. There were a dozen seconds left on the clock for the first half. The Warriors might as well just pack up and go home. Not that anyone in his right mind would want to go to the Bronx right now. At least not until there was a cease-fire.

Byron reached over and hit the mute button on the remote.

"You were really upset when the game got preempted," Byron said as his hands slipped the tie from her robe.

"I was looking forward to a decent massacre." Angel nipped at one of Byron's triangular ears.

"The president was talking about a massacre." Byron rolled over and stretched on the couch under Angel.

Angel sighed and lowered her face until their noses touched. "Political games. At least with football, there isn't the pretense that it means anything."

"That's rather cold."

"So I'm a cynic." Angel slid back on to Byron's hips and nuzzled his chest.

"A few years ago I would've argued with you."

Angel rested her chin on Byron's chest. Somehow their clothes had ended up as a nest underneath them. The silent comm was the only light in the room.

Byron placed his hand on the back of her head, and began stroking the length of her back. "Let's change the subject."

"You were just telling me how cold I was." Angel found one of his nipples under his chest fur and teethed it.

Byron smiled his incredible smile, and Angel felt his tail wrap around her midsection. "I was mistaken. You're actually very warm."

Angel reached between his legs and said, "So're you."

Lei didn't come back until the following morning, and for that, Angel was very grateful.

# CHAPTER 3

The first Wednesday in November, she ran into Balthazar on her way home. The ancient forty-year-old lion was her downstairs neighbor, and she didn't see him come out very often. But when she made it to the stairs, she heard a whispery growling voice from behind her, "Missy?"

She turned around and saw the old lion, sitting in a wheelchair behind the half-open door to his apartment.

"Yes?" She felt a little uncomfortable as she approached him. She had never really talked to Balthazar before. Her only contact with him had been the sound of his comm drifting through the door.

"Come closer, hearing's shot." He waved her over with a hand that arthritis had twisted into a nearly useless paw. It was an uncomfortable reminder of her own mortality—and how the more the pink gene-techs fiddled with something, the more age would ravage it.

Angel walked up to the door.

Balthazar had been a huge morey. Had he been able to stand, he would have been close to twice her height. His eyes were clouded, his teeth were chipped, but the mane was still regal. Even in decline, the leonine moreau had the bearing of royalty.

Which was why Angel nearly burst out laughing when she saw that the blanket that covered his legs was covered with cartoon characters. She kept a straight face and asked, "Can I help you?" She was still in waitress mode.

She stood in front of the lion, looking up at him even though she was standing and he was seated. He coughed a few times, and asked in a hoarse whisper, "Angel?"

She nodded, trying to avoid staring at the old blanket. Gray rabbits, black ducks, other things too faded for her to make out. The blanket looked almost as old as Balthazar himself.

"You're with that fox who's been in and out for the last week."

"Yes, yes." And she was getting impatient because that fox was probably waiting for her upstairs.

She could see his comm in the living room beyond him. It was playing some sort of animation, a black duck going on about how something was "despicable."

"He left you something."

"What?" Angel found her attention drawn back to the old lion.

"Here." With some difficulty, he pulled out a plain-wrapped package the size of a wallet. There were no markings on it at all. He passed it to her.

Angel hefted the package, feeling a little confused. "Byron left this with you? Why didn't he just give it to me him—"

"Said he had to leave." The lion erupted into another fit of coughing, shaking his head, and rippling his mane.

Angel held the package and was enveloped by a very bad feeling. "Thank you for holding this for me."

"Cost me nothing."

Angel nodded and headed toward the stairs.

"Missy?"

She turned back toward the lion.

"None of my business, but I don't trust him, too smooth."

"You're right. It's none of your business."

Balthazar grunted and began to wheel his chair back into the apartment. Before the door shut completely, Angel thought she could make out a chanting refrain from his comm, "Rabbit season, duck season, rabbit season, duck season . . ."

She had no idea what it meant, but it didn't make her feel any better.

The package was still sitting on the coffee table in front of the comm, unopened, when Lei came home. Lei asked about it, and Angel had the bad sense to tell her.

"Why haven't you looked in it?" Lei asked her, picking up the small plain-wrapped bundle.

"I don't—" Angel retreated into the kitchen. She didn't want to look at the thing. She'd yet to get to the point where she had a lock on what she was afraid of. Instead of thinking about it, she started to fix herself dinner.

Lei didn't leave it alone. When a few minutes passed without an answer from Angel, she followed her into the kitchen.

"Open it," Lei said, brandishing the package. Her brown-furred canine face was twisted somewhere between a growl and an amused smirk.

"Let it rest," Angel said as she tried to get past her and put her bulb of soup in the micro. A thin brown-haired arm blocked her. Playing defense, Lei had the advantage of a much longer reach and about 80 centimeters of height—if you didn't count Angel's ears.

Lei slipped in after the arm. "I won't until you open it up and read the thing."

Angel tried to break through one last time and only got a noseful of canine-smelling fur.

Angel tossed the bulb on the kitchen floor in disgust. It bounced once. She had wanted it to burst open. She stormed out of the kitchen and threw herself down on the couch. "Mind your own business."

Lei followed her out to the living room and tossed Byron's package on the table. "I don't understand you. What's your problem? What did Byron do?"

Angel shook her head. "Nothing, I just *know* . . ."

Lei paced in front of the couch, tail swatting the air. "Know *what?* He's handsome. He's charming. He has money." Lei paused and made a sweeping gesture. "He likes you better than he likes me, God knows why. He's—"

"Too good to be true."

"What?" Lei stopped pacing and turn to face her.

Angel looked at the small bundle on the coffee table. "Someone had to wake up."

"Bullshit!"

Angel shrugged. "Par for the course."

Lei sat down and hugged Angel's shoulders. "Don't you see how silly you're acting?"

"It's not silly."

"How long have you two been going out?"

Angel reviewed the dates in her mind to get the passage of time straight—the football game, the Hyatt Memorial, Golden Gate Park, Chinatown. . . .

"Nine days." Only nine? Yes, today was November fifth, only nine.

"And this is the second night you haven't spent together?"

"First. Wednesday we never made it back here."

"So I managed to get one good night's sleep out of that nine days—"

"We're not that loud."

"You're stressing 'cause you aren't going out tonight?"

"Well—"

Lei shook her head and chuckled. She rubbed her knuckles in the space between Angel's ears. "What're you going to do, graft yourself to him? Maybe he just had the urge to go to the john a few times and hold it himself."

Angel sighed. Lei was right. She knew Lei was right. But she couldn't shake the feeling that something was wrong. "So I'm not rational."

"He didn't do anything to bring this on? Did he?"

"No."

"He didn't break any plans you had tonight, right?"

"We haven't planned anything in advance yet. Just seems to happen."

"So what's eating you?"

Angel reached for the package. No, he never said one damn thing that could explain the awful feeling she had in the pit of her stomach. "I don't know."

Maybe it was what Byron didn't say. "He's keeping stuff from me."

"Ah," Lei shifted around so she was sitting on the coffee table and propped her muzzle in her hands. "He's married."

"No!" Angel leaned forward and tried to stare Lei

down, but her roommate's expression told her that she wasn't serious. Still, the suggestion made her nervous.

Maybe the problem was that she was so caught up in someone she knew so little about. She'd been so sure she'd dived into this of her own accord. Why did she feel that she had lost control somewhere?

"What, then?" Lei was asking. "Tell me."

Angel sighed. "Everything. Nothing. What does he do for a living?"

"He hasn't told you? Have you *asked* him?"

Only the once, Angel thought to herself and cursed. If only he didn't make her so self-conscious. As if she constantly had to cover for the fact that she was raised on the streets, a well-used rabbit who'd been homeless for half her life.

Angel flopped back on the couch and stared at the ceiling. "Moonlit strolls, romantic dinners, dancing—with my feet, dancing—watching the sun set in the Pacific and watching it rise over the bay, talking, talking, talking . . ." And nothing ever got said, she thought. Nothing but the right things to say.

Lei tapped her on the shoulder and Angel lowered her head to face her. "Well, open the damn thing."

"I'm afraid to." Too soon into this and Angel had an uncomfortable emotional attachment that seemed too fragile.

Too much, too soon.

"Don't be a wuss."

Angel glared at Lei and ripped the wrapping off the package.

At least a dozen ramcards fell out, all emblazoned with a holographic blue and white thunderbolt—the San Francisco Earthquakes logo.

"Holy shit." It was all Angel could manage to say. She stared at the tickets, feeling real silly.

"Your expression is priceless."

"Box seat season tickets, the fifty yard line, where the hell did he get—?"

"I wish I had a camera."

Angel picked up a note that'd fluttered out of the package. In Bryon's flowing script it said, "By now, my little angel, you've peeled yourself off the ceiling. There are two sets of tickets, and while I am NOT an Earthquakes fan—no matter how much you threaten me—you *better* take me to the Denver game.

"I want to be with you right now, because there is a very important question I have to ask you. However, I have to deal with some leftover responsibilities first, then I can think about the future.

"Love, your Byron."

Angel let the paper slide through her fingers.

"What?"

" 'Important question—' " Angel said, suddenly unsure of how she felt. "Am I misreading that?"

Lei picked up the note and began reading it.

" 'The future?' " Angel felt her heart accelerate and told herself that she was getting irrationally emotional again.

"Oh, my," Lei said.

Angel got off the couch and walked to the door, paced back, walked to the window. "Is that all you have to say? 'Oh, my?' "

"He could be talking about anything—"

Angel stared out the window. "Damn." Angel rested her forehead against the glass.

Lei walked up behind her. "What's the matter? You look worse off than before."

Angel shook her head. Why couldn't he wait a little while? Why'd he have to force things so damn quickly?

"Angel, you're crying . . . "

"I'm not crying!" In a much quieter voice she said, "I'm not ready for this."

Lei rested a hand on her back. Angel felt herself shake under Lei's hand and realized that she *was* crying. "Damn it. I don't want to lose him—"

"Shh, you aren't going to lose him."

Angel stood there, crying, unconvinced.

Thursday morning, Angel wasn't ready for the breakfast crowd. As her shift drifted toward noon she was so distracted that she confused orders at least once, giving a young tiger a plate of greens and giving a trio of white rabbits the tiger's plate of bleeding hamburger. She could scratch two tips right there.

Sanchez rode her even harder than usual, even coming out of his little shoebox manager's haven to order her to pick up the pace. All the time her mind kept drifting off the orders and on to Byron.

Foxy knew she'd freak if he popped the question unprepared. Of course he did. And she *had* to live in one of the three states that recognized moreau weddings as legit. The only state that recognized interspecies marriage—even the Catholic Church in its latest liberal wave had yet to go that far.

If she still lived in Cleveland, she wouldn't even have to think about it. But then, in Cleveland, she'd have more pressing worries—like stray gunfire.

It was unnerving for her to realize that if she was going to marry anyone, Byron'd be it. Worse, he obviously knew it.

Yeah, right. She was going to marry anyone? Bloody fat chance, as Byron would say.

"Yo, fluffy!" came from part of the rodent brigade of the lunchtime crowd. "Where's my fries?"

Spuds for the spud. Obviously she had to stop whatever she was doing so a fleabitten member of the rat patrol could get his daily allotment of grease. She almost served the ratboy a handful of abuse, but Sanchez had come out of hiding to lord it over his lunchroom kingdom and his look said, *He's a customer—*

Angel returned Sanchez's look with one that said, *Yeah, a rare breed here,* and got the rat's fries from the kitchen.

Byron and her, she thought. It was too soon.

She shook her head. Whatever happened, she'd be asking the same question a week, a month, a year from now. And she was getting older. Balthazar was an uncomfortable reminder of that. She was doing well for her age, but twenty was three years the far side of middle age for a rabbit.

At least with Byron she wouldn't have to worry about kids—unless they wanted to go to a Bensheim clinic and make some.

Angel had a vivid mental image of a litter of rabbits

being infected by Byron's seductive Brit accent. It brought a smile wide enough to make the old cut on her cheek ache.

Was she really thinking about this, seriously?

"Where's my ketchup, fluffy?"

Angel looked at the black rodent and wondered if it was some genetic quirk that made all rats assholes. Angel looked at him, street kid, pissed at the world, age pushing double digits. He was making points with his friends here by harassing the help. Rat would probably die of old age before he had to work for a living.

The fries were steaming from the fryer and Angel had an urge to insert them into that shiny pink nose of his. Instead she said, as sweetly as she could muster, "Just a moment." She couldn't bring herself to say "sir." It'd dock her a few points in Sanchez's book, but at this point she didn't give a damn.

She was heading off to get a bottle from another table—the rat had probably stolen the one that was supposed to be on his—when she found herself facing two pinks.

From a decade plus on the streets she ID'd the pinks as pure cop the instant she laid eyes on them. Not just the fact they were pinks in a morey joint. Cop emanated from the shoddy suits like the bald one's cheap cologne. The barely hidden shoulder holsters didn't help. A matched set, and from the way they spaced themselves—out of arm's reach from each other—there wasn't much love lost between the two.

The one on the right was Asian, jet black hair, razor mustache. The other was balding, rumpled, and carried a gut that could have comfortably hidden Angel in its girth.

She was still in waitress mode, so she asked, "Can I help you?"

"We're looking for a Miss Lopez," said the Asian.

The urge to simply bolt for the door and disappear became overwhelming. Why'd Frisco PD want her? She was clean—except for the damn gun in her underwear drawer. Angel began cataloging all the shit leftovers in Cleveland. There was a lot of six-year-old crap nobody had tagged her for yet.

She was thinking of stonewalling when Sanchez bellowed. “Get your butt moving, Lopez.”

So much for stonewalling. The balding one pulled out an ID and flashed it at her, too quickly. “Detectives White and Anaka, San Francisco PD. We need to talk to you.”

Angel bent around the Asian and grabbed the ketchup squeeze bottle off the table. “What about? I’m working.”

She was going to go about her business and get the rat his ketchup. But something about the way the two cops smelled made her hesitate. There was a little too much nervousness hanging in the hair around them.

Instead of delivering the bottle, she stood and waited. The cops’ manner was beginning to worry her.

“Miss Lopez,” the balding one asked, “do you know a vulpine moreau by the name of Byron Dorset?”

She didn’t even feel the bottle slip out of her fingers as she asked them what had happened.

# CHAPTER 4

Byron was dead.

She had known it from the way the cops acted, even before they told her that he'd been killed in some hotel in the Tenderloin. When she went with the two detectives, she said nothing, even as Sanchez asked her what the hell was going on. She was in the cops' unmarked green Plymouth before she could begin to think.

Byron was dead.

She couldn't shake the phrase. It kept running through her mind over and over.

*Get a grip,* she thought. A cynical part of her brain was telling her how insane this all was.

Why?

Angel's mind locked on that word like a mantra as the cops shot down Market toward the police station. The fat pink, White, tried to be comforting, but his words didn't jell into anything coherent—just another noise, like the engine and the abused suspension. Anaka said nothing.

Why?

Why him? Why now? Why did this have to happen before she knew what she felt?

Maybe the cops were wrong and it wasn't him. To most humans, moreaus all look alike, right? Even cops. Even to some cops who worked the moreau districts—

Angel shivered when she realized that they were going to ask her to identify the body.

Could she handle that?

Damn it, of course she could handle it. She'd seen corpses before, some of them her friends. She'd led a fucking street gang. She'd seen more death up close than some morey veterans. She was tough, a survivor. . . .

She never should have let someone get that close to her.

The new, supposedly earthquake-proof, police headquarters squatted on the foundation of the old post office. It tried, too hard, to look contemporary with the surviving structures in the cluster of civic buildings across Market. The Plymouth slid into a tunnel that fed into the parking garage. Even in the car Angel could feel the temperature drop and smell the ozone of a few hundred confined vehicles. The lights buzzed, and the echo from that made the scene feel unearthly.

Anaka parked the car near the bottom of the hole. The garage was a concrete tomb. It was dark, hard, and cold. White led her out. Anaka had stepped out of the car to follow them, but White stopped him. "Go check with the coroner—"

"But—" Anaka began to say.

"Meet us back up on three."

Anaka stepped back into the car, slammed the door shut behind him, and pulled away.

White put a hand on Angel's shoulder and maneuvered her toward the elevators. Angel stayed pliant, saying nothing.

They entered the elevator and White flashed his badge at a sensor. "Detective Morris White, third floor."

"Confirmed," the elevator responded.

Angel took a few breaths and tried to find her voice. "Where are we going?"

The doors slid open, and White led her to a desk, behind which sat a bored looking uniform.

White acted a little uncomfortable. He addressed the uniform first. "I have an appointment for a vid room."

"Detective White, right?" The uniform held out his hand. White handed over his badge and the cop ran it through a scanner. "The lawyers are waiting for you, 5-A."

"Lawyers?" Angel asked, forcing herself to regain a little touch with reality.

"We want you to ID our suspects." They walked past the desk, and down a long corridor. They passed doors every ten meters or so. One door near the end of the hall hung open. White paused in his walk down the corridor. "Are you up to this?"

"Me? ID the suspects?" Angel spoke slowly. She'd agreed to go with the cops, mostly out of shock. She still didn't trust police, and she was beginning to wonder exactly what was going on here. Who the hell could she identify? She barely knew Byron.

*Yeah,* said the cynical part of her mind *so why are you so torn up over this?*

*I might have married him,* she answered herself.

*Out of love,* replied the cynic, *or because he was the only person to ever show any interest in a well-used lepus that barely scraped herself off of the pavement back home?*

"Let's talk inside," White said, taking her nonanswer as a yes.

White led Angel the rest of the way to room 5-A, and shut the door behind him. The room was a stark white rectangle. The far wall was covered by ranks of vid screens. A long table squatted in front of the screens. Two empty chairs faced the table and the screens beyond. Two chairs at either end of the table were filled.

Both occupants wore conservative dark blue suits. The one on the far right was a redheaded human woman who was idly tapping at a wallet computer. The other one was a moreau ferret. The ferret turned a sinuous gaze on the two of them and shot White a chuckle. "You finished prompting the witness?"

White sighed. "Miss Lopez, let me introduce Mr. Igalez from the public defender's office."

The ferret whipped a nod.

"And Mrs. Gardner, Assistant District Attorney."

Gardener glanced up, and her head moved in a nearly imperceptible acknowledgment.

There was a third person in the room. A uniformed cop sat at a control console next to the door. White didn't introduce him. From the way the seats were arranged, Angel couldn't see him when she sat down.

White sat down next to her. They faced a wall full of test patterns. He pulled a microphone over to face her. "I want you to understand, you're here as a witness, not a suspect. But you do have the right to have your own lawyer present."

*Yeah, right, a morey with a lawyer. A morey waitress ex-gang member with a lawyer.* She wondered where Igalez came from, and who he was defending.

Angel sighed and asked, "What do you want from me?"

Gardener, the DA, started. "We want to know about the events of October 27, 2059."

After a long pause, Angel finally asked, "Monday?"

It all slipped into place. *The Rabbit Hole.* That's who White's suspects were—

The three punks who'd jumped her!

She'd been feeling numb, in shock, ever since White and Anaka had picked her up. However, she had no idea how truly pissed she'd been until she had something to focus her anger on. Angel bit her lower lip until she tasted blood. She wanted to kick something.

She'd see those skinheads fry.

The questions went on about *The Rabbit Hole,* and the punks who'd attacked her. The DA asked calm, sometimes leading questions, while the Public Defender was hard, angry, trying to rip any hole in her story, and, failing that, trying to cast her in the worst light possible.

The questioning was accompanied by a rapid drumbeat that Angel only realized belatedly was her own foot pounding the ground, hard.

Igalez got to her. Not that he made her admit anything, but having a fellow moreau try to make that fight look like she'd provoked something. . . .

"Are you saying that crushing that man's testicles was not excessive force?" asked the ferret.

"Three bald punks were about to spike me like a football." Her pounding foot doubled its speed against her volition. The table vibrated in time to it and Angel realized that White was staring at her.

"You could see no other way to remove yourself—"

Angel jumped on to the chair, tensed like a spring. She leaned toward him. "You ever been raped, Igalez?" She was amazed how calm her voice sounded.

"Miss Lopez—" White said. He put a restraining arm on her shoulder.

*"Have you, Mr. Public Defender?"* The pounding was now her own heart, and the smell of the blood from her lip seemed to fog the room. She was riding a razor-thin edge here, and be damned if she wasn't pushing the envelope.

Gene-techs all over the world had designed moreaus for battle, and most designs had some combat mode written into their genes. All Angel really needed was to get pissed enough and she'd go crazy on her own adrenaline.

"No—" From the way the ferret looked, he could smell how far he'd pushed her. The fear he broadcast, and the sound of his own heartbeat fed into Angel's state.

It was like a wind at her back, pushing her to *move.* She'd reached a point where she'd fired every cell of her body to scream *threat.* "A ferret—kinda like you—tried to rape me once. If I'd kicked him in the balls, he might still be alive." She jumped. White didn't expect the move, and she was so hyped that she was across the table and on Igalez before anyone else could act. By a supreme act of will, all she grabbed was his tie. "I let him get too close." Her nose was only a few centimeters from the ferret's. She could hear other people in the room scrambling around the table. Every sense was sharpened on a metabolism her anger had driven to just this side of panic.

She gave Igalez her best smile. "I had to chew through his throat."

Some sense started leaking in, and she began to force it all back. Her body wanted to rebel, but it recognized that she was still in charge, barely. She let go of his tie and he dropped back into the seat. "The scar on my cheek's from a chunk of his cartilage."

She backed off, barely able to admit to herself that what she'd just done had scared her as much as it had Igalez.

White was about to grab her, but she hopped back into her seat without assistance. "Excessive force, my ass."

Had she really been about to do to Igalez . . .

It took a few seconds for everyone to return to their seats. Even the uniform by the door had vacated his post.

The color had drained from the Assistant DA's face, and her hand shook her wallet computer slightly. White glared at her, wiping sweat from his balding skull. The uniform's hand hung a little too close to his weapon.

Angel shook. Losing control like that wasn't good. The only person who knew how close things had come was Igalez, the only other morey in the room.

And Igalez looked truly spooked.

"Are you contending," Igalez asked, regaining his composure and spending a few seconds loosening his tie, "your belief at the time was that these humans were going to—"

"Beat me up, rape me, kill me, and bugger me up the ass? In that order? Damn straight," Angel said quietly, trying to hide her own discomfort.

The questioning was subdued from that point on. Dates, facts, times. Igalez didn't go into motivation or justification again. They covered the fight at *The Rabbit Hole* two or three times, and only briefly did they go over the time between then and now. The fact that they didn't ask her much about relatively recent history struck her as odd, but she didn't dwell on it. She was too shaken.

When the questions ended, White said, "Now, what we'd like you to do is identify the three men who attacked you."

White waved back at the uniform and the test patterns dropped from the screens; Angel faced a wall of faces. Over twenty of them slowly rotated in front of her—

"First of all, I told you, they were all bald."

In response, the pictures with hair froze as the computer erased the hair, pixel by pixel. After a half second, she was facing a wall of bald humans. Angel stared, looking for Earl, Chico, and the black dude. Earl was the first one she recognized; he wore a face she'd never forget.

"Freeze number twelve. That's the guy I kicked."

Twelve froze and the Assistant DA said, "We're more interested in the other two—"

"Can we avoid prompting the witness?" The ferret stepped on the DA's speech.

Angel ignored them and studied the black faces on the

wall. She didn't know his name, but ten days ago he was standing closer than White was now.

"Six, number six." Six froze, facing them expressionlessly. "That's number two—"

"Are you sure?" asked the ferret.

"What did you say about prompting the witness?" the DA said.

Angel couldn't find Chico on the wall. "Are there any more pictures?"

In response the entire wall changed, and she looked at another army of bald faces. Chico was almost dead-center, staring at her. "Fifteen, that's the fucking bastard, fifteen."

Fifteen froze. The other faces blanked and the other two came back, flanking Chico. "Now we want you to be sure—"

"Those are the bastards who attacked me."

"You chose rather quickly—" the ferret started.

"That's them." She stared down Igalez. "The scum you're defending'd kill you for not being human."

White put his hand on her shoulder. "I think we're done here." White led her out of the room, and Angel was glad to get out of Igalez's presence.

Anaka was waiting by the desk, looking impatient.

She'd been right. They needed her to identify the body. They took her to St. Luke's Veterinary. She sat in the back of the car, numb, silent, while Anaka and White talked about what cops talk about.

They were going to stick her face-to-face with Byron cold on a slab and Angel wasn't sure she wasn't going to lose it. Hell, it felt like she'd lost it already. It was a damn close thing with Igalez.

She was stronger than that, though. She had more control.

Hoped she had more control, anyway.

*Stop brooding on it,* she told herself. *Soon the whole thing will be over. Over already, really.* Byron was a slab of meat and there was not thing one she could do about it.

Anaka and White argued around her, oblivious.

"I'm telling you," Anaka was saying, "Ellis is hiding something."

"I don't want to deal with your conspiracies today." White sounded more resigned than argumentative.

"Why's she doing the Dorset case? She's not a vulpine expert."

"Who gives a shit, Kobe? Our job's to bust the Knights, remember?"

"And if something's funny about the autopsy—"

"Damn it, Kobe, if we do this right, the skinheads will plead, roll over on their masters, and we'll never have to bring up the body . . ."

Angel was almost tempted to ask if that was so, why they needed to put her through this. She didn't. Who cared what kind of internal politics these cops were going through, she just wanted to get the damn ordeal over with.

The pair argued with each other all the way to the hospital. After a while Angel stopped listening.

The detectives took her to Byron's resting place, the morgue in the basement of St. Luke's Veterinary. The morgue's white tile walls echoed sounds to unnatural lengths. Cheap pine-scented disinfectant didn't quite cover the smell of dead flesh that'd sunk into the walls.

Angel was cold down here.

Byron lay on a stainless-steel table. As soon as Angel saw the body, there wasn't any doubt that it was him. Blood had caked on his fur, but it was the same face. . . .

"I love you, Byron," she whispered for the first and only time.

She said it so quietly that she was unsure if she had said it at all.

"Is it him?" Anaka asked for perhaps the third time.

Angel was still trying to find her voice.

She kept thinking how cruel it was. The slash on his neck had cut halfway through his throat and up the side of his face, pulling his cheek into a slack grimace. She was glad for whoever it was that had closed Byron's eyes. If Byron's eyes had been open, she was sure she'd go running off screaming—

After an eternity she managed to drag her gaze from

the corpse. She nodded at the cops. She screwed her eyes shut, but it felt like the image of Byron on that table had glued itself to the inside of her eyelids. She felt White's hand on her shoulder. "Let's take you home."

The cops took her back to the Mission District. White drove this time, Anaka next to him, leaving her alone in the back. For most of the ride they sat in silence, which was fine with Angel. She was still trying to deal with it, not just Byron, but her reaction to it—

She should be able to handle this, but she was on the verge of falling apart. *Come on,* she told herself, *you only met him ten days ago.*

They paralleled Market on Harrison, traveling toward the Mission District. As they made the turn south, Anaka finally asked a question.

"Miss Lopez, would you know *why* Bryan Dorset would want to meet with those two?"

"What two?" Angel whispered. She didn't want to deal with more questions.

White sighed.

Victorian architecture began to slide by the car as Anaka tackled Angel's hill. The cockeyed angles of the old homes made Angel's head hurt. She put her face in her hands.

It was wrong.

Not just the offense of someone killing Byron. There was something else that was wrong—

White pulled the car up in front of her place, between the Antaeus and the Jerboa. Angel looked at Anaka before she left the car, "What are you talking about. Meet who?"

"He was killed in a hotel room rented by the Knights of Humanity—" Anaka began. "The information that led us to the body also said that there was a meeting scheduled within a hour of the time of death."

*A meeting? Why?*

"No." Angel said, backing away from the car. "I don't have a damned idea why he'd want anything to do with those sleazeballs. What information—"

Anaka chuckled. "You don't know? It's—"

"Time you got some rest," White said, and drove the car away.

Angel watched the car leave and smelled something worse than the morgue scent that clung to her fur. . . .

# CHAPTER 5

Angel didn't bother going back to work, didn't even call Sanchez. It seemed pointless—

Everything seemed kind of pointless.

She sat on the couch, turned on the comm, and tried to stay numb. By seven she was watching Sylvia Harper, the senior senator from California, from behind a forest of beer bulbs. It was the third time they'd put up bites from Harper's speech in the Bronx. It was about Angel's tenth beer.

Angel thought to herself, not for the first time, that the woman had guts to be human and anywhere near the Bronx.

"—the twenty-ninth amendment was not a mistake. Some people think that, because of the violence that is tearing at our cities, the United States should have never opened its arms to you, the nonhuman.

"These people forget what America represents. The ideals of liberty, equality, freedom—"

*La-te-da,* Angel thought. She might be some dumb uneducated bunny—but she knew *some* history. The grand ol' United States always had that effing "liberty" at the expense of someone—morey, Amerind, or blacks like Sylvia up there.

Angel wondered if Sylvia was grateful that the moreys took the bottom rung for her.

The station jump-cut to another sound bite.

"When we tolerate slavery, we destroy ourselves. A lesson we must constantly relearn. Not just the slavery of physical bondage. It's easy for us to say you cannot own another person, that you cannot *make* another person.

"But what will destroy us is *mental* slavery. The slavery of bigotry. The slavery of discrimination. The slavery of nonhuman ghettos that are allowed to spiral into poverty and despair. The slavery that allows a human being to say that because you are a different species, you have no human rights."

*"Human" rights, there's a nice bit of ethnocentrism. Great, Sylvia, and you wanna be president?*

Angel took another swig of beer. The room smelled like a yeast culture, but at least she was getting a buzz.

Angel heard Lei come in during the lead-in to the next story.

"Angel . . ." From the sound of Lei's voice, she knew about Byron.

"Shh," Angel responded as she downed the last bulb, the bottle of Ki-Rin. Right after Harper, the news went local. Still leading the local news was the murder of a moreau. Only in San Francisco would Byron's death be a lead story. Human suspects helped make it the lead.

"Angel, I'm so sorry." Lei sat down and put her arm around Angel.

"I knew I was going to lose him." Angel threw her empty beer bulb at the screen. It bounced off.

Lei squeezed her shoulder, and for once remained quiet.

"Laid his throat open. I had to ID his body." The comm prattled on about martial law in LA. Angel closed her eyes on the aerial shots of the fires. "How could he be so careless?"

Lei stayed quiet.

"They're psychos, and they're *pinks*. How'd they get *close* enough to do that?"

Lei rubbed the back of Angel's head between the ears. "You need some rest."

Angel buried her face in her fur. "It's so unfair."

"I know."

"I miss him."

"I know."

Angel had a restless sleep, and upon waking, sat herself in front of the comm again. She called in sick, almost cussing out Sanchez. Then she turned on the news and tried to think clearly.

Byron was still news. Now the vids had planted a camera in front of the seedy hotel on Eddy Street where he'd been killed. The voice-over said a pair of human members of the Knights of Humanity were being held for suspicion in the knifing.

They made her ID *three* suspects, and it hadn't looked like a knife wound to Angel.

Then again, news was fucked more often than not.

Byron's letter was still sitting on the table. Angel picked it up while, on the comm, Father Alvares de Collor, a moreau jaguar, was talking about making Byron's funeral a show of moreau solidarity.

*There is a very important question I have to ask you,* Angel read, *but I have to deal with some leftover responsibilities first, then I can think about the future.*

"Leftover responsibilities," Angel repeated, aloud. "Some future."

Dawn light began to filter though the bay windows behind the comm. Angel could hear Lei wake up and start her shower.

" 'Unfinished business.' "

What the hell *had* Byron done for a living?

The news switched to an update on the fighting in Los Angeles. Like New York, other than a few fires here and there, things were static. The moreaus had carved themselves out the heart of the city, and local politicians were calling it a civil war. The National Guard had yet to go in, and Angel got the impression of a blast crater ringed by troops pointing their guns into the hole.

The Guard had good reason not to press the standoff. The Moreau Defense League had heavy armor on both coasts. On Manhattan, the blackened wreckage of the Nyogi tower testified to the last Federal push into the Bronx.

LA was supposed to be next on the Sylvia Harper urban violence tour. To Angel, it seemed a pointless gesture. Harper might chair a committee on interspecies violence, but no pink politico was going to calm things down there.

To a lesser extent, violence was occurring in every city with a large concentration of moreaus.

*Not here,* Angel thought. *San Francisco is different.*

At least it felt different before a bunch of bald pinks jumped her.

What the hell did those cops mean, he was going to *meet* with those punks? And Anaka acted like she should have known where they were getting their infor—

Angel slapped her forehead for a fool. Of course there were only two suspects in Byron's death. Earl must still be in the hospital after what she'd done. In the hospital and being pumped for all he was worth. Earl was the cops' source.

"Damn it, Angel, what are you doing up at this hour?"

"Trouble sleeping."

Lei was half dressed for work, swishing her tail, and tapping a digitigrade foot. She stepped over and picked up the remote for the comm and switched off the news. "Are you going to keep torturing yourself?"

"That's not it. It—"

Lei shook her head and pulled on a blouse.

"Something's wrong about Byron's death."

"Tell the cops. It's their job. Then stop worrying about it." Lei leaned over and turned Angel's head to face her. "Dear, you don't need any *more* reasons to feel bad." Lei rubbed noses and stepped back. "I'll be back right after work to see how you're doing, okay?"

"I'll be fine."

"Sure?"

"Sure." Angel nodded.

She waited until Lei left, then she put her face in her hands and shook. Did it really matter? Byron was gone, and that was that. Even if there was something strange about what was going on, it wouldn't bring him back. Those two pinks were scum anyway. Who cared?

Angel could smell her own blood and realized she was biting her lip.

*She cared.*

And she was going to drive herself crazy thinking about it. Lei was right, it was the cops' job. She should take her problems up with White or Anaka— If she could figure out what was wrong.

She called the Frisco PD and the reaction of the uniform answering the comm made her grab a robe. It had slipped her mind that she was calling humans and they considered it polite to wear some sort of clothing on a comm call.

Little details like that were slipping by her.

They transferred her call through three or four departments before someone realized that someone might actually want to talk to her—in that respect, Frisco wasn't any different from Cleveland, New York, LA, or anywhere else. . . .

Sun was beginning to leak in through the bay windows and the omnipresent fog by the time she got through to Detective White. The pink didn't seem any less obese. If anything, he seemed even bigger cramped into the screen on the comm.

He was in the middle of eating breakfast out of a mass of Chinese fast-food containers littering the desk between him and his comm. White had just speared a chunk of beef with a chopstick. The sight made Angel feel a little ill.

"Miss Lopez," White said between bites. "What can I do for you?"

Angel sucked in a breath. "You people sure those guys I fingered were the ones who did Byron?"

White was in the middle of swallowing and started coughing. He ended by hacking up a chunk of meat and spitting it into the container he was eating from. "*Jesus Christ.*" He dropped the container and pulled a dirty-looking handkerchief to wipe his face. "You're not going back on your testimony—"

"No, but I—"

White was shaking his head. Angel saw something hard begin to surface in his expression. "You *will* press assault on these guys—"

"I will, but—"

White leaned back, and Angel could hear the stressed office chair creak over the comm. "Whew, you scared me, lady."

Angel pulled the green robe around her and sat on the coffee table, scattering empty beer bulbs. "What the hell's going on here?"

"Miss Lopez, we want these guys—*all* of them. Your testimony on the assault is what we got. Without that—" White clasped his forehead and shook his head.

"Damn it, what *have* you got about the murder?"

White leaned forward. "What are you asking, Miss Lopez?"

"How do you know *they* killed him?"

White was silent for a long time. Eventually he said, "They killed him."

"How do you know?"

He rubbed his forehead. "I know that because half a million moreaus in this city believe it's true."

"What?"

White looked really angry. "We have them dead on the assault charges. They're guilty as sin."

"The murder?"

"We have enough to get things past the grand jury."

For the first time, Angel began to realize just how little the cops must have. "The bastards who did this might still be out there, and you—"

"We *have* the bastards who did this." White stared at her. "And if you want to see the guys who were going to 'beat you up, rape you, kill you, and bugger you up the ass' put away, don't do anything to jeopardize our case."

"What case?" Angel asked, and cut the connection.

"Great!" she yelled at the ceiling. Not only did White do nothing to settle her fears, but he as much as said that it didn't matter. The SFPD had their men, job done, let's break out the wine and fucking cheese. If we can't pin murder one on the geeks, we can put them away for a year or two for talking mean to this here rabbit.

Angel walked to the bay window and looked northeast, toward downtown. "The system sucks!" She slammed her fist into the windowframe. "It ain't just when it's against us! It *always* sucks!"

Angel turned her back on the city and slid to the ground. She sat there for a long time, thinking that she might as well've stayed in Cleveland.

Angel didn't realize she had fallen asleep until the comm woke her up by buzzing for her attention.

"Who the hell?" she mumbled, debating about letting the computer answer it. She decided against it. "Got it!" she yelled. The comm heard her and obliged by putting the call through.

"Hello, is there anyone there?" said a slightly familiar voice. She wondered where she'd heard it before.

"I'm coming," Angel said, pulling herself up from in front of the window. While she had slept, full daylight had come to burn off the fog for a while.

She had to limp around the comm because her foot had fallen asleep. For the first time in what seemed like two days—or was it only one—she realized the mess she must have looked. She hadn't cleaned her fur since—

Who the hell was this guy?

Large spotted feline, a Brazilian jaguar. The jaguar's eyes followed her to the front of the comm, golden eyes with tiny pupils. The large cat wore a grave expression, carefully avoiding either a show of teeth or creasing his muzzle. It wasn't until she saw the priest's collar that she realized who it was.

"Father Collor?" It was an easy guess to make. There were only three ordained nonhuman Catholic priests in the States at the moment. Alvarez de Collor was the only feline. Angel felt stupid for missing who it was. She'd seen him on the news just this morning.

"Angelica Lopez?"

Oh, great. "This is about Byron, has to be—"

"You're Miss Lopez?"

"Yes, yes." Angel rested her head against the top of the comm. Let the priest get a great shot of her robe, she didn't care. "What?"

"Miss Lopez, I apologize for breaking in on your grief—"

"Cut to the point, padre."

There was a long pause. "I need your permission to make funeral arrangements for Mr. Dorset."

Silence hung in the air for a long time. Angel pushed herself away from the comm and looked at the feline priest. "What the fuck?"

The priest made a visible effort to ignore the vulgarity. "We need to show a united front to the kind of people who did this—"

*"What the fuck?"*

"As his fiancée, you're his heir and only next of kin."

*"Is this some kind of sick joke?"*

"Please, can we discuss this calmly—"

Angel's head was whirring as she began to figure out how the pieces of the priest's little world slid together. "You made a statement to the press."

"Miss Lopez—" He was starting to show signs of distress. His eyes were darting past the comm's screen, as if there were spectators out of Angel's view. This was obviously not going as he'd planned.

"Before you had any—before you even talked to—" Angel realized she was pacing around the coffee table, trailing the robe behind her. She stopped and faced Father Collor. *"You want to turn this into a circus!"*

"That isn't it at all." He was looking to the left and right. Angel was positive now that there were people off-screen, and he was looking at them as if to say, "This isn't my fault."

Angel wanted to kick something. She brought her fist down on an empty beer bulb, and traces of froth splattered over the table, the wall, and the comm. "How'd you get a hold of my comm?" The bill was in Lei's name, Angel wasn't listed in any directories.

"I assure you—"

"Father, go chase another ambulance." Angel cut the connection.

The world seemed to be conspiring to piss her off. Who the hell did that self-righteous feline think he was? Byron wasn't even Catholic—

One of the jaguar's statements began to sink in.

"Fiancée and sole heir?" Angel felt a little dizzy.

She sat down on the couch. How the hell did she suddenly become Byron's fiancée?

The comm rang and Angel answered it, somewhat afraid of what it might be.

The call announced itself as being from Krane, DeGarmo and Associates. Sounded like a bunch of pink lawyers.

That's what it was.

The lean black-haired human who'd called her was Paul DeGarmo, Byron's lawyer and the executor of his will. What the jag priest had said was half-right anyway. She was Byron's single largest bequest.

DeGarmo didn't seem to find this odd at all, even though Angel had only known the fox for nine days.

What the hell was going on here?

She silently took the security codes for Byron's car and his condo. She nodded politely when DeGarmo told her that the body was going to be released on Monday and some sort of burial arranged. He told her a lot of financial details that slipped right by her—estate taxes and such.

All she kept thinking was that she had taken one step into Byron's life and suddenly she was in charge of all that was left of it.

# CHAPTER 6

Angel reread Byron's note for the tenth time since she'd parked the car. The words had begun to blur and lose their meaning—and she was no closer to understanding why Byron might want to meet with those bald psychopaths. It still made no sense.

Angel shoved the letter into her jeans with the Earthquakes tickets. It was no help, and she knew it by heart already.

"What the hell am I doing here?" she asked no one in particular.

She was sitting behind the wheel of Byron's BMW in the parking lot of St. Luke's Veterinary. The engineered-leather bucket seat was jacked up as far as it could go, giving her a view down the sloping blue hood at the moreys coming and going.

It was Saturday afternoon—no work, nothing for her to do but brood on Byron's death. Brooding had brought her here. She was still unsure why. She was unsure of a lot since talking to DeGarmo yesterday.

Everything she was doing felt odd, disjointed—as if someone else was making the decisions and she was just along for the ride. She only felt in touch with her surroundings when a knife edge of emotion slid briefly through the haze. More often than not it was a spasm of grief or self-pity.

But with increasing frequency it was anger. Irrational anger at silly things, like the ease with which she'd retrieved Byron's car from the impound lot. For the first time in her life, cops were being reasonably nice to her, and it felt like she was being bribed—all the cops in San Francisco wanted her to be a nice little rabbit and go along with the program. Most of all, anger at the increasing fraction of her life that was getting public airtime. Father Collor was only the first person to try to make political hay out of Byron's death.

Angel hated politics.

She kept an eye on the Ford Merovia sedan parked across from her BMW. It was the reserved spot for Dr. Pat Ellis, the doctor who'd signed Byron's death certificate. The doctor who Detective Anaka, White's Asian partner, seemed so suspicious of.

Why didn't she just call the doctor?

"What the hell am I doing?" she asked herself again.

The Merovia started, and Angel watched the feed cable automatically withdraw from the curb outlet. Angel saw a woman approaching with a little black remote control in her hand. Must be the doctor.

Ellis was approaching human middle age. Her sun-bleached hair was shot with gray. Her blue eyes were clouded by corrective surgery. She wore a suit whose sharp lines seemed to be working at cross purposes to the plump roundness they contained.

Angel got out of the BMW and moved to intercept Ellis.

Ellis didn't seem to notice her at first. The doctor kept walking to the quietly idling Merovia. Angel had gotten within a few meters before Ellis looked up at her. The doctor's expression showed surprise, and for a second she wielded the remote control at Angel, as if it was a weapon.

Angel stopped, "Dr. Ellis?"

"Y–yes." Ellis responded, looking around the parking lot, as if she expected to be ambushed or something. Angel could smell fear.

"I'd like to talk to you for a few minutes."

Ellis kept looking around the parking lot. "Who are you?"

"Angelica—"

Ellis wasn't looking in her direction. "Yes, I remember, you identified the body."

Angel nodded. "I want to talk about Byron."

"Not here." The doctor opened the door to the Merovia and retreated inside.

"Where, then?"

"Get in," Ellis left the door open for her.

For Angel, things had gone from disorienting to just plain weird. The doctor's paranoia was beginning to rub off on her. Angel slipped into the car, casting a glance over the parking lot at St. Luke's to see if she could find what Dr. Ellis was looking for. Angel didn't find it.

Ellis zigzagged through half of the new city south of Market. Angel didn't see any sign of the people Ellis must have thought were following her. Every time Angel started to talk, Ellis told her to wait.

Eventually, Ellis parked the car a block east of Franklin Square. "Let's go for a walk around the park." Ellis said, and Angel could tell she was making an effort to sound calm.

"Okay." Angel stepped out of the car and on to the sidewalk. They were surrounded by construction now. The skeletons of new buildings covered the area between Twentieth and the Central Freeway like an iron forest. A combination of earthquake and economic recession made this area one of the last to be rebuilt. It was getting close to seven, and the silence was ominous. Construction had ceased for the day, and the street was empty of cars and people.

Franklin Square itself was getting a facelift—which meant that sidewalks were torn up, piles of dirt covered by black tarpaulins were scattered at random, the park was clogged by construction equipment, and pipes from the old sewer system lay in choked stacks by the entrance.

They began to circle the park, and Angel asked, "What are you afraid of?"

"You wanted to talk about Byron Dorset, so talk about him."

They were walking down a deserted stretch of Sixteenth Street, and Ellis was still looking around as if she was being followed.

"I want to know how he died."

"You saw the corpse. Massive trauma to the neck—"

Angel grabbed the doctor's arm. "You know what I mean. I want to know what sliced him."

Ellis stopped and shook her head.

"News called it a knifing," Angel continued. "What kind of knife tears out that much of someone's neck?"

"It wasn't a knife."

"What, then?"

Ellis looked around again. "I can't be talking to you."

"What was it?" The fear-scent was floating off of Ellis and embracing Angel. It was hard to be that close to someone so wound up and not see eyes peering out of the darkness. What was Ellis afraid of?

The doctor looked torn, and very upset. It was getting hard for Angel to take. She grabbed the doctor by the elbows and shook her. "What killed him?" she shouted.

The fear-smell became sharper, less generalized. Angel could hear the doctor's pulse and breathing accelerate. For a moment, she seemed more afraid of Angel than she was of anything else. "I retrieved feline fur and nail samples from the wound."

Angel let go of Ellis. Suddenly she felt that it wasn't a hill she was standing on, but the crest of a rolling breaker that was dropping out from under her.

"Don't talk to me again." Ellis turned and ran back to her car. So much for a ride back to St. Luke's.

"A morey?" Angel asked herself.

"You're where?" The perennial look of concern crossed Lei's muzzle.

"Frisco General, you know, Potrero—"

"I know where the hospital is. What are you doing *there?*"

"I'm not there, really. I'm in a car across the street." A foghorn sounded from the bay.

"If you're calling to reassure me, you aren't doing it by evading the question. What possessed you to walk down there?"

"I said, I have a car."

"What . . ."

"Look, Lei, I'm fine. I just didn't want you to worry about me not being home."

"Well, I'm worried—"

"I'll explain when I get back." Angel cut the connection before Lei could object.

What *was* possessing her to come here? Did she think the cops would allow her to talk to Earl? Did she think that he'd actually talk to her?

But, damn it, she wanted to know what Earl had given up to the cops. What he'd said that had put two pink Knights away rather than the morey that'd slashed Byron.

And Earl was in stable condition at San Francisco General Hospital, according to the incessant news reports. Of course, the news didn't call him Earl. They called him "a third alleged assailant." Alleged was right, considering that Earl, pink number three, was in the hospital when Byron got sliced open.

Everything about Byron's death was beginning to smell.

As if cued by her thought, she began to smell something odd for Frisco General—moreys. Lots of moreys. She closed on the front of the hospital, and she could see cop cars scattered everywhere, flashers cutting through the humid darkness. An aircar from BaySatt News was hovering over Potrero Avenue, pointing at some disturbance.

Angel slowed her walking and began to listen.

"Chanting?"

A group of a few dozen moreaus, mostly canines and foxes, were holding a sit-down protest in the lobby of the damn hospital. It sounded like they were chanting hymns to the cops.

Angel stopped her approach as police vans started driving up.

*Like hell they're going to let a morey in the building now.*

Angel had an inspiration.

She avoided the lobby and walked around to the Emergency entrance and the ambulance bays. No moreys here, as Angel had hoped. The protest was aiming for media attention, not at really disrupting the hospital's operation.

What it *did* do was disrupt security.

With all attention on the fracas out front, Angel managed to walk in to the Emergency Room, slip past the nurse's station, and make it to the elevators without being challenged. That was the easy part. Now she had to find Earl and get into his room.

In all the movies she'd seen where this was a problem, the hero always slipped into a lab coat and walked around the hospital unchallenged. Unfortunately, the hero was never a morey.

Before the elevator came, she heard a familiar voice coming up behind her. The voice of detective Kobe Anaka, the Asian cop.

*Oh, shit.*

She only had a second to think before Anaka and whoever he was talking to—the other voice was much too even and mannered for his partner, White—turned the corner and saw her. She backed away from the elevator, felt a door behind her along the opposite wall, and darted through it just as Anaka and a tall gray-haired human in a white coat came around the corner.

Damn it. She had backed into a closet with no extra room, even for her. She was wedged up against a hard plastic cleaning robot, and she couldn't close the door enough. The door was ajar, with the ten-centimeter gap facing out into the hall, toward Anaka and the doctor. She didn't want to climb up on the robot because the only place to stand seemed to be a touch-sensitive control panel and she'd probably turn the damn thing on by accident.

She was saved from discovery by the elevator. The elevator she'd been waiting for arrived just as Anaka walked into the line of sight with the closet. As if in response to Angel's frantic wish—he and the doctor walked into the elevator with apparently no thought as to why an empty elevator had stopped on this floor.

As soon as the doors of the elevator closed, Angel allowed herself to breathe again. In response, the closet door swung open. She left the closet with the cynical thought that at St. Luke's they had morey janitors rather than these robot things, and the moreys were probably cheaper—

Then it hit her. She needed to find Earl. It couldn't be

a coincidence that Anaka was here. The cop had to be here to see Earl.

Angel felt like a fool as she looked at the indicator for the elevator. It was going down—*down?*—and stopped at S-3. They were keeping Earl in the basement?

She wished she had paid attention to what those two had been saying; then she might know whether or not this was a wild goose chase.

Instead of waiting for the elevator, she bolted for the stairs. Inside the echoing concrete stairway, she took the steps half a flight at a time. If she was lucky, she'd reach the subbasement while Anaka and the pink doctor were still in earshot.

The last two flights were blocked by a chain and a sign reading, "authorized personnel only." She only noticed because she almost ran into it.

The door to the third sublevel opened on an empty corridor. Angel didn't see any of the directory holos saying "you are here." Angel guessed the assumption was that, if you were down here, you were supposed to know where you were going. A map wouldn't have been much help anyway, since she didn't know where they were keeping Earl.

Angel listened. The tile on the floor and the walls gave a distorted audio picture, but she was pretty sure she couldn't hear more than half a dozen people roaming the halls. Most of those seemed stationary. After some thought, she could pick out footsteps way down the hall on her right. The subdued voices were difficult to make out, but Angel bet that they were Anaka's and the Doc's.

She followed them.

If she didn't blatantly walk in front of a nurse's station or a security booth, she might be all right. There wasn't much she could do about the cameras that panned the corridor—except hope that the protest out front had captured everybody's attention.

She was following the two away from the biggest concentration of human noise. "Too much like the morgue," she whispered to herself. She was reminded of Byron in the basement of St. Luke's. The too-cold walls, the disinfectant that didn't hide the smell of blood and decomposition.

Eventually, her cautious pace lost her the audio clues to where Anaka and the Doc had gone—and with the disinfectant everywhere, tracking by scent was useless.

She slowed even further, but kept going.

*What now?*

She turned a corner and bumped into a gurney.

The top edge hit her at about neck level, and under a sheet, she felt a cold foot hit her face. She fell backward, and the gurney rocked forward slightly on locked wheels.

Angel rubbed her face and slowly got to her feet.

"Fuck. It *is* the morgue." She slapped herself on the forehead for saying that out loud.

She could smell the body on the gurney now—blood, shit, and death. The corridor beyond ended in a massive pair of double doors. That was where most of the odor of decomposition was hanging.

"Wrong number," she said, slightly disgusted with herself. Now she could either continue this fruitless search for the third punk, or she could slip out and pretend this never happened.

Never happened was starting to sound good.

Then she heard a familiar voice—Detective Anaka's.

*They had been going this way . . .*

Through the double doors she couldn't make out exactly what was being said, but she suddenly wanted to see what was going on. Especially because Anaka sounded royally pissed.

Angel walked up to the doors, but the windows were much too high for her to look through. If she opened the door, even a crack, the people inside would notice her right off. She draped an ear against the door. Anaka was saying, "What do you mean, accident?"

"An error in the computer. It's rare, but it happens." It was the pink Doc's voice.

"Do you know what your 'error' does to our case?"

"I'm sorry—"

Angel wanted to see what was going on, but she needed nearly another meter of height to look through the window. She looked around her, and her gaze rested on the unattended gurney.

*How morbid,* she thought, smiling.

She unlocked the wheels and rolled the gurney in front of one of the doors. Then she climbed up on the corpse. Something slipped out of her pocket, but she barely noticed when she saw the scene on the other side of the small window.

She already had suspicions about what she was going to see, but it was still something of a shock.

Anaka was standing in the room beyond, running his fingers through jet-black hair. "How the hell could this—"

Doc, in surgical garb *sans* mask, was seated on a stool in a corner of the room tapping at a small computer terminal. "The computer forgot that he was a flush addict."

"How the hell did the computer 'forget' that?"

Angel stared at the centerpiece of the room.

Earl, the third pink goon, rested, naked, on an operating table under a frosty white light. His eyes were open and staring. His abdomen and waist were a study in browns, reds, and blues—his genitalia purple and swollen. Quite dead.

"Oops," Angel whispered.

"If we knew that, things like this wouldn't happen. Somebody flubbed his file, a random power spike, maybe it never was in his file to begin with. As it is, with his flush-weakened nervous system, the muscle relaxant we gave him pushed him into cardiac arrest."

"You're not making me happy."

Angel decided she was overstaying her welcome. Her reason for being here was on a slab. No sense waiting for someone to pick her up for trespassing.

She climbed off the gurney and headed for the elevators.

If Earl was dead, could they try to hang a murder rap on her? It *was* self-defense, and they'd never even charged her with assault.

But . . .

For the first time, Angel began to worry about her own furry hide.

She made her way to the elevators at a dead run and told the computer "ground floor" three times before it understood her. Ellis' paranoia had slipped in and had taken root. She was convinced that Earl's death was no "accident." It was a rock-solid gut feeling that also told her to get out of the hospital *now.*

The doors opened on the corridor of the Emergency Room, letting in sounds of nonhuman singing and sirens. She turned the corner and started to bolt for the exit.

And ran straight into a pink cop. At least that's what Angel pegged him for when she began backing up. Human, two meters, suit, wearing a nearly invisible white crew cut that made him look like one of the Knights if the light was at the right angle. His skin was pale, nearly translucent.

Under his arm was a bulge that spoke of artillery that was ten-millimeter or better—maybe even a machine pistol. As Angel continued to back up, she saw that the suit was too expensive for a local boy, and decided the guy was Fed.

She could see a throat-mike peeking out from behind the knot in his tie, and the nearly-invisible earpiece.

She had just decided that she was in really big trouble when she realized that the Fedboy's smell was out of sync. Hunting excitement tinged by just a touch of fear. He wasn't even looking at her.

He pushed Angel out of the way and made for the elevators. It gave her a chance to see beyond the Fed's sunglasses. Angel thought she saw red irises.

The encounter had lasted less than a second, and she was not one to question good fortune. She split Frisco General, deciding that sneaking into the human hospital had been an all-around bad move on her part.

# CHAPTER 7

It was close to midnight when Angel made it home. Lei's quiet, regular breathing told her that her roommate was asleep in the darkened living room. Angel found Lei curled into a brown ball on the couch, tail wrapped around her muzzle. The comm was in the middle of a pop-political broadcast with a panel of commentators indulging in verbal mud wrestling.

"—Harper is the only potential presidential candidate who's advocating peace—" one of the ones to the left was saying.

"Appeasement you mean." An off-screen voice stepped on his line.

"Merideth's approval ratings have been in free-fall since the crisis began," he continued, ignoring the interruption. "The Democrats are in the worst position they've been in since the CIA scandal. If her Committee manages to reach some diplomatic sol—"

"You must be kidding, Fred. No one seriously thinks a NOA party candidate can win the presidency—"

Angel walked in front of the comm and heard Lei stirring behind her. After a long yawn Lei said, "Finally came back? What did you think you were doing?"

"I don't know."

On the screen, a balding pink was leaning into the camera frame to berate somebody. "You remember what you said about the Greens, Dave? The country's ready for a candidate like Har—"

Angel shook her head. "Wanted to talk to the punk I put in the hospital."

Lei sat up and stretched, Angel could hear her joints pop. "What could he possibly have to say?"

"—the None-of-the-Abovers are a lot more radical than the Greens," The one woman on the show was saying.

"I don't know," Angel said, "the bastard's dead."

"What?"

"—ideth avoided getting tarred with the same brush that hit the rest of the Democrats during the CIA indictments in '54. He's bounced back from worse numbers—"

"I accidentally walked into the morgue. The guy was laid out colder than—"

"Sure it was the same guy?"

"—had over two years to recover for the '56 election, with a better economy, and this 'alien' business isn't helping him—"

Angel walked around the coffee table and sat down next to Lei. "How many tattooed pinks you think check in there with their dicks looking like overripe eggplant? It's him."

"Didn't see anything about it on the news."

Angel picked the remote off of the table and put her feet up. The argument on the comm was reaching a fever pitch with three or four people shouting at once.

"—Gregg and the Constitutionalists are the Democrats' only real rivals—"

"—believe those 'aliens' were cooked in some gene-lab—"

"—ideth had any sense he'd resign now and give his successor a cha—"

"—NOA never held more than ten seats, and that was fifteen years—"

Angel changed the comm to a sports channel, and hit the mute button. "News is fucked, news's always fucked. The police're probably scared shitless about what news of another death'd do."

"How'd the guy die?"

"Some computer glitch."

Lei shook her head and Angel could hear her tail batting against the couch. "Why keep digging? What's the point?"

Angel was silent for a long time before answering. "If I just sit around, I might have to start *thinking* about this crap, and I'm not ready for that."

"You might have to."

Angel waited for an explanation.

"Half a dozen reporters called while you were out. It's not going to be long before you have to talk to them."

"Why me?" Angel tried to sink into the couch.

"And that priest what's-his-name—"

"Collor called again, great. Any other good news?"

"Well, this lawyer—"

"DeGarmo?"

Lei nodded. "Wants to know about funeral arrangements for Mr. Dorset."

"Byron."

"Huh?"

"Never mind." Angel sighed.

"So, are you going to tell me where you got this car?"

Angel turned to see Lei staring at her, muzzle cradled in her hands.

With Sunday came a stormfront sweeping in from the northwest. When Angel glanced out the window, the steel-wool stormclouds seemed to be parked in a holding formation across the Golden Gate and over Oakland. The spires of Downtown were still sunlit, carving light holes in the dark horizon. All backed by the bone-white eggshell that had swallowed Alcatraz.

Daily, hourly even, the city was becoming more surreal.

A chain of lightning flashes began to her right and shot back to the west.

Angel looked back down to Twenty-third. The Dodge Electroline van was still there. "He hasn't moved."

"You're going to let one guy and a van trap you here all day—"

"He's been pointing a vid unit up here."

Lei walked up next to her and waved out the window. "You can't avoid reporters forever. They're like children, the more you deny them something, the harder they go after it."

Angel turned away from the window as the sound of thunder reached them. She didn't want to mention the fact that she thought that the van wasn't a reporter. The van was much too generic—a solid unmarked gray job. And the guy with the vid unit bore an uncomfortable resemblance—down to the reddish eyes—to the Fedboy she'd run into at Frisco General.

Angel shrugged. "What the fuck? Like you said, it's inevitable."

Angel walked back to her room and opened her underwear drawer.

In the drawer, under a collection of pink-designed clothing she owned and never actually used, was a Beretta 031-S nine-millimeter automatic—a matte-black carbon fiber design that fired caseless ammo. She emptied a few dozen rounds of ammunition out of a sock that had been balled up near the back of the drawer.

Lei's voice came from behind her. "What the hell is that?"

Angel didn't look up. She arranged the various components on the clean area on top of the dresser. "You should know what a gun looks like."

"What are you doing with one?"

"Cleaning and loading the damn thing."

Lei watched for a long time as Angel did her best to undo a few years of neglect. When she began to load it, Angel said, "Don't worry, Lei. I'm not about to take potshots at some vid guy."

"Thinking of getting yourself into trouble, aren't you?"

Angel rummaged in her closet until she came out with a loose blouse that would cover the gun when she shoved it in her jeans. "All I'm thinking about is the possibility that a screw-loose morey who offed Byron might still be out there and might have enough reason to do me—"

Lei looked unconvinced.

"Believe me, I am trying hard to avoid becoming a charter member of the paranoia parade." Angel walked out of her room and back to the bay windows. The stormfront was still stationary, and so was the van. "It ain't easy."

Lei stayed by the door to Angel's room. "What are you going to do?"

"Right now? Visit Byron's condo. Nice low-risk activity that shouldn't attract anyone's attention."

"I'll go with you—"

"You don't have—"

Lei walked up and put a hand on Angel's shoulder. "To keep you from doing anything stupid."

Angel sucked in a breath, about to say something, and thought better of it. She spared a last glance at the pink in the van with the camera and said, "Let's go."

Down the stairs to the front door, Angel added, "I wish I knew where they got my address and the comm number."

"It's their job."

As they passed the first-floor apartment, Angel heard the ghost of Balthazar's comm. The explosions and boinging sound effects made everything feel that much more surreal. Angel thought about the old, nearly blind lion sitting alone in his apartment, watching the same cartoons over and over again. For some reason, all the humor had leeched out of the image. Now it seemed nothing if not tragic.

It seemed that even Balthazar wasn't immune to the change sweeping her life—even if it was only her perspective.

Angel opened the door and stepped down to the sidewalk. The Fedboy/cameraman, who had intermittently pointed a vid out the driver's side window on the van, was nowhere to be seen. The van was still parked across the street, and the only noise was the distant thunder—

Angel felt her hand creeping toward her waistband. She restrained herself. She looked up and down the street. A few moreys were gathered at an intersection up the hill.

"*Angelica Lopez!*" came a call from down the street. Angel turned with Lei to see a too-perfect-looking hispanic pink making his way up the hill toward them. Following him was a spotted-white ratboy with a remote vid setup. In an instant, the reporter was upon her. The rat was focusing the camera and Angel had the bad feeling that they were on a live feed, because the hispanic was already turning toward the camera and saying, "Daniel Pasquez, here with a BaySatt news exclusive—"

"Fuck this." Angel made an end run around the camera, stepping over the camera rat's naked pink tail.

The rat panned after her and Angel felt a hand on her shoulder. Angel slowly turned to see Pasquez. "Miss Lopez—"

"Get your hand off of me."

"Miss—"

"I'm not here to boost your ratings. Move the hand or you'll shit your own teeth for a week."

Pasquez gently let go of her shoulder. "If you could please give me a few minutes—"

Angel turned and walked to the BMW. Lei had beat her to it. Apparently the press didn't think she mattered. Behind her she heard Pasquez saying, "Don't you want your view heard?"

Angel gave him the finger without looking back. "What an asshole," she said as she hit the combination on the BMW, letting her and Lei in.

Lei got into the passenger seat. "Do you think spouting off at him was a good idea?"

"I don't give a shit." Angel floored the car and rocketed down the hill, leaving Pasquez and the ratboy running for whatever vehicle they were using. "When I find out who leaked my address—"

"Where exactly are we going?"

"South Beach Towers."

Lei let out a whistle of air from the side of her muzzle.

Angel weaved the BMW past the construction clinging to Sixteenth as she aimed for the coast. Without realizing it, she turned on to Mission and drove toward The Rabbit Hole.

"Jesus Christ." She had to slow down because there were fire engines crowding the street. Traffic had slowed to a crawl. Angel could smell the smoke through the air recyclers before she even saw the rubble where the bar used to be.

"The bastards burned the place down."

"It could be an accident—"

"Bullshit." Angel hit the comm on the dash and started scanning through channels hoping to catch some word on what was happening.

She had to stop because one of the ambulances ahead

of her was lifting off. As the ambulance cleared ahead of her, she *saw* what was happening.

The comm latched on a news station. "—of arson. This bar was the scene of the alleged attack police believe—"

The pink Angel saw across Mission was white, slight of build, and wore a leather jacket. She had a flaming sword tattoo and a stupid smile on her face. She was almost hidden from view in an alley across the street from the chaos.

She was totally bald.

Damn it!

Horns blared behind the BMW. Lei said something, but Angel didn't listen. Instead, she popped the door on the car and dived out after the pink.

Angel cleared the twenty meters separating them in five running steps. She was in the air in a ballistic arc aimed at the pink's neck before the woman turned to notice a crazed rabbit pouncing on her.

The pink's eyes went wide, and she started raising her arms.

"Shi—" she began to say.

Then Angel landed on the evil twitch with both feet. The flames across the street roared in her ears and Angel had to shout to hear herself. "*You fucked shitheads!*"

Angel's head throbbed with sirens, the roar of flames, the smell of smoke, air heavy with humidity from the hoses, and the vicious pink face framed by wet, dirty sidewalk—

Pinky tried to push her off, but Angel grabbed both sides of the bald head and put her foot into the pink's throat. Pinky gagged and pushed harder but Angel had her fingers firmly hooked around Pinky's ears. A jagged earring was cutting into Angel's hand.

"*You want to burn? You want to fucking burn?*" Angel let go of one ear and reached for the Beretta. "*You wanna see Hell?*"

Pinky's eyes opened even wider as she saw the gun. She redoubled her efforts to dislodge Angel, but fighting and trying to breathe at the same time seemed beyond her.

"*Angel!*" called a voice from behind.

Angel brought the gun out of her pants.

"*What are you doing?*" The voice was Lei.

Christ, what the hell *was* she doing? Was she going to turn this pink twitch into street-pizza with the cops only a few—

Angel whipped her head around to look back at the fire. Thank God, she thought. Everyone was still intent on the torch *The Rabbit Hole* had become. It and three adjacent buildings.

If she didn't draw any more attention to herself, she wouldn't be up on charges for the gun she was waving around. What the hell had she been thinking?

She took her foot off Pinky's neck, letting her roll away. Pinky made a croaking noise, and there was a slight tug from Angel's left hand.

Angel had kept a grip on the jagged earring.

"Crazy freaked hairball," Pinky managed to croak.

"Let's go, Angel." Lei grabbed Angel's arm.

Angel slipped the gun back into her waistband. "Fuck this shit."

Pinky looked her right in the eye as Lei led her out of the alley. "We know who you are."

"Bullshit."

"Come on, Angel." Lei kept dragging her back to the BMW.

When they reached the BMW, Angel could hear Pinky croaking, "A flaming sword of righteousness—" Then the door closed.

Angel floored the car as fast as she could move, past the bottleneck.

"What is possessing you, girl? You looked about to kill—"

"I was."

"Are you going to start blitzing out on me? If you are, I'd like to know. You going to jump any human you run into now—"

"She wasn't *any* human."

"Then *who* the *fuck* was she? And why were you tap dancing on her neck?"

Angel turned down Beale, under the old Embarcadero Freeway on-ramp. As the BMW passed under the new

Oakland Bay Bridge, she said, "She, or someone like her, set that fire."

"How the fuck do you know that?"

"You saw. She's Knights of Humanity—"

"So-fucking-what? Is it suddenly open season on every freako nutball group out there? That's half this city, Angel. I don't think you have enough bullets."

*"Don't you see what's happening?"* Angel slammed on the brakes and a green GM Maduro laid on the horn and swerved around them.

"What?"

"They set that fire in retaliation. Someone else is going to retaliate for that, it's going to keep going, someone has to, to . . ." Angel leaned her head against the steering wheel. Why did she feel that she was spinning down into some dark abyss? She told herself that the smell of smoke that was clinging to her fur was making her dizzy.

"Has to what?"

Angel felt her eyes watering. "God, I don't know."

Lei hugged Angel's shoulders. "You've been stressed out. It's understandable. Let's go find that condo you inherited and get you something to drink, all right?"

Angel nodded, and took a deep breath. "Sorry, Lei. I've been losing it lately."

South Beach Towers was at the corner of Stanford and Townsend, right on the coast of the bay. In fact, it sat right on the terminus beyond which the Embarcadero and a few million tons of landfill slipped underwater in the '34 quake. Now that she could see it without the benefit of fog, Angel thought the look of the city might improve immeasurably if the white concrete and black glass neo-Aztec building joined the last half-klick of Townsend under the bay.

Angel parked the BMW in the reserved garage and led Lei up to the building.

The combination that DeGarmo gave her let her into the lobby, and she had to spend a few worthless minutes explaining the situation to the security personnel. The rent-a-cops were nice and professional enough that Angel could pretend that it didn't matter that she wasn't human.

Even so, Angel could smell the tension. The veneer was cracking on these guys.

It took a few minutes to double-check and clear Angel through to the elevators. They gave her a personalized ID card and promised that she was now on the computers and wouldn't be hassled again.

On the elevator ride up, she asked, "Did you see it?"

"What?" Lei asked.

"Those guys. They feel it, too, in the air."

"What's in the air?"

"Violence. We aren't immune here. People are beginning to realize it."

"You're just paranoid."

The doors whooshed open on the fifteenth floor, where Byron had his apartment. "Lei, I think it's only a matter of time before all Hell breaks loose."

"This isn't New York or Los Angeles. I think you're too close to all this. You're losing perspective."

Angel led her down a corridor to apartment 156. She tapped in the combination on the keypad next to the door. "What's so different about San—"

Angel stopped talking as the door swung open on Byron's apartment.

They both stood there, silent, staring through the door.

"Shit." Angel finally said.

"I'll go call the police," Lei said.

Angel nodded, not really listening. She walked into the room, stepping over cushions that had been tossed from the couch and shredded. The coffee table was in three pieces, the glass top shattered. The wall-to-wall pile carpeting had been cut neatly into five-centimeter-wide strips, as had the upholstery on what remained of the furniture.

Angel could smell a faint animal musk hanging in the air. Canine or feline, she couldn't tell. It had taken a while to fade, but she knew it wasn't Byron she was smelling.

*Yes,* Angel thought, *Lei had to go to the lobby.*

That was the comm there, and there, and there— Angel thought she even saw a piece of it on the balcony.

Angel walked through the rubble to the remains of the wet bar and hoped the folks who trashed the joint had left her that drink.

# CHAPTER 8

They were seated out on the patio, under a blackening sky, and Angel was having a tough time figuring out what else could go wrong.

"Did you notice anything missing?" Anaka asked.

"I told the first cops. It wasn't my condo." Angel refused to sit down or even look at the Asian cop. Anaka was just the latest in a series of uniforms, detectives, and lab guys who were busy tearing the wreckage apart. She'd given a statement to one of the uniforms, and she didn't want to go over it again. "Same damn questions, again? Why not zip off and leave me alone—"

She heard Anaka inhale as if he was about to retort. Instead, he hit her with another question. "When was the last time you were in this apartment?"

"Week ago Wednesday. Answer to that hasn't changed in the last half hour."

"It is possible that the humans we're holding—"

Angel whipped around. "The *hell* I'm supposed to know if a trio of hairless geeks could've managed a little party time here?"

Anaka was rubbing his temples. "Miss Lopez, I wish you'd be more cooperative."

"Why you bothering? You have your suspects. They're going down. Your job's over." Angel walked up to Anaka. With him sitting and her standing, they were eye to eye. Under the smell of the lightning, the cop was shedding stress and tension like old fur.

"Sure," she said with an insincere smile. "The fuckheads did *this* too, make life easy for yourself."

"I'm trying to do my job here. There's more to this—" Anaka looked around and stood up.

"Yeah, like I make a shitload of difference?"

Anaka didn't look like he was paying attention. He was looking back into the apartment, where the police were still sifting through debris. The forensics people were dusting the place and sweeping an UV laser around in their search for biological material and prints—paw and/or finger.

Anaka stepped over to the door and slid it shut. Suddenly Angel was reminded of Dr. Ellis. She remembered the rather tense byplay between the two pink cops. White didn't want to deal with Anaka's "conspiracies." Anaka had suspected—

"Something funny about the autopsy." Angel said.

Anaka whipped around. "What do you know about that?" Suddenly she could see all of Ellis' paranoia mirrored in Anaka.

"Ever find out why Ellis the not-a-vulpine-expert was assigned to cut up the corpse?"

"No." Anaka warily backed away from the doors. "I've been trying to contact Ellis on the substance of the autopsy."

"Did she mention a morey did him?"

"What? How do you know that?"

"Ellis told me when I cornered her yesterday. About to crap her pants, too." She was glad to see somebody *else* look confused. Even though the expression on Anaka's face only lasted a second.

Anaka nodded as if something just made sense to him. "Falsified the autopsy, then she panicked. *That's* why she's disappeared . . ." Angel was about to ask him about what happened to Ellis, but he went on, changing the subject. There was an edge of fear, or paranoia, in Anaka's voice. "This is bigger than you know."

He said it with such conviction that Angel backed up to the railing. Chain-reaction lightning shot across the sky, and for the first time she noticed how fatigued he looked. The rumpled suit he wore was the same one he'd been wearing in the morgue. Might have been the same suit he'd worn to *Ralph's.* "What are you talking about?"

Anaka walked up next to her as the peal of thunder reached them. The wind began to pick up, and the few last remaining shards of sunlight raced south, across the bay.

"The first big quake, it was the fires that almost killed this town." Anaka stared out at the water, towards the dome. His voice became harder and more distant. "In '34, it was money. The quake, martial law, the recession, the civic restructuring . . . This town was bought and sold like it was a public auction. Cops rented out as hired thugs, firemen paid protection money—"

"What's your point?"

Anaka turned toward her. "I'm not an enemy."

"You're *part* of that machine."

"No." Anaka shook his head. "For twenty years— A quarter century since the quake, and things haven't changed."

Another bolt of lightning tore open the sky, and a minute long roar of thunder followed close on its heels, vibrating the railing Angel leaned against. A drop of moisture struck her square on the nose.

Anaka was going on now, like Angel wasn't even there. "The DA's office is rushing a conviction on the shoddiest evidence I've seen since the National Guard stopped shooting looters."

Rain began to gently patter the balcony, and the rumblings were closing the gap on the flashes.

"They say they want to shut down the Knights—" Anaka was raising his voice now. All she heard of the rest of his sentence was: "VanDyne Industrial?"

"The ones who rebuilt the Pyramid?" she shouted over the storm.

"And the cable cars, and half of downtown between Market and Telegraph Hill. They own this building, and most of the condos overlooking the bay." The rain finally cascaded upon them in full force, sheeting across the balcony in rhythmic waves. "*Byron Dorset worked for them,* and if there's a central cog in the San Francisco 'machine' it's VanDyne."

"Does that have anything to do—"

Anaka shook his head. "I'm working on it. Help me."

He slid the door open and rushed inside, Angel on his

heels. In the apartment, the only thing Angel could smell was her own wet fur. "What about Detective White?"

"He's a good cop." There could have been an edge of sarcasm in his voice.

"White doesn't like you, does he?"

Anaka shrugged. "Few people in the department do, I'm used to it."

She looked at the cops and the forensics guys who were packing things up. Apparently their job was completed. A balding black human walked up to them and addressed her. "The place's all yours now, though I'd suggest you take pictures for the insurance companies before you clean up."

"You're done?" There was a slight hint of disbelief in Anaka's voice. "That was damn quick, Beirce."

The man turned to Anaka as if he'd just now bothered to notice him. He ran a hand through what was left of his hair. "And what're *you* doing here? No meat lying around—you *did* make Homicide, didn't you? Paint's still wet on that suit."

"Since when does it take less than an hour to dust up a crime scene?"

"Fuck you. Just because you wear civvies now don't mean you tell me my business."

"Listen—"

"No, *you* listen. I do what I have to do and get out of the lady rabbit's hair—"

"Fur." Angel said.

"Whatever. So, *Detective* Anaka, I suggest you pack your paranoia and do likewise. And if you need a report, you know where you can file it."

Beirce turned around and left the apartment, leading a platoon of men carrying equipment. The uniforms followed, leaving Anaka and Angel alone in the living room.

"What did you *do* to that guy?"

"Me?" Anaka shook his head. "Nothing." Anaka sighed. "I'm going to go before my partner starts missing me, but we'll need to talk later."

"Sure," Angel said, "for all the good it'll do."

"One thing though." Anaka pulled something out of his pocket. "Would you stop poking around on your own?"

"Huh?" She tried to look innocent.

He handed her a folded up paper that she instantly recognized. It was Byron's letter, wrapped around the Earthquake's season tickets.

"Where?" Angel asked as she reflexively stuck her hand in the pocket of her jeans. She began to remember feeling something drop while she was watching Earl's corpse.

"You dropped them outside the door to the morgue."

She took the tickets and the letter and replaced them in her pocket. "I'm sorry. I don't know why I—"

"Just *don't* any more."

She shook her head and felt stupid. She was way out of her depth and felt like things had flown totally beyond her grasp. She didn't say anything as Anaka let himself out.

The BMW kicked up a sheet of water over the sidewalk as Angel pulled up to her house.

"The van's gone," Lei said.

Angel looked at the spot where the gray Dodge van had been watching their apartment. Nothing. "They probably saw what's-his-name get shit for footage and gave up." It would be comforting to think they'd just been reporters.

"I suppose."

They both got out of the car and ran for the door, splashing across a sidewalk that was becoming a shallow river. The storm was still gaining in intensity. The rapid-fire lightning flashes were now simultaneous with the thunder.

The door was open.

"Shit." Angel pulled the Beretta out of her pants.

"You didn't ditch that thing?" Lei asked.

"Why?"

"There were a dozen cops—"

"I was an innocent victim, why search— Damn it, did you leave the door open?"

Lei looked at the door which had swung inward with a slight touch from Angel. "I don't know. I could've in all that confusion when we left."

A blast of wind slammed the door into the interior hall. Angel covered the hall and the stairs with the gun.

"Who're you going to shoot? Balthazar could've—"

"Almost forty, barely leaves his apartment during weather like this?" Angel stepped into the hall and started edging up the stairs, leading with the gun.

Lei followed, keeping a respectful distance behind her. "Are you going to shoot some overeager reporter?"

"At least make him crap his pants. Close the door."

Lei pushed the door shut with her foot. Angel asked, quietly, "Do you smell anything?"

"Besides us?"

Angel nodded. Lei shook her head no.

Maybe she was wrong and all she could smell was her own wet fur, but Angel could swear she could smell something else. Something else that was alien to this house. Neither canine, lepine, or Balthazar's leonine scent. Not an animal smell at all.

*Fake pine?*

The door to their apartment was closed. There seemed no sign of any forced entry. Angel backed up and leveled the gun at the doorway. She waved Lei over. "Open it. Then stand back."

"Is this smart?"

"Do it."

Lei stood next to the door and punched in the combination. Then she stepped back and cowered as if she expected some sort of explosion. The door swung open a few centimeters, and Angel stood for nearly ten seconds, waiting.

She could feel her own pulse in her neck, and there was the copper taste of excitement in her mouth. Her breath tried to burn her nose.

She took a deep breath and dove through the door.

Through the door, she swept the gun to cover the living room from the kitchenette, past the bay windows, and then to the hall to the bedrooms. She rolled into the hall between the bedrooms and covered, in turn, her room, the bathroom, and Lei's room. It took all of three seconds to see the apartment was empty.

Angel slumped against the doorframe to the bathroom,

hyperventilating, pointing her gun at the floor. Lei took a few tentative steps into the living room. "Safe?"

Angel nodded, panting.

"Would you *please* put the gun away?"

She nodded again, unable to get the breath to talk, and clicked the safety on the Beretta. She went and tucked it back in the underwear drawer. There was a nearby lightning strike that shook the house. The lights flickered.

She stood, leaning against the dresser in her room, catching her breath. The shower started, and she realized how wet and miserable she was. She walked back to the bathroom and sat on the john. "Leave some hot water," Angel told Lei through the fogged-glass partition.

As she waited for the shower, Angel kept telling herself that it wasn't paranoia. There really was something rotten going on here. It was perfectly reasonable, what she just did. Someone—she wished she knew who—could have been waiting for them.

She put her head in her hands. Yeah, but jumping that pink Knight on the street today, that *wasn't* reasonable. A fine line she was treading here, and at the moment she didn't know exactly what side of it she was on. It didn't help matters that city employees were feeding into her paranoia.

Detective Anaka just about flat out said that all the corrupt forces in the city government were conspiring to pin Byron's murders on the two punks. Dr. Ellis said Byron got clawed by a moreau, covered the fact up, and disappeared.

And Byron worked for VanDyne Industrial.

What the hell did that mean?

What could a Brit fox named Byron Dorset be doing for one of the major stockholders in the San Francisco civic machine?

And what was he doing on Eddy Street? Was he really going to meet a bunch of bald schizo pinks in their own apartment? If so, why'd he get whacked by a morey?

Anaka was right, this was all *his* job. She wasn't equipped to do any half-assed investigating. She was just a piece of street trash from Cleveland who barely had enough smarts to keep her hide intact. Just thinking about all of this made her head hurt.

The only person she knew who was equipped to unravel something like this was down in Los Angeles behind a blockade of moreaus and National Guard. Even then, she'd be lucky if Nohar remembered her.

So, was she going to sit on her ass and wait until she talked to Anaka again?

"Yeah, right." Angel said with all the sarcasm she could muster. Okay, skulking into other people's buildings was a bad idea. But she'd be damned if she stopped trying to figure things out. Even if she was a half-assed investigator, she was the only one she could trust.

Besides, she had to straighten out Byron's affairs. If certain questions came up in the process, no one could blame her for asking—right?

The dryer came on for a few minutes and then Lei came out of the shower. "It's all yours."

Angel grunted a monosyllable.

Lei leaned forward and rubbed noses. "I understand, but you *could* try and relax a little bit."

"I'll try," Angel said as she shrugged out of her wet clothes.

# CHAPTER 9

San Francisco awoke to a positively ugly morning. The sky was asphalt black. The wind was trying to shake the windows apart. A hazy fog evolved into rain so heavy that Angel could barely see across the street out her bay window.

As far as Angel was concerned, the weather was the least ugly part of her day. She made the mistake of waking up for work, eating an abbreviated breakfast, and driving down to *Ralph's* to start her shift—all pretending that last week hadn't happened.

She should have known better. In a universe that allowed her to drive up to *Ralph's Diner* in a hundred K worth of BMW, nothing could be normal. As she drove toward the diner, she could see something odd was going on, even through the rain. There was too much traffic hovering around, especially for this early—*Ralph's* never had much of a breakfast crowd—and way too many cars for this weather.

Angel rolled past without stopping. She could read the logo of several news services. She pulled to the curb and played with the expensive comm set into the dash. She punched up the BaySatt news feed, and there was Daniel Pasquez, male hispanic archetype, doing the live feed from *Ralph's*.

"Great."

So much for trying to lead a normal life.

She pulled the BMW over at the crest of a hill. She flipped a few switches on the dash, and the small screen of the BMW's built-in comm activated for outgoing calls.

Having a car with a full comm unit, *that* she could get used to.

She called in sick to *Ralph's.*

The response was typical Sanchez. "Why aren't you here?"

"I'm not coming in."

Sanchez did not look pleased. "What do you mean, 'not coming in'? Where're you calling from—" Angel could see lights behind Sanchez, they were covering his little manager office. What did Sanchez think he was doing?

"I mean I am not coming in. And where I'm calling from is none of your business."

"Damn it, what do I tell these reporters?"

Angel just stared at the screen. Was this greaseball serious? "What?"

"You're just going to blow this opportunity—"

Damn it. Sanchez *was* serious. All he saw in all this was a chance to get some free advertising. The fact that this was her *life* that was being screwed with didn't seem to occur to him. Either that, or he assumed the sad proposition that his every employee lived and breathed that lickspittle job as much as I'm-the-manager-and-have-no-life did.

"You're right, Sanchez. I shouldn't call in sick."

He looked visibly relieved. "Thank—"

"I quit."

*"What!"* The look on Sanchez's flabby face was almost worth the months of irritation she'd endured.

"I said I quit. I'm tired of your flabass dimestore greasepit. I'm sick of getting shafted on hours because you're boffing Judy. I'm sick of someone who only serves moreys because humans wouldn't stand him. Go wait on tables yourself—your customers will fucking love you."

To make everything clear, she gave him the finger and hit the mute button. It was wonderful to watch, even without the sound. Sanchez's face went red, and he began shouting at her, spraying the screen. It was nearly ten seconds before he seemed to realize that he was coming down on her in front of reporters.

So much for his free publicity. Angel knew that if the

reporters couldn't get a hold of her, they'd be perfectly willing to give airtime to her manager throwing a rod.

She killed the comm and turned the car around to go home.

It was an odd feeling. She had never thought she'd miss that job, of all the shit places to work she'd been in, but her sudden unemployment worried her. Another part of her life she'd thought stable had crumbled so rapidly that she was still coming to grips with what she'd done when she got back to her apartment.

The calls started around eight, about the time she got back home.

At nine, reporters were calling every ten minutes.

After a while, the opportunity to bitch the media leeches out was outweighed by the annoyance factor and by 10:30, she just told the comm to lock out all the incoming calls.

Amidst the forest of reporters, a few calls came from moreaus. All of those ended up being representatives of Father Collor and his people. They wanted her to think about nonhuman solidarity. She told them all to fuck off.

One call came from a bald human. He only stayed on screen long enough to say: "We know who you are."

The news off the comm wasn't much better once she got over the novelty of seeing her ex-manager getting it over the public net. There'd been a half-dozen incidents of cross-species violence in the city overnight, primarily concentrated in Chinatown during a power failure. There had only been one minor injury, but property damage was estimated at fifty thousand dollars. The vids panned down a street of broken storefronts, and one taxi that had the windows busted out.

They said that the incidents were probably the result of the suspected arson of *The Rabbit Hole.*

At noon, she killed the comm entirely.

They were going to release Byron's body today. DeGarmo wanted to hear about funeral arrangements, too—

"Ahh, shit."

She didn't want to do this. But it had fallen on her head, and who was she kidding if she said she had something better to do? Better she do this than let it fall to someone who wanted to use it to make some political point.

And she'd be damned if she let that happen.

She turned the comm back on and called DeGarmo.

If she'd wanted to, she probably could have orchestrated the entire procedure over the comm. Somehow, that wouldn't have felt right. She had no desire to see Byron's corpse again, but she didn't think she could let him pass from St. Luke's unaccompanied. DeGarmo offered to supervise things for her. But, in the end, there was no way she could stay at home.

So, at 3:30 she met DeGarmo in the parking lot of St. Luke's Veterinary.

When Angel drove the BMW into the half-flooded parking lot, she saw DeGarmo for the first time in the flesh—a tall human, wearing a black trench coat that shone from the rain sheeting off of it. He hung back in the halo cast from sodium lamps mounted next to the ambulance bays. His hair was a matte-black crew cut that enhanced the thinness of a too-lean face.

Angel got out of the car and made for the shelter of the ambulance bays. It wasn't until she was up next to the lawyer that she realized exactly how tall he was. His waistline was just about eye level on her.

DeGarmo was holding out his hand by the time she reached him, Angel shook it with both of hers.

"I'm pleased to finally meet you in person, Miss Lopez."

"Call me Angel," she told him. "I'm sick of 'Miss Lopez.' Ain't mine, the INS picked it for my grandmother."

DeGarmo gave a noncommittal shrug. "We need to get your authorization to move the body. Then we can go to—" DeGarmo looked at a small palm-held computer. "Cabrillo Acres Funeral Home."

He looked up from the computer. "Can I ask why all the way down in Pacifica?"

"First place I called that handled moreaus."

DeGarmo led her into the building where a group of paramedics were standing around a u-shaped desk. As they approached, Angel asked DeGarmo, "How'd you end up in this? What's your angle?"

"Mr. Dorset retained me to handle this."

"How much did he pay you?"

"Don't worry, none of it is from the current estate."

"So when do *I* have to pay you something?"

"As long as it involves the settling of Mr. Dorset's affairs, you don't."

What kind of estate were they talking about? She'd avoided asking DeGarmo about that because it seemed tacky. She wondered about it all the way through the authorization procedure. Then there was the fact Byron did all this bequeathing to her in the nine days prior to his death.

DeGarmo acted as if that was normal.

Once she'd satisfied the bureaucracy, they rolled out a gurney with the sheeted body on it. It smelled of cold rot and disinfectant. It made Angel cringe inside. There was a ground ambulance waiting for the drive to Pacifica. Angel and DeGarmo flanked the body as the medics rolled it toward the waiting meat wagon.

"You can ride down with me," DeGarmo offered.

Angel shook her head. "I'll go with him." She patted one of Byron's sheeted hands—

"Hold it," she said.

"What?" DeGarmo and two medics said simultaneously.

Angel took in a deep breath. She smelled wet fur, blood, disinfectant—and something smelled wrong about the body. And there was something radically wrong with the shape of the hand under the sheet.

"Lift the sheet."

"Do you really want to do that?" asked the medic pushing the gurney. She was a hispanic woman, and her young human face had a look of concern on it. "I don't think you—"

"I need to see him." There was a terrible sinking feeling in Angel's gut. "Lift the sheet, now."

The four of them stood at the points of the compass around the body, blocking the door to the ambulance bay. The hispanic medic gave a questioning look to her partner, who shrugged. She shook her head, as if she thought it was a really bad idea, and lifted the sheet.

*"What the hell kind of fuckup is this!"* Angel screamed at the medic, before she'd even taken her hand off of the sheet.

It wasn't Byron. It wasn't even a fox.

Laying under the sheet was the body of a brown-furred canine who looked like he had taken a shotgun blast to the neck.

"Who the fuck is this?" Angel yelled.

The hispanic woman covered the body again and reached out for her. "Please, it's just some sort of mixup. I'm sure we'll be able to—"

The other medic practically ran back to the desk and picked up a receiver and began talking rapidly to someone.

Angel shrugged away from the woman. "Damn straight it's a mixup. Jesus-mother-humping-tap-dancing-Christ, *you lost him.*" Angel backed up and turned to the lawyer. "Can you *sue* these shitheads?"

At the sound of that, the nurse running the station got on another receiver and began talking to someone. The medic pulled the gurney and the unidentified corpse back into the hospital.

DeGarmo tried to calm her. "I'm sure this will be resolved in a few minutes."

"I don't like this shit," she said. "Too many people are *fucking* with me! Byron's been on the comm more times than the president and they *lost him.* What're they running here? *What?* Just because he's a morey means he's fucking interchangeable?"

They stuck her and DeGarmo in an empty waiting room and it took half an hour for the hospital's chief administrator to come down and "explain" what had happened.

The guy was a pink, of course, middle-aged, white, fat, bald, and sweating enough to look like he'd just come from the rain. She could smell the stress and fear off of the guy from ten meters away. The man's emotions were as subtle as a toxic waste dump. He had a salt-and-pepper mustache that seemed to grow whiter as he talked to them.

"It seems, Miss Lopez, that there was a computer error."

"What the fuck happened to—" DeGarmo put a hand on her shoulder to restrain her outburst.

She knew it was bad, whatever it was, otherwise they wouldn't have sent the boss down here. And Dr. Varberg—that's what it said on his ID tag—wouldn't look like he was about to crap his pants.

"Byron Dorset's ID number was transposed with that of another patient, a John Doe gunshot victim. That's why you picked up the wrong body."

Angel sucked in a breath and kept her voice level. "Okay, so what happened to Byron?"

The room was very quiet. Somewhere out in the hospital a public address system spouted something incomprehensible. It took a long while for the answer to come.

"John Doe's body was scheduled—" Varberg paused and rubbed his forehead with a pudgy hand.

"What happened to the body?" Angel said, getting up from her seat and trying hard to keep an even edge to her voice.

"It was cremated at 9:30 this morning." Varberg said quietly.

The scene froze, DeGarmo seated to Angel's right, Varberg standing in front of her. The air seemed to hang dead around her, making it hard to breathe. She tried to say something, but it only came out as a squeak.

"Miss—"

She shook her head violently and slammed her foot back into the chrome-vinyl chair she'd spent the last half hour sitting in. The chair buckled and bounced halfway up the wall behind it, tearing out a chunk of drywall. Varberg backed away, cowering, as if he expected to be next.

Angel took a few deep breaths, and looked back at DeGarmo. He had vacated his seat and was staring at the wreckage of Angel's chair.

She found her voice. "I've got money, right?"

DeGarmo looked at her and did a good job of regaining his composure. "Yes, I've filed the appropriate tax f—"

"Good. I'm retaining you to talk to this asshole." She pointed at Varberg. "Get what's left of Byron. File complaints, charges, whatever it is you do. Make his life hell." Angel walked to the door and yanked it open. "I've got a few calls to make."

She left to the sound of DeGarmo saying, "Does the hospital have an attorney I can talk to?" Then the door slammed shut.

She pushed her way to a public comm in the emergency room. She'd finally had enough bullshit.

It took her nearly ten minutes to get her call through the various extensions at BaySatt news, but she finally found herself facing a too-perfect hispanic face.

With a demonic grin that reawakened the pain in her cheek she asked, "So, Mr. Pasquez, you want a fucking-A exclusive?"

For close to an hour, Angel vented her spleen at St. Luke's, the cops who cared for little but busting the Knights, the reporters who were trying to make her life hell, the cops, the Knights themselves, the cops, Father Collor, the cops. . . .

She lost count of how many people she'd piss off if this aired, but for a while it made her feel better.

When 8:30 rolled around, Angel said, *"Five million?"*

She and DeGarmo were sitting in a rear booth of *Ralph's,* not because Angel was nostalgic, but because it was the closest place to St. Luke's she could think of—only a few blocks south.

The press was gone, and the place was occupied by a scattering of soaked moreys huddling in from the rain. DeGarmo was the only human other than Judy. Judy seemed unaware of this morning's events, and Sanchez was nowhere to be seen.

Lucky on all points.

A few rats in one corner turned to look at her when she shouted. Angel thought she recognized the black one.

DeGarmo nodded. "After estate taxes the net assets

that Dorset left you is about a hundred fifty thousand short of five million." He sipped his coffee impassively, as if he handed news like this to people all the time.

Angel sat, staring at the lawyer. She should be—she didn't know what she should be feeling. A cynical part of her mind kept saying she should be shitting a gold brick and bouncing off the ceiling. She'd just struck the lottery, her ship had come in, she was set for life. . . .

The problem was, the news had finally knocked out whatever feeling of stability she had left in her life. If things could change so damn quickly, *nothing* was certain.

She must've been staring quite a while because DeGarmo lowered his coffee. "Are you all right?"

Angel blinked. Was she all right? Could she even *know* if she was all right? "I'm fine, I guess. I need to get my bearings."

"I know it's quite an adjustment. One of the things Mr. Dorset hired me for was to get you over that hump, should it be necessary."

Admirable prescience on Byron's part.

What a fucking wonderful guy.

Angel started to realize exactly how pissed she was at Byron. He let her get blindsided by everything, without any warning, up to and including this damn will.

"Why didn't he tell me?"

"Pardon?"

"Damn it, if he made a will just a few days before—"

DeGarmo held up his hand. "Ahh, I see where you got the impression. No, Mr. Dorset was my client for ten years. His current will has been in force for most of that time."

"But he just met me—"

"He had a habit of changing the name of the bequest every time he entered a relationship. He named you the primary heir a week before he died. He changed the will frequently. I doubt the proximity of the change to his death represented anything sinister."

She was beginning to feel numb. "He changed it a lot?"

"Do you want to talk about this?"

"How many times?"

DeGarmo removed the palm computer from the breast pocket in his suit and referred to it. "Twenty-seven times in ten years. All female moreaus, California residents. All of them now receive a token bequest of forty thousand dollars."

She tried to do the calculations in her head, and failed. As if losing Byron wasn't enough, if the general chaos wasn't enough, there was a sinking feeling that what she'd thought of as something special might have been something routine, pedestrian, casual.

"Did he mention anything about a possible engagement?"

DeGarmo arched an eyebrow.

Angel closed her eyes. All this fiancée bullshit was people making assumptions. Byron never was going to propose anything.

"Miss Lo— Angel?"

"I'm fine." *I'm not crying,* she thought. She shook her head and tried to compose herself. "You looked at his estate. You were his lawyer for ten years. What did he do for a living?"

"He worked for VanDyne Industrial."

*Tell me what I don't know.* "What did he *do* for them?"

"The occupation he listed for the IRS was delivery. Other than that, I don't know specifics. I only helped him manage his money. How he managed such large compensations from VanDyne, I don't know."

"And you don't know jack about what he delivered."

DeGarmo nodded and sipped his coffee. "I know enough not to want to know."

# CHAPTER 10

When Angel made it home, her head was still swimming. DeGarmo had managed to blow whatever certainty she had left in her life. She was so distracted that she was halfway in the door and shaking the rain out of her fur before she heard human breathing from the darkened living room.

Her head shot up. She could barely smell the man over her own wet fur, but she knew it was Detective White before her eyes adjusted. It took a conscious effort to keep her hand from drifting to the gun in her waistband.

White sat on the couch in the living room, lit by the flickering light from the comm and the occasional lightning flash. The vision of the balding lump of rumpled humanity on her own couch was surreal enough to trigger a frightening wave of vertigo. Lei was nowhere to be seen.

"What are you doing here?" Angel asked, one hand clutching the top button of her soaked blouse. The last time she had seen this man in the flesh had been when she IDd Byron's corpse. Then, he'd tried to be comforting. Even when she had called him at the station—making him hock his takeout Chinese breakfast—the iron that had crept into his voice held barely a hint of the tempered glare that locked her on her entrance.

"Do you have any idea what you've done?" White hit a button on the remote and the picture on the comm froze. The reflection in his gray eyes made them molten lead bearings. The heat of his anger had sunk into the walls. Angel could smell it.

She glanced at the frozen picture on the comm and saw Pasquez's face.

Angel's latent paranoia was returning in full force.

Thank the lord that humans couldn't pick up on the scent cues, otherwise the way she was tensed could probably be used as just cause to blow her away.

"Where's Lei?"

"Frankly, I don't give a shit."

Christ, what was going on here? *Well, you knew you were going to piss people off talking to Pasquez,* she thought.

"How'd you get in here?"

White gave her a hard little smile. "I'm a cop, you little twitch. I can override any electronic lock in my jurisdiction—and I want to know what the hell you were thinking of when you talked to Pasquez."

"I have a right—"

White stood up and threw the remote down on the coffee table. *"I am sick of people's fucking rights."* He walked up to Angel, who still stood in the open doorway, dripping. She noticed that White had been in the apartment long enough to dry off. "You think you have the right to make all sorts of half-assed accusations? Where do you get off?"

She backed up a step. "Do you have a warrant?"

"I'm not here to arrest you. Just want you to know how grateful I am." He stood in front of her now, tensed to the breaking point. Angel was very careful not to move. "We *had* the Knights. Thought a morey shit like you'd appreciate that. But you had to shoot off your mouth, didn't you? Not only screw the case, but you stir up shit in this town from Internal Affairs and the mayor's publicist, to every shit-for-brains radical who's got a gripe against the city."

She was ripe with the scent of her own fear. "I'd like you to leave," she said with as calm a voice as she could muster.

White nodded. "I'm going. But ask yourself if you want to see Chino Hernandez and Dwane Washington out on the streets again. Because they're *all* the Knights we got now, and you pull any more fancy bullshit, they're going to walk."

He stepped up to her and raised her face with one finger under her chin. The finger was warm, soft, and hairless. The contact made Angel nauseous.

"This town's ready to take a header. Don't help push it—" White let go of her chin and moved past her out into the hall. As he started down the stairs, he added, "You might fall off the same cliff."

Angel stood there, shivering.

After a while, she calmed down and closed the door behind her. White had reminded Angel of a seminal truth—she did *not* like cops. Angel walked to the comm and unpaused the program White had recorded. It was Pasquez all right, him and his BaySatt news exclusive. The basic theme of which was, "what was the city trying to hide?"

As Pasquez rambled on in the background, she turned on the light in the living room and saw that White had been a fairly busy boy. On the coffee table must have been every single ramcard that had been left in the house. The cards were scattered like some mad rainbow-sheened game of solitaire.

Predictably, behind her she heard Father Alvarez De Collor's voice. Pasquez was asking Collor about the mess, in his capacity as the "voice of the nonhuman population." Apparently, "the nonhuman population"—she wished the media sometime, somewhere, would use the word moreau—wanted the real murder suspects prosecuted. Collor made the assumption that the killers were human, and implied that they might be cops. *Now there's the voice of peace,* Angel thought.

The nonhumans wanted empowerment. The nonhumans wanted to do to the Knights of Humanity what the Knights wanted to do to them. The nonhumans wanted better jobs, better housing, better medical care. The nonhumans wanted an end to discrimination.

If the nonhumans didn't get all this now, with a cherry on top, then, Collor said, "Los Angeles is not that far away."

Angel turned to look at the comm and got the closing shot of Collor in his full regalia. His priest's collar, and the full combat getup of the Brazilian strike team he used to belong to, way back when. That wasn't new, that was all Collor's radical priest schtick. What was new was the fact that the holster had a sidearm in it this time.

It had been federal law for two decades that it was a felony for a moreau to possess a firearm. Collor was smiling at the camera with a perfectly vicious show of teeth on his feline face. The expression dared anyone to pick him up for the offense.

"Great," Angel said.

Then the scene shifted and Pasquez was in an even more interesting interview.

The first thing she could see was the red flag with a white circle. In the circle was a stylized H that could have been a hacked representation of a double helix. It was the flag of the Knights of Humanity.

The camera faced a seated individual whose face was obscured by BaySatt's computer. He was human, and in contrast to Collar's field-grunt attire, this pink was wearing a stylized officer's uniform done up in urban camouflage.

Pasquez introduced him as "Tony X," prime mover and shaker of the Knights of Humanity.

"Oh, Christ," Angel said, it was already being cast as a war. This exclusive by BaySatt news just seemed an exercise in picking out the leading players in the soon-to-be televised drama.

Angel walked around the coffee table, staring at the screen in fascination, as if it was an oncoming car, or a canister containing some deadly biological weapon.

"We had no part in the death of Byron Dorset," said a computer-altered voice. "Individuals don't matter. The Knights are interested in the destiny of the species."

"You've been accused of promoting violence."

"Any violence the Knights are involved in is defensive in nature."

"Are you saying that the twelve alleged attacks on unarmed nonhumans in the past week were all cases of the Knights defending themselves?"

The computer-altered voice gained in intensity. "We are under assault, every human being in this country, by this plague of genetic *waste.* Anything the Knights can do to help this country wake up is an effort to save the race."

"You've been accused of advocating genocide—"

"Do you know what these things are?" Tony X stood up and walked to a table. He pulled aside a sheet of canvas that was on top of it to reveal a terrarium. Inside it was a black object about the length of Tony X's arm. "Look in here. This is an example of what we're harboring in this country."

Pasquez didn't interrupt as the camera zoomed in on the flopping creature in the tank. The thing was black and chitonous, it had faceted eyes, and a meter-long ovipositor that oozed an emerald-green fluid the consistency of semen.

"The same labs that made our furry neighbors, produced this atrocity." Tony X prodded the thing from offscreen with a metal rod. The bug creature erupted in a manic frenzy of thrashing that sprayed the sides of the terrarium with green, and it ended up wrapped around the rod and trying to stab it. "For the same purpose. To kill."

The camera pulled back to reveal Tony X standing behind the terrarium. Angel was feeling queazy. Importing that kind of macro gene-engineered monstrosity was about as illegal as you could get.

Tony X went on. "It is only a matter of time before this country erupts in the same kind of conflagration that destroyed Asia, before we are cut down with the same plagues that depopulated Africa, before the nonhumans, the half-humans, the hairballs, take over." He withdrew the slime-coated rod from the terrarium. "Genocide? We advocate survival. The survival of the human species."

Angel closed her eyes and put her face in her hands, one displaced thought running through her head—the hope that Tony X's bug never got loose.

The Tony X interview went on another minute and a half, but she didn't really listen to it.

Instead, she sifted through all the ramcards on the coffee table. What did White think he was doing? Did he play all of these? What the hell was he looking for?

The door to the apartment opened and Angel jumped to her feet and turned around, scattering ramcards everywhere.

Lei was standing in the doorway.

"Lei, damn, you scared the crap outa me."

"Hello to you, too."

Lei walked in and started gathering up ramcards.

"Where were you?" Angel asked.

"Friend of mine's in the hospital. Some damn pinkboy Knight jumped her in Chinatown last night. The comm's been so tied up that I only found out when I got home from work."

Angel took a handful of ramcards from Lei. "Is she all right?"

Lei nodded. "Yes, only a bump on the head from a tossed brick. They're just keeping her for observation. By the way, I wanted to ask you about these ramcards. What were you doing with them all day?"

"It wasn't me, it was—" Angel came up short. Paranoia parade or no, something was *very* wrong with what Lei just said. "What do you mean 'all day'?"

"I come home from work and all these cards—" Lei wrinkled her nose and swatted her tail in agitation. The look of agitation made her canine features almost feral. "Who's been here?"

"One of the Detectives, White. You came back from work and—"

"Ramcards all over the table, the place smelling of disinfectant, the comm on. What the hell are you doing, Angel? I've been giving you slack because of the shit you've been through. But some of these cards are personal. What were you doing in my room?"

"No one was here?"

"I walked in, saw the mess, got my call, walked out. Now tell me, what right did you have to— Are you okay?"

Angel shook her head and sank into the couch. It wasn't effing paranoia any more. She was in something, deep. She only wished she knew exactly what it was.

"What's wrong?" Lei asked.

"I haven't been here since noon. I didn't take out those ramcards. I left the comm blocking out all incoming calls. *I* didn't reset it."

"You said Detective White—"

"He left and came back? And, what you say you smelled, disinfectant?"

"Yes—"

"Someone covering their scent? That sound like a cop?"

Angel remembered the fake pine she smelled when they had come back from Byron's condo. Someone had been here, twice. She shivered.

They called the police. It was well after lunch on Tuesday when the cop came. Cop, singular. It was quite a different story from the break-in at the condo. The uncharacteristic deference the cops had been showing seemed to have evaporated. It took Angel an hour to get the complaint in, and it took the cop—one lone uniform with a vid unit—twelve hours to get there.

Apparently, she was no longer high on the priority list.

Not that the cop who showed was bad. He took footage, cracked his gum, and talked incessantly about the cops holding Chinatown and the Tenderloin together, about the Knights of Humanity—whom he called neo-skinheads—about Father Alvarez De Collor—about whom he expressed some ambivalence, being Catholic himself—and even the presidential bid of Sylvia Harper.

Not once did the uniformed cop mention Byron Dorset and his untimely death.

The cop took an hour to record the apartment, and another fifteen minutes to take her statement. When he left, he slipped around Detective Anaka, who was standing in the doorway.

"Can I come in?"

Angel shrugged. "Your partner didn't bother with invitations."

Anaka walked in. He smelled of dirt and sweat, and his suit was even more rumpled than usual. "Sorry about White." He sighed and collapsed into the couch.

"Please, sit down." Angel told him as she cleared the table of ramcards.

Anaka leaned forward and rubbed his temples. Angel walked around, putting things away. She activated the drapes on the windows, letting in some sunlight that had taken over in the abdication of the storm. Throughout, Anaka remained silent.

After nearly ten minutes of waiting, she couldn't take it any more. "What? You said you were going to talk to me, so talk."

"There's not much to say—" Anaka sighed and stared at the ceiling. "They suspended me."

Angel opened her mouth, closed it, opened it again. Angel didn't want to hit him with her primary question, *Why come here, then?* Instead, she asked him, "What happened?"

"Over four months of stacked-up sick leave and vacation time. They said I was overworked." Anaka ran a shaky hand through his black hair. Even his razor mustache looked frazzled. "I guess I do put a little too much of myself in my work. Haven't missed a day in years. . . ."

"I'm sorry—" Angel was increasingly uncomfortable. She wasn't used to total strangers coming to her for comfort. Much less cops. What the hell was she supposed to do?

"Only a matter of time, really. I'm too much a pain in the ass. I keep digging where people don't want me to dig." Anaka kept shaking his head. "People in the department have been waiting for an excuse to get me off the streets. Folks in the council have been plotting against me for years, waiting for an opportunity."

"Yeah. Right." Angel never liked anyone who said that people were plotting against them. It always sounded like the guy speaking was one step ahead of the white coats and trank guns.

*Come on,* Angel berated herself, *give the guy a break. He's a drum major and you're a cheerleader, but you're both in the same parade—about to be run over by the same float.*

After a long period of silence, he looked up. "Do you have anything to drink?"

She wanted to get Anaka out of her house, this seemed the perfect excuse. "Sorry, we haven't had a chance to go shopping."

"Oh." Anaka didn't look like he was moving.

Angel walked up to him and grabbed his elbow. "Why don't we go somewhere and get something?"

DeGarmo had given her a coded ramcard with a withdrawal limit of fifty thousand dollars. She figured she could spare a little of that to get Anaka out of her fur.

# CHAPTER 11

Angel took Anaka to an anonymous bar wedged between Haight Asbury and Japantown. A dark musky place that, if it didn't quite welcome moreaus, didn't turn them away.

She and Anaka sat in a booth far to the rear of the place. Angel gnawed on a succession of stale pretzels while Anaka ordered beer bulb after beer bulb. For once, Angel didn't know what to say.

"Didn't get much of anywhere," Anaka was saying. "First, Earl, our little songbird, dies of computer error. Then Dr. Ellis disappears after a perfunctory autopsy and the fox's corpse gets cremated—because of a computer error."

Anaka shook his head.

Angel kept gnawing her pretzel, wishing for something tougher to work out her tension on. Anaka was staring consistently at the table, his eyes seemed focused at some point beyond the holo-menu hovering under the surface.

"Two sequential computer screwups at two different hospitals? One kills a suspect, one destroys the victim's corpse. That's too much. And now Chico and Dwane are plea bargaining on the assault charges."

"You need to stop thinking about this— Damn it, what is your first name?"

"Kobe." Anaka looked up from the table with tired eyes. "You, of all people, should understand."

"Damn straight I understand, but when was the last time you slept?"

Instead of answering, Anaka downed the last of his beer. He stabbed at the menu, ordering another.

Angel tapped Anaka on the back of his hand with half a pretzel. "You need some sleep."

"Perhaps you're right," Anaka yawned. "Tired people make mistakes, and I can't afford any mistakes now."

"Huh?"

Anaka's beer arrived and he popped it open. "Well, isn't it obvious why they suspended me?"

Angel looked at his tangled hair and the circles under his eyes and held her tongue. *Pretty damn obvious, if you ask me.*

"I was too close to what's going on in this town. They took me down the same day I started digging into VanDyne. This close to the source of the corruption in this town—" He spread his hands like a man explaining the blatantly obvious. "I *can't* stop now."

Angel got a sinking feeling. She wouldn't trust White on a lot of things, but White seemed to think his partner was a bit of a nut. Angel had to admit, Anaka looked like a bit of a nut. "*Why?* You don't have a personal stake in this."

Anaka glared at her. "My job's my life. That's as personal as you get."

The silence stretched. Anaka drank quietly.

Eventually Angel realized how deeply she'd cut into him. "Sorry. Lei says I've been reacting weird to stress lately."

Anaka smiled. "Don't worry, the system hasn't succeeded in screwing me yet."

Angel had seen that kind of bravado before. She'd seen it mostly in moreys who were about to go ballistic after the gang that roached their best friend, lover, parents, car, whatever— "You're going to take on VanDyne all on your lonesome?"

Anaka shrugged.

Angel shook her head. *Great.* Anaka was convinced that the ex-Byron Dorset was working for the evil empire that ran this town. Even so, Anaka seemed to be trying to recruit the ex-Byron's ex-lover in some left-handed fashion.

When she started listening to him again she heard, "—what you went through in Cleveland."

"How the fuck—"

"The FBI has a whole division that keeps track of moreaus with criminal records." He shrugged. "I read your file."

"You have no idea how safe I feel now I know the Fed is protecting my rabbit ass," Angel felt a wave of paranoia that Anaka would probably have taken for granted. "What'd it say?"

"Led a small gang. Gang was wiped out by the original Zipperhead gang in '53. Almost skinned alive by—"

"It's called shaving." she whispered. It was why the fur on her legs was off-white. If it hadn't been for a tiger named Nohar, she would have bled to death in a sleazy motel east of Cleveland.

"Not much else I could access," Anaka said, interrupting her train of thought.

"What?"

"The Fed can be sticky about releasing information to local departments. That was it. The FBI wouldn't release *any* of the file they had on the Zipperhead gang. Even though from all accounts they just about self-destructed six years ago."

"Great." Angel could picture some Fed bureaucrat at a terminal, highlighting parts of her life and hitting the delete key in the name of national security. Angel drank her own glass of water.

Anaka rambled on, and Angel let him. She was only half listening. The pink cop wasn't telling her anything new, or that she couldn't figure out herself. *Of course* someone was after something Byron was involved in.

The question was, what someone?

White would think that the someone was the Knights. Anaka would think that the someone was VanDyne. Father Collor would say it was the cops. Pasquez would do a five-part report on the cover-up in the civic government. Lei would tell her she was being paranoid—

The missing Dr. Ellis pinned the murder on a feline morey. But, with the doctor missing and the body so much ash, Angel might be the only one who had that particular tidbit of information, without a shred of evidence to back it up.

However, Earl—that bald bastard of all people—had sung loud and clear to the cops that the Knights were meeting Byron when he got offed. And Byron got offed in the Knights' own hotel room in the Tenderloin.

But the lawyer, DeGarmo, fed credence to Anaka's paranoid fantasies by saying the Byron *had* worked for VanDyne, in something that the amounts of money involved suggested was a little left of legal.

None of that even approached the question, *why?*

Her mind was going all over the place and she hadn't even taken a drink. She ran her hand over her ears and tried to fight the sense of creeping unreality.

An hour later, she was helping an exhausted and inebriated Anaka to his house in Pacific Heights. She had to drive him in the BMW, and the best she could do for coherence was getting the address out of him.

Somehow she managed. She got lucky on most counts. Anaka's house was on the crest of a hill, so all the tilting he did was alcohol-related. It was on the first floor, so she didn't have to help him up any stairs. Lastly, it didn't have a combination, but an expensive palm lock and retinal scanner. A half-dozen bolts chunked home, opening the armored door.

Anaka's place was a study in austerity—polished wood floors, stark white walls, light fixtures hidden behind frosted-white globes with no personality whatsoever.

Anaka was more of an anal neat freak than Lei. In fact, when he collapsed on the futon that was the one piece of furniture in the living room, his rumpled form seemed an affront to the rest of the apartment.

"Thanks for the lovely afternoon." The sarcasm was lost on Anaka, who had probably lost awareness halfway to the futon. She found herself debating whether or not it would be a good idea to leave him alone.

She shook her head. What did she care. The guy was a nut. Just *look* at this place. The only decoration was a large plaque over the futon on which was mounted a Steyr AUG assault rifle. Angel didn't want to know if it was some sort of replica, or a working model.

She sat on the bare wood floor, across from the futon, and thought.

What *was* she going to do? Anaka had seemed to be her one potential ally in the whole Frisco establishment, and he'd just been canned.

Even if she ignored Anaka and his rampant paranoia, even if she decided to ignore the fact that Byron's killer was still out there, someone was still after something. Someone had trashed Byron's condo, and someone had been through her own apartment.

Why?

It was clear that she wasn't going to be able to relax until she'd fingered who'd killed Byron and who'd done the break-ins. The problem was, she had no idea how to proceed.

All she knew was that it was allegedly the cops' job, and the cops didn't seem to help at all.

"Damn it." She wasn't any great brain. Her greatest intellectual achievement was teaching herself to read. She knew how to run a small-time protection racket. She knew how to wait tables in a cocktail bar. She knew how to defend herself when the shit got thick. But this—she needed help.

She knew who to call for advice. The inspiration struck her so hard that she felt a need to pounce on it immediately, as if hesitation would lose her the ability to do anything constructive.

Kobe Anaka's comm was as sterile as the rest of the nearly-empty apartment. It was a black cube resting on a glass table, the only thing to mar its smooth black lines was the necessity of the screen. The screen was so flush with the box she thought the designers would have gladly done without it to achieve a sort of archetypal black cube.

Angel saw no sign of a remote control.

"Comm on," she whispered.

The comm responded voicelessly. After a blue flash as the picture activated, the screen stayed blank, waiting for her.

She didn't like voice-activated comms, and what really irked her was the lack of an obvious manual control. She was left to try and intuit what the thing parsed for commands.

It finally responded to her plaintive cry of, "help."

The comm responded with a menu, a screen full of options.

No wonder the designers left out the damn remote. There were about four dozen options on this thing. And that was the first of five pages.

The layout made it clear that the screen was touch-sensitive. Which made her life easier. She didn't want to have to spend all day shouting at an unfamiliar chunk of electronics.

She started calling Los Angeles with only a slight twinge of guilt about running up Anaka's phone bill. Only a twinge. It was buried under the need for her to do something now, and the creeping sense that her comm at home and in the BMW couldn't be trusted, not for this.

Every time she told herself that she was worrying needlessly, she came back to the fact that person or persons unknown had read every single ramcard in her apartment. Bugging her comm line didn't seem that much of a stretch.

Detective Anaka probably swept for electronic surveillance the way some people shampoo the rug. Even if it was only a case of her catching some of his neuroses, she felt better using his comm. Besides, she figured she could pay him back eventually.

And she needed to talk to Nohar.

Nohar Rajasthan might be able to give her some advice, even though she hadn't seen him since he left Cleveland. He'd seen her through some shit back in her home town and saved her life twice over. Had circumstances been different, Angel could have seen him in Byron's place in her life.

Angel sighed to herself and thought that maybe she had something for big guns.

It took her four tries to get into the Los Angeles public directory. The first two times she only got electronic garbage, an asynchronous beeping, and a screenful of scrolling blue and red lines. The third time she got a computer and the Pacific Bell logo asking her to only stay on if her call was an emergency situation, and then cut her off.

The fourth time she got through to dead air.

Five was a dim low-res representation of the directory listings for Los Angeles. Angel put her request through, hoping that she spelled Rajasthan correctly.

She got the number and it took another half-dozen tries to get through to it. The fighting in LA was making hash out of the communication net in the city. It would be impossible to get through to Nohar if his comm was on the other side of the National Guard. She was pretty sure that there was a data embargo to inner Los Angeles, though the only folks it really hurt were the media types and the people who wanted to find out if cousin Ed in East LA had bit the big one.

Lucky seven, she got a hazy Pacific Bell logo. The red, blue, and green parts of the animated logo were all a fraction out of sync with each other. It melted into blurred computer text that said something like Rajasthan Investigations.

Nohar answered the phone.

God, he'd changed. The massive feline face had—aged.

It made Angel uncomfortably aware of her own mortality. Moreaus weren't given to long life, and rabbits were given less than most. If she'd been a rat . . .

"Angel?"

His voice was barely audible through the shitty connection. But it was Nohar, all two and a half meters, three hundred kilos of him. The tiger's fur had lost some of the sharp definition between the lines, white hairs were beginning to scatter themselves across his face, and there were now deep lines above his broad nose, but it was Nohar. Up to and including the subtle expression of disbelief.

"Yes. Angel. From Cleveland."

The picture fuzzed and jarred as Nohar must have hit his own comm. "Surprise to hear from you."

"I'm in Frisco." Angel raised her voice in case Nohar was having as much trouble hearing her.

"What can I do for you?"

Angel took a deep breath and dove into the story. Even

when she only hit the high points, it took a long time to make herself clear over the inferference on the line. She ended with Detective Kobe Anaka's involuntary retirement.

"You want my advice?" Nohar said as the red part of the image separated and began slowly sliding to the right, pixel by pixel.

"Yes."

"Blow Frisco. Go north, Seattle."

"Kit, you must be kidding."

"I'd tell you that if you weren't in trouble. Do you *like* urban warfare?"

Angel sighed. "I can't leave this hanging."

"Why?"

"Look, I'm staying. Now can you give me an idea about—"

The picture faded into incomprehensible snow.

"Nohar, you still there?"

"Yeah," came a small fuzzed voice. There was the scream of some feedback overlaid with static. "Can you hear me?" Nohar's voice was gravely distorted and barely audible. "I maxed the gain on this, but the vid's shot."

"Yes. Do you have anything useful to say before the line dies?"

"Okay, after what you—ffff—looking for something. Did Byron give you anyt—ffff—" Nohar's voice was fading in and out wildly now. Black pixels were starting a shotgun effect as the signal's data degraded.

"I can't make you out."

"—can't hear you any more. If you—ffff—en call Bobby Dittrich in Cle—ffff—can tell you people to—ffff—ver they are—ffff—eem to be looking for data—ffff—Dittrich in—ffff—hope you—ffff—tty signal—ffff—fuck it—ffff—"

The screen went dead black and the sound died.

After a few seconds the Pacific Bell test pattern came up informing Angel of technical difficulties. She shot a dozen calls down to LA, none successful. All her calls came up with the same test pattern and the information that the data flow into LA was temporarily blocked.

She supposed she was lucky she'd gotten through at all.

Well, Nohar had told her to get a hold of someone named Bobby Dittrich in Cleveland. At least it gave her something to do.

# CHAPTER 12

It took Angel a while to find Mr. Dittrich. Fortunately, whatever urban violence plagued her home town hadn't affected the data lines into the city. Her only problem was sifting through a succession of different Bobs, Bobbies, Roberts, Robs, and Bobbis. Not to mention a half-dozen Dittrich's who only bothered with a single first initial.

Her tenth call was forwarded to a place called Budget Surplus. The call was answered by a chubby, red-bearded human. "Budget Surplus, can I help you?"

On the bottom of the video, under Anaka's comm's date-time-status stamp, the picture was scrolling a hyper-fast line of gibberish. Something that looked like neoelectronic hieroglyphs was whizzing by under this Bobby's face.

"You know a tiger named Nohar?"

"May, may not. Who're you?" There was a weighty look of suspicion in this pink's eyes, but there was an impish smile under the red mustache.

A square block of the scrolling hieroglyphs froze. The block was to the far left, and the remaining line of pixel gibberish redoubled its speed.

"My name's Angelica Lopez—"

"Angel?" One of the pink's eyebrows arched.

Two more blocks of garbage froze, traveling from left to right. The rest of the line was now a total blur, it was changing so fast.

"Yes. Nohar told me, sort of, that I should talk to you."

"Now why—" Dittrich paused and his gaze flicked downward. It was the first sign that he could also see the line of strange flickering characters on the bottom of the screen. As he paused, a few more blocks froze. He looked back up. "—would you be forwarded to someone of my talents?"

"Well—"

"Shh." Dittrich said quietly, raising a hand to his lips. He was staring at the scrolling line on the screen. Three more blocks of it froze, the line of gibberish seemed almost to form a coherent pattern. Angel could hear Dittrich say to himself, "I love this."

The rest of the line suddenly fell like a row of dominoes. The bottom line of the screen froze.

Suddenly the picture blanked, briefly became a negative version of itself, turned black and white, and re-reversed.

The picture was now a substantially lower resolution black and white image of Dittrich grinning from ear to ear.

"What the hell was that?" Angel asked, hoping that she hadn't somehow busted Anaka's comm.

"A little security." Dittrich shrugged. "I'm in a sensitive line of work."

"What did you do to my comm?"

"Oh, that. The lower quality pictures frees up the data signal to handle all the encryption data."

"What?"

"I did a long-distance reprogramming of *your* comm's computer. Don't worry it's not permanent. And—" Dittrich glanced off to his left, "—unless your name is Kobe Anaka, that's not your comm."

Angel sighed. "You do know Nohar, right?"

Dittrich nodded. "And you're the hell-bunny he scraped off the remains of Musician's Towers way back when."

Angel opened her mouth to say something, but instead simply nodded.

"Any friend of Nohar's . . . What can I do?"

She took a deep breath and dove into the story again. Dittrich stopped her when she got to the pile of ramcards on her dining room table. "Whoever they are, they're looking for some sort of data file."

"Okay." Angel said, unsure.

"They haven't found it yet."

"How's that follow?"

"There's nothing at the condo, and at your apartment they're interrupted before they can put things back—hmm. You know what it sounds like to me?"

"What?"

"Your Byron was a data courier. He moved things VanDyne didn't trust to the data net. Stuff too hot for anyone to trust to a wire. High-risk, high-reward, easily could make a few million doing that. Did he give you anything on a ramcard? A movie, music, software, love poetry—"

Angel's hand found its way into her pocket. The season tickets were still there. She pulled them out of her pocket and looked at the rainbow-sheened cards with the Earthquakes' logo on them. She stared at them with growing realization. "You bastard, Byron." All that time, was she just being used?

Dittrich nodded. "I think Nohar wanted me to give you a line on a fellow hacker out there on the coast."

"Yes, someone to help sort out this mess."

"Before I do so— A warning from an old hand at the information game."

Angel looked up and waited for Dittrich to go on.

"Data that valuable's likely to be just as dangerous."

Angel left Anaka asleep on his futon. She'd decided that it was pretty much a sure thing the cop was going to sleep through the rest of the day. Alcohol and exhaustion had finally caught up with the man.

Over and over, Angel thought about the damn tickets. She did not want to think that Byron was using her like that, planting crap like that on her—

The more she thought about it, though, the more it was starting to look like Byron was acting the playboy. While she had been taking things seriously, he'd been taking it as just another fling. She was just another female he'd charmed, the only real distinction being that she was the last.

She hadn't been in a relationship, she'd been in an effing lottery.

She surprised herself by actually considering not accepting the money.

"Come on, let's not be a fool twice," she said to herself as she hit the switchbacks on Lombard Street.

"Oh, God," she said as she hit the first turn. She started cursing rapidly in Spanish as she slowed to a crawl and maneuvered the large BMW down the insane curves. She would have avoided this stretch if she'd been thinking.

She had one brief close call with a Dodge Portola pickup on the last turn. A long, red-flagged length of white PVC pipe that hung out the back of the truck bed actually swept over the front hood of her car, barely missing the windshield. It took all the self-control Angel had not to slam on the brakes in the middle of the turn.

She came out the other end of the bend without impaling her car on the pipe.

Cursing herself, she continued down Lombard, and almost ran down a cable car trolling through the intersection at Columbus. The BMW froze, half in the intersection, as the car passed by in front of her going at its slow, sedate, pace. It caught her attention that there was not a single moreau on the car.

Horns began to blare behind her.

She turned down Columbus and suddenly, for the first time since coming to Frisco, began to worry about the neighborhood. Nob Hill and points north were solid pink. Always had been solid pink. That usually didn't bother her. . . .

Today was different.

She drove down Columbus, toward Chinatown, toward the Pyramid, and she could feel the pinks looking at her. She could feel the drivers around her thinking she didn't belong in that kind of car, didn't belong this far north of Market.

Suddenly, this city didn't seem so different. Frisco might not have any concrete barriers blocking off access to the morey neighborhoods, it might not have a morey curfew, it might even have one or two morey cops, but the eyes that followed her down Columbus Avenue could have been from Cleveland, or LA, or New York.

She was sitting at the light at Montgomery, just in front of the Pyramid, and something hit her windshield.

Angel heard a smack, and some liquid splashed across her field of view. She looked to the left, and she saw a knot of pinks on the crosswalk. One of them had thrown a bulb of coke, or coffee, or some dark beverage at the BMW's windshield.

"Go home," she heard one say.

There were seven or eight of them, and what scared Angel was the fact that they weren't skinheads. They looked like fairly normal pink adolescents.

They had crossed to stand in front of her car, and they stopped.

One gave her the finger, two others put their hands on the hood and began rocking the car up and down on the shocks.

"Oh, shit," Angel whispered. She checked to make sure the doors were locked. As she did, the humans began to surround the car.

"Where'd the rat steal this—"

"Don't want your kind here—"

"Looking for some kind of trouble—"

The humans began to hit the car with their fists.

The light changed and the car behind her began to lay on the horn. Christ, Angel thought, couldn't he see the mess she was in? She punched the BMW's comm to call the cops, but the damn thing only broadcast static. She looked up and saw a pink with a denim jacket and a T-shirt with an "Alex Gregg in '60" logo on it. He was whipping the end of her severed antenna across the hood of the car.

One of the pinks jumped up on the hood and started to jump up and down, and Angel heard a window behind her shatter.

That was fucking enough.

She slammed the BMW into reverse, flooring the accelerator and turning the wheel. The rear wheels bit pavement and her car shot back to the left, across the double yellow line. The computer on the BMW began to flash all sorts of collision avoidance lights and traffic warnings at her.

The pink on the hood took a header backward and fell headfirst into a storm sewer drain. Two pinks on the left jumped back, out of the BMW's way and into the other lane.

An old Dodge four-door was turning in from Washington and slammed on the brakes in the center of the intersection to avoid running down one of the pinks. A motorcycle crunched into it broadside. The cyclist tumbled over the hood of the Dodge and landed on a few of the pinks who were still standing in the crosswalk.

There was a crunch as the BMW kissed fenders with the car behind it, then Angel shot backward in the opposite lane, up Columbus the way she'd come. There was screaming from behind her, and she saw that one of the pink kids had put his arm through her rear passenger side window. He was now hanging on to the door, his other hand frantic for some sort of handhold. Angel grinned as she shot backward through the intersection at Jackson—fortunately, the light was with her—and slammed on the brakes just on the other side of the light.

The pink tumbled from her door, and Angel made a squealing left turn on to Jackson.

It might have been a dumb idea, but she looped around Jackson Square and came down Washington to view the destruction from the other end. She shouldn't have been worried about the kids. They deserved what they got. However, she still found herself hoping that no one got seriously hurt. If nothing else, she didn't want any more trouble with the cops.

She drove by the intersection in front of the Pyramid, and everyone seemed to be standing around, ambulatory— Except for the kid who'd taken the header into the storm drain. He was lying in the street, unmoving.

Angel didn't stop to give the survivors a chance to tear her apart.

She turned down Stockton and followed the length of Chinatown as the night darkened around her.

When she hit the tunnel, she realized she was shaking. She took a few deep breaths and told herself that she'd deal with it later. She'd talk to the cops later, too, after she found the contact Dittrich gave her.

What the hell was happening to this city?

She left the claustrophobic confines of the tunnel and the night seemed even darker now. She was surrounded by post-earthquake Chinatown, south of the so-called Gateway Arch. Nothing around her now was more than twenty years old. It was all chrome pagodas and flickering neon. There seemed to be something quintessentially Asian about garish street signs.

And here, where Chinatown was busy crowding Market, there were moreaus. Lots of moreaus. A quarter of the refugees from the Asian war were nonhuman, and half of those were Chinese. Angel drove by towering ursoids, the typically long-limbed Asian rabbit strains, dark-haired canines, as well as some exotic species that she couldn't place.

The name Dittrich had given her was Kaji Tetsami—a name that didn't belong down here. A Jap in Chinatown was about as out of place as a rabbi at a mosque. But, as she turned on to Post Street to approach a postmodern steel and glass neo-Asian monstrosity, she realized that her navigation wasn't off. The address Dittrich gave her *was* in the southwest corner of Chinatown. The rich part that held a lot of descendants of old Hong Kong refugee money.

The address was, in fact, the neo-Asian monstrosity she was approaching. It was a residential tower that took up most of a city block, and if her estimate of the thing's height was correct, Tetsami lived close to the top of the building. Maybe *the* top.

She pulled into the parking garage, and was stopped by a transparent, probably armored, barrier. She sat and idled, wondering what the hell she was supposed to do. She didn't see a comm box around, only two lanes of concrete and one video camera.

"Please lower your window," came a voice from nowhere.

Angel did so, looking for where the voice was coming from. The sound was amplified and echoey in the concrete chamber, but she couldn't locate the source, even with her oversized ears.

"Name?"

"Angel Lopez," she said, trying to find the guard, the voice pickup, or the speaker. She ended up deciding that it was all in the camera.

"Who do you wish to see?"

"Kaji Tetsami."

There followed a long silence. It grew to such a length that she thought that their speaker or their voice pickup might be broken.

"I'm here for a Mr. Tetsami. Hello?"

She got no response.

She had shifted the BMW into reverse and was about to pull back out of the garage when the transparent door rolled up into the ceiling.

"Parking space five-zero-seven," said a different amplified voice.

Angel pulled into the garage, and noted the door closing immediately behind her. She took one turn into the structure and saw a guardhouse. It sat behind armored windows and had a human watching a few dozen vid screens. As she passed it she noted an open door behind the rent-a-cop. She saw part of a rack and at least three shotguns and a small submachinegun.

She drove through the garage past Porsches, Mercedes Benzes, other BMWs, a Ferarri, a Maduro—

The lane split into two ramps. The one going up had a sign saying "050-499." The one down said "500+." The one down was labeled "authorized personnel only."

She turned down the lower ramp and began the descent. Another armored door was raising as she approached. She drove past it and found herself in a much smaller sublevel of the garage.

The BMW was barely ten yards into the garage when she saw the dozen armed rent-a-cops lining the walls. They all had their hands on their weapons and, as Angel looked back behind her, the door was already closed.

"Oh, shit," she whispered to herself.

# CHAPTER 13

"Get out of the car," said one of the guards.

Angel didn't argue. She stepped out.

"Step away from the vehicle and keep your hands in sight."

The troops wore black. Their only insignia was an ID card clipped to their breast pockets. With the body armor and the automatic weapons, they looked more like a mercenary unit than building security. They were all human, except the one shouting the orders.

Their leader was one of the rare results of genetic tampering on humans. At a distance, he could pass. But his smell was all wrong for a pink. That, and his joints were too big. When he moved he moved *wrong*. The platform the engineers designed for the guy's hyped strength and reflexes was disturbing for her to watch in action—and she wasn't even human.

The guy was the first frank she'd seen since Cleveland. Franks were, as a rule, more insular than moreys. Most of the pinks who hated moreaus were positively terrified of frankensteins. It seemed to be a racial characteristic. The pinks' fear of the franks led to a UN resolution banning genetic experimentation on humans long before the war. Only a few countries dabbled in it after that, and only a few products of that managed to get over the border.

Franks were rare.

A small chromed door opened at the far end of the garage, and out stepped another one. This one was different. He was short, as short as Angel, and as bald as one of the Knights.

The tampering on his genes was more subtle. It didn't ring in his odor, which could blend in with any pink crowd without Angel noticing. It was more in the shape of his skull, the length of his fingers.

Like the guards, he wore black, but his black was a suit that could have cost a few grand. He wore black down to the buttons on his shirt, down to the gloss-black rings on his fingers, down to the metallic frames on the thick tinted glasses he wore.

Occasionally, Angel saw light reflected in those glasses that didn't originate anywhere inside the garage.

"Names," he said.

"What?"

"Names have power, Angelica. Names are to conjure with." The man walked up to her, and she saw a number of the guards visibly tense. "Names open doors." He nodded slightly back where he had come.

She was beginning to get the picture. "I—"

The man raised an incredibly long finger to quiet her. "It is a novelty for someone to walk up to the front door and ask for me. I am . . . curious."

He was close enough that she could see the display that scrolled across the inside of his glasses.

"I was told you could help me."

"Someone has knowledge . . . who?"

Angel swallowed and decided to go through with it. It was silly, but apparently Bobby Dittrich knew what he was about. "He said to tell you that 'The Digital Avenger knows your hat size.' "

The scene froze. The bald man had an oddly-shaped head, and Angel was afraid that she had committed a lethal insult.

Instead, the man laughed. Really laughed. He shook his head and clapped his hands once. In response, the guards melted back through the chrome door he had come from. All but the other frank, who stood, gun lowered, at parade rest next to the door.

"Angelica," the bald man said, "you have some odd friends."

"So you are Mr. Tetsami?"

"Please refrain from using that name from now on. It makes people nervous."

"What should I call you?"

"Mr. K, if you need a name. Intriguing that you should find your way to me. But come to my office." Tetsami, or Mr. K, waved ahead of him, toward the chromed door.

He led her through a spotless white corridor, lit by indirect lighting. They passed doors, but they were few and far between. It became obvious, after a while, that there was a gentle slope downward and the corridor extended way beyond the confines of the building above.

"Where are we?"

"Shall I tell you?" asked Mr. K. He glanced sideways at her and smiled. "In the early thirties, when they started work on the ill-fated Mill Valley Ballistic Launch facility, this city started an optimistic northern spur to the old BART system."

"North to *what?*"

"After the earthquake, exactly."

The corridor ended, and they started descending a stairway that led into a circular chamber whose floor was fifteen or twenty meters below them. Their corridor entered near the arched ceiling and the stairway took a right angle and hugged the side of the curving wall as they descended.

The room was huge. It could have been thirty meters in diameter, all white walls and blue carpeting. Diffuse white light came from a starburst pattern of fluorescents that pointed radially from the center of the slightly domed roof.

The room itself dwarfed its contents. There may have been a dozen terminal stations down there, only a few seemed to be occupied at the moment. The silence, especially to Angel, was unnerving. Acres of blue carpeting seemed to smother any sounds, so other than a diffuse high-frequency hum from somewhere, the only real sound seemed to come from the footsteps of the people around her.

Central to the room was a black machine. It was contained in a cylindrical case whose transparent walls ran floor to ceiling. The container dwarfed the black machine while simultaneously drawing all attention directly to it.

It was made of four metallic slabs resting crosswise on

a black toroid that formed its base. As they descended, and Angel could make out more detail, she saw the top of the toroid was divided into wedge-shaped panels and that the rectangular slabs didn't quite touch in the center. In the gap, she saw hundreds, perhaps thousands, of neatly arrayed cables running from the inside of the rectangular slabs and down through the hole in the torus.

She could also see the Japanese writing on some of the panels, and a very understated Toshiba logo on the sides of the rectangular sections.

"Jesus, is that a Japanese mainframe?"

Mr. K snorted. "Mainframes are for payrolls— That's a Toshiba ODS 3000."

"I thought that kind of stuff was fried when they lost the war."

"You can't destroy technology, only hide it a while."

Angel stopped at the foot of the stairs, looking at the Jap computer. "How the hell did you get one?"

"Quite simple. I imported it myself, before the war."

"But wasn't that—"

"Oh, highly illegal and a major threat to Japanese national security. Especially with someone trained to use it to its full capabilities. If I was caught, they would have shot me for a traitor." Mr. K pulled gently on her arm and pointed to a door halfway along the curving wall. "My office, I believe we have things to discuss."

Angel allowed herself to be led to the office. Seeing that large a chunk of Japanese technology in one piece, in working order, had stunned her. Angel knew that a lot of the stories of Jap technology had to be so much bullshit and wishful thinking, but there was still a mythic quality about the stuff the island nation had done with silicon, superconductors, nanotechnology, biological interfaces . . . .

The only real problem with old Jap technology was that there was only so much it could do when the Japanese faced an army ten times the size of its own. The Chinese lack of pinpoint accuracy didn't much matter when they lobbed a ten-meg warhead.

What the hell could that Toshiba do? It was probably

more powerful than some of the stuff that was buried in the Pentagon.

Angel went straight from that and into free fall. At least that was what it felt like, walking into Mr. K's office.

When the door opened in front of her, she suffered dizzying vertigo caused by the gigantic holo screen behind the desk. The screen was on, projecting a screen of solid sky-blue. It was as if she found herself falling upward.

She blinked a few times and the feeling passed.

The door closed behind her, leaving the frank guard outside. Mr. K sat himself behind the desk and motioned her toward a chair that was a single flat piece of upholstered plastic that had been molded into a chair shape. It didn't look stable, but she sat in it without tipping it over.

"So," Mr. K said, leaning back in his chair and looking at her over the top of his glasses—his eyes were a deep violet—"what can we do for each other?"

Angel began to relay the story, but he stopped her. "I'm quite familiar with the basics. Sometimes the news services can produce something . . . enlightening. I would like to know your needs—your *specific* needs."

Angel thought about that.

"I need to know who killed Byron and who's been trashing apartments."

"And to that end?"

"I need to know what the hell Byron was doing." Angel pulled the football tickets out of her pocket and tossed them on to the desk. "And I need to know what, if anything he hid on those ramcards."

Mr. K nodded. "Good. I like specifics. Now we need to discuss the terms of this exchange."

"Huh?"

"My payment, Angelica. I came to this country because I do not work for free."

"Oh, if you tell me how much you—"

He clucked and shook his head. "No, no, you can't afford to pay me money."

Angel grinned slightly. "I do have some money—"

He nodded. "Something under seven million I suspect."

Angel gaped.

"Perhaps you see now. I deal with corporations for the most part, only the very rare individual. Computer time on my machine is effectively priceless. Conservatively, it's fifty-thousand a minute."

She closed her mouth slowly.

"However, I do not deal only in—or even primarily in—money."

"What do you want?"

"I want free access to whatever information he was transporting." He reached over with incredibly long fingers and rested them on top of the cards. "Acceptable?"

Angel looked down at the season tickets under Mr. K's hand. "What makes you think he was carrying *anything?*"

Mr. K smiled. "I knew him."

Of course. Why the fuck not? It wasn't like she ever actually *knew* the damn fox. She just let the vulpine bastard seduce her into this mess.

"What do you think he was transporting?"

"I have no idea."

Angel shook her head and snickered. "You'd do this for something that might turn out to be worthless?"

"It is valuable to someone, which means it is valuable to me. Sometimes I take a low-risk gamble."

"Okay." Angel said. She really didn't care what Byron was transporting, what she wanted to know was what that information could tell her about whoever was fucking with her life.

Mr. K picked up the series of ramcards.

However, Angel wasn't stupid. "On two conditions, though."

His hand stopped moving. "It is you who are coming for help."

"Yeah, but if that info's worth it, I want a piece of the action."

His hand began to lower. "This, I don't know. I do not like needless complications."

"Tell me you can't afford it."

"Tell me you really need it."

"It's the principle, Mr. Tetsami."

He frowned at the use of his name. "And the other condition?"

"If you're taking those tickets, I want them replaced. I want to go to the game on Sunday."

Angel slammed the door when she got home. Somehow she had managed to avoid running down any innocent bystanders.

She had to ask Mr. K about Byron, and she had her suspicions about what she might have found out, but the truth had sliced her open like an unknown feline morey had sliced open Byron's neck. What really pissed her off was the fact that her reaction meant that she was still harboring some secret delusions that her time with Byron had meant anything.

What it had meant to Byron, apparently, was that she was a convenient mail drop.

The really disgusting part of all this was the fact that, by the time he'd slipped her those cards, she'd been so gooey-eyed that she would have willingly stashed anything for him had he just asked.

"What a fucking day."

"Angel—" Lei stepped out of the living room and walked up to her. Lei looked flustered and her tail was swatting so frantically that no shin within a meter of her would be safe. Angel barely noticed. She was fuming about Byron.

"The bastard was *using* me! He always was. It was his effing MO. He handled this hot data, found some squeeze to get close to and planted the stuff till he wanted it—"

"Angel—" Lei grabbed Angel's shoulder and shook it.

"What?" Angel snapped back.

Lei cocked her head back into the room. Standing there, in Angel's living room, was Detective White, belly spilling over his belt like an impending avalanche. White wasn't smiling. Flanking him were two uniforms who looked a little nervous.

Angel shouldered past Lei and looked the detective in the paunch. "What the fuck are you doing here again?"

"I'm here to arrest you."

"What?"

"Hit and run at Columbus and Washington at five fifteen this afternoon."

# CHAPTER 14

While the cops hassled her through the bureaucracy, Angel tried to isolate the moment at which her life started going wrong. It was an unprofitable pursuit because her thoughts traveled back from the current disaster in an unbroken chain of events that began two decades ago when her mom visited a Bensheim clinic to get inseminated.

That was depressing.

*No,* she thought, *what's depressing is the fact I still need to find out who killed Byron, and the guy was an asshole, a con artist, and God knows what else—*

If their positions had been reversed, Angel was pretty sure that Byron wouldn't be overly upset about her death. In fact, she had a morbid fantasy about what her funeral would be like. She could see Byron picking up Lei at the wake.

It was upsetting that that half-blind lion, Balthazar, saw Byron clearer than she ever did.

Her mind continued in its self-destructive spiral as she got more and more irritated with the cops.

At least, for once, she actually had a lawyer to call when they gave her access to a comm. That screwed with their program a bit. Moreys weren't supposed to have bail, or lawyers. When she called DeGarmo and told the cops to engage in some experimental hermaphroditism, they shuffled her away into a holding cell.

With a bald human.

From a logistical point of view, it had to be intentional on the cop's part. The stainless steel gate on the cell slid aside and they tossed her into the bare concrete, and she knew they wanted some sort of incident so they could continue to hold her after her lawyer showed.

Even though she knew it was what the cops wanted, she couldn't help but say, "Hey, it's the firebug."

The small white human looked up at her for the first time.

"Shit!" The female pink stood up and went over to the gate, giving Angel a wide berth, and began yelling, "You can't put it in here with me—I've got *rights!*"

"Pleased to see you, too, shithead."

"That rodent, it tried to kill me, you can't—"

"If you don't watch your effing pronouns, I *will* kill you."

It soon became obvious to the pink that the cops weren't particularly interested in her dilemma. She turned around to Angel, who had taken her spot on the one cot in the three-meter-square cell.

"Stay away from me," she said.

Angel never realized how sleazy the smell of human fear could be. The fact that she'd touched this hairless wonder at one point made her want to wash her hands.

"Ain't moving, pinky." Angel smiled. "But I hope you have a lot of self-control." She looked at the john next to the cot.

Pinky slid down, along the bars, until she was sitting on the ground. "You don't touch me."

"Don't worry, I don't feel like spending an hour picking shit from my claws."

Pinky winced, even though rabbit claws weren't much to worry about. "You just don't touch me. I got friends."

"Yeah, I know. A bunch of screaming freakazoids with so much heat conduction from the head that they suffer brain damage. If you're the best and the brightest, I don't have much to worry about."

Pinky just sat there, glaring.

Angel continued, "Stood outside the bar grinning until they picked you up, didn't you? Scary example of the master race indeed. Kinda drafty up there, ain't it?"

Pinky was getting real pissed. It was getting damn close to the incident the cops wanted, and Angel was about at the point where she wouldn't care. If the twitch jumped her, she could kick her through the bars and there'd be one less scumbag in the city. By all rights they should give her a medal for something like that.

Pinky glared at her, but she was into self-preservation. "You keep talking. When we have the power, your kind will be swept aside."

"The Knights? You must be kidding!"

*"I'm not talking about . . ."*

It was amazing how quiet it could get down here. It was a new block of cells that smelled of machine oil and fresh concrete and only slightly of urine. Their nearest neighbors were two cells away.

The near-silence—bullshit continued elsewhere in the block—was filled by the realization that Pinky had said something significant.

It was like slow motion, as Angel swung her feet to the floor and Pinky pushed up to her feet.

"Who *are* you talking about?"

"Don't come near me."

For the first time in a long while, Angel was aware of the new scar on her cheek. It was nearly invisible now, and she only felt it as a slight tightness on her face. She realized she felt it because she was grinning like a maniac. Angel could feel her heart pounding in her ears, and she hoped the smell of blood was from the scar opening up on her cheek.

"You can tell." She was approaching Pinky slowly, but she could feel the muscles in her legs tightening. "Just between you, me, and the hookers three cells down."

"You can't."

"Who's going to stop me, you freak? You're so proud of your friends in high places. Why don't you tell me who they are?"

She backed Pinky up. It was beginning to hit her how silly the scene must look. After all, in the looking-fierce competition between moreaus, a lepus would come dead last.

Even so, the bald twitch had a right to be scared. Angel was beginning to feel a real strong desire to tear something apart. Angel could feel the anger ratcheting her nerves tighter and tighter.

Pinky found a corner and stuck. Angel closed on her. "Come on," Angel said, "impress me with these friends."

*"Don't touch me."*

"Must be a good reason they're letting you all twist in the wind."

*"Get away."*

"Tell me—" Angel was now as close as she could get. Her toes were touching Pinky's boots. She slowly raised her heels and tilted forward until she had raised her muzzle level with Pinky's face. "Tell me these people and I'll leave you alone. Roll over. Looks like something you'd be good at."

Angel stood there staring at the twitch. Pinky stayed quiet.

"No? Do you want a description?" Angel leaned in. Her smile still hurt. She was shaking with the restrained desire to go fully off on Pinky's bald little head. Angel was reminded of the scene with Igalez. Never mind, she could handle it. "First, I eat your nose." She dragged her tongue across Pinky's face, tasting sweat and fear.

As Angel licked across the bridge of her nose, Pinky's eyes rolled up and she emitted an inarticulate moan. She shoved Angel away and threw herself at the bars. "Get me out of here! Just get me out of here! I'll admit to anything, just get me away from that animal!"

Angel was about to say something more—perhaps even jump Pinky and show the twitch a *real* animal—but at that moment all hell broke loose in the cell block. All the empty cells opened simultaneously, and cops in riot gear started pushing in a mass of moreaus of both sexes. The cops lined themselves up against the wall, holding up stun rods—a sort of glorified cattle prod—as a wall of fur washed past the cell.

Damn, Angel thought, these weren't gang members, or the kind of folks she expected to see in such a roust. For one thing, the moreys wore too much clothing. There was a definite linear equation that related income level with the amount of pink clothing a morey wore. Angel actually saw a few ties.

Most of the moreys looked to have been through some rough treatment. A few were bleeding, and one or two had to be helped along. The smell of urine was being overpowered by the smell of wet fur and blood.

Angel's body stopped screaming for combat, and the tension started to leak away from her muscles.

Pinky freaked, especially when the passing moreaus began to notice her.

"Oh, God, I'm gonna die." She crawled into a fetal position under the cot.

"I suppose," Angel said, as she rubbed an ache in her thigh. "If you're lucky."

The tide of moreaus let up for a few minutes, and a pair of cops pushed through to the door of their cell. The door slid open.

"My lawyer here?" Angel wanted to get the hell out of this place.

"I know fuck about your lawyer, rabbit," said one of the cops. "This just became a segregated cell block."

The other cop reached in and got his arm around the firebug's chest. "Come on, Berkeley. You're getting transferred in with some of your friends."

Pinky began kicking and screaming. "You aren't going to take me out there!" One kick landed in the other officer's crotch. The cop was in full riot gear and it only pissed him off.

"Cuff her!" he told the other cop as he grabbed both legs. They left the cell in less than five minutes, Pinky trussed up between them like a Christmas present.

They barely cleared the cell door before Angel's cell began filling up with more wet moreaus. Angel immediately lost sight of the big picture, suddenly being surrounded by taller people. All she had a chance to do was claim the section of cot next to the john before the place got too full to move.

Though she couldn't see her progress, Angel could hear the firebug make her exit. Pinky left on a crest of moreau growls and insults and a buzz or two from the cop stunners—apparently when someone wasn't quite satisfied with verbal abuse.

There was a rush into the cell, then Angel's world stabilized somewhat. She was surrounded by a mixed group of canines plus one of the occasional exotic breeds that she hadn't seen before.

The exotic was the closest to her height, shorter and looking like a cross between a rabbit and a rat, so she addressed him.

"Raining out there?"

He shook his head. "No, they're using fire hoses."

Apparently, two conflicting demonstrations, pink and morey, happened to meet in front of City Hall. Predictably, bad things happened. From the description, a melee erupted in the lobby of City Hall itself, causing a shitload of damage from the fight and more so from the firehoses they used to quell the violence.

The cops ended up busting everyone in a five block radius.

The exotic, a chinchilla, hadn't even been a part of the demonstration. He'd just been driving down Van Ness when the cops stopped him. Angel just had the dumb luck to get embedded in what must be a logistic nightmare for the Frisco legal system. A tidal wave of moreaus washed in, only to leave by an anemic trickle.

The cops called names out of the cell block by some equation that must have involved species, the first letter of your last name, and a dart board somewhere. It seemed to Angel that they called a name every ten or fifteen minutes, and it caused no lessening of the crowding whatsoever.

Hourly, rumors spread back from the cell nearest the door. First that they were all going to be set free. Next, that they were all going to be prosecuted with a two-year minimum sentence. Then, everyone they found with a record was going to be shipped to Oakland. There were rumors that there were two dead, ten dead, fifteen dead. They said that no one really died even though the newsvids said so.

Rumors that Father Alvarez De Collor was coming, that Sylvia Harper was coming, that the media was coming, that no one was coming because the cops were keeping everything a secret. They let the humans go. The Fed was already involved. . . .

As time passed and Angel felt more and more isolated

from the outside world, it became harder and harder to segregate out even the obvious bullshit. When she'd been there ten hours and the rumor passed by that the cops were going to shoot all the moreys and dump them in a mass grave in the Presidio with the help of the Army Corps of Engineers, Angel felt unreasonably nervous.

The last rumor Angel heard was something about President Merideth's aliens from Alpha Centauri. She never caught all of it because that was when her name was finally called.

The population density had lessened to the point where she could make it to the door of the cell without actually climbing over people. In the previous hours she had actually seen people literally passed over the heads of fellow inmates.

When she reached the door, there was the lean form of DeGarmo, looking like he had gotten about as much sleep as she had. He was accompanied by a cop in riot gear who held the remainder of the cell at bay as the gate opened.

"Finally," Angel said as she walked out of the place that had been her home for a good fourteen hours.

DeGarmo shrugged. "For the record, bail was posted ten hours ago. But the city is suffering a bureaucratic meltdown. System wasn't designed to handle this many people."

As they walked to the cell block entrance, the door before them opened, letting in another two cops. One was holding a wallet computer and reading off of it. "Jesus Montoya."

As Angel left, she distinctly heard two different moreau voices say, "Over here!"

One cop shook his head and put a hand up to a helmeted forehead. "Shit. Now what?"

When Angel made it outside, she was blinded by the unexpected intensity of daylight. She turned to her lawyer. "What day is it?"

"Wednesday, close to noon."

"Thanks for getting me out of there. I thought it would never end."

"A feeling affecting many people in that building.

Something you should be thankful for." DeGarmo walked her a distance to the curb, where the BMW was waiting.

"Don't the cops want this for evidence or something?"

DeGarmo smiled. "All they ever really had you for was leaving the scene of the accident. The injured parties never pressed, especially when I informed them of the possible assault charges *they* were facing."

"What about the city?"

DeGarmo ran a hand through his black crew cut. "That's what you should be thankful for. They're so overwhelmed with cases that it was fairly easy to get them to drop what was essentially a nuisance. Especially when I pointed out I could shoot down the charges in front of any judge in the state."

Angel shook her head. "Damn, again, what do I owe you?"

"You'll receive a bill."

"Yeah, right." Angel punched the combination and opened the BMW. "Did I thank you?"

DeGarmo nodded.

It was a measure of how strange Angel's universe had become, the fact she was regarding a lawyer as a person and not as some hypothetical amoral construct to be lumped in with cops and politicians.

"One last thing," he added as she got behind the wheel. "I've gotten St. Luke's to release Mr. Dorset's ashes. They've gone as far as offering to pay for the funeral arrangements—"

Angel yawned. "Look, can you hold that thought?"

"All right, but arrangements should be finalized."

"Tomorrow, okay? When my biological clock has reset. And after I've gotten some sleep."

"Tomorrow." DeGarmo extended his hand and Angel shook it.

*Yes,* Angel thought, *before this week is out, that bastard Byron should be put to final rest.*

She rode the accelerator all the way home.

# CHAPTER 15

Eight hours later, Angel was driving circles around the remains of *The Rabbit Hole* and wondering what had happened to her life.

She'd dug up a relic from Cleveland, a music ramcard, and had the cardplayer jacked up to full volume on the BMW's comm. It was morey music—mostly the screams of clawed guitars—garage bands that no one outside of Cleveland had ever heard of. Unlike most of the synthvid crap that clogged the comm channels on the West Coast, this music had once existed outside of a computer's memory.

The screaming chords and pidgin Arabic lyrics were a reminder of when her life had been understandable. Angel wanted to withdraw into the back alleys that had bred her, back when she knew the rules, back when she was going to live forever and the world was a half-dozen city blocks.

Back when she didn't have enough sense to worry about tomorrow.

*Must really be fucked up if you're nostalgic about living in a burned-out building and a neighborhood that chewed up and spat out a good friend of yours every month or so.*

Fucked up was right. This mess was infecting everything. Every facet of her life was becoming distorted.

Even Lei.

Angel slammed a fist into the side of the steering wheel.

Even her best friend, damn it. Her *only* friend in this town. What was worse, she hadn't seen the argument coming until she found herself in the middle of it.

The transition had been so seamless that Angel still couldn't figure out exactly what had happened. Lei had come home, and, at first, Lei was happy to see her back.

At first . . .

Down Market to the coast, up Mission to the scene of the fire—she'd been driving randomly, trying to clear her mind, and she'd been caught in this loop for the past fifteen minutes like a damaged ramcard, repeating the same four bits over and over. Market, Beale, Mission, and Second.

Angel could understand Lei's point of view. No one should borrow trouble. She shouldn't keep involving the cops and screwing with Lei's life. Angel had tried to be reasonable, but somehow their voices kept getting raised.

A visit by an Asian gentleman in Mr. K's employ hadn't helped matters. Angel then had to explain how she'd become tied to someone with major league involvement in the shady side of the computer underground. The vindictiveness that revelation had unleashed made Angel run away from the apartment, into the BMW.

She'd been cruising south of Market for nearly two hours now.

Angel had needed to clear her head, and while she could have gotten the same air by walking, she felt better with a few tons of armor around her. That and the Beretta—Lei had made it very clear that she didn't want a gun in the house anymore. Angel had slipped the gun under the driver's seat.

Angel tried to think, even though she didn't really want to.

She turned off Second again, passing the corner of Chinatown, and thought of Mr. K's message.

*Dear Miss Lopez,* the letter went, *find enclosed the tickets I agreed to replace. Two are not the originals, I'm afraid, since forging the primitive copy protection of the NonHuman Football League is infinitely easier than reproducing the subtle encryption that masks the data covering two of the ramcards you gave me. . . .* The letter went on for a whole page like that, the upshot of which was that it was going to take *days* of computer time to unravel the data, and even then only if Mr. K had the right algorithm in the first place.

This whole situation had her in a dark foggy room with only a few solid objects she could get a grip on.

No question that Byron was a data courier. Between Mr. K fingering his MO, the anomalous data on two of the tickets Byron gave her—the ones, ironically, for the Denver game—and all the veiled references to "delivery" from Byron himself, Angel was finally clear on what he did for a living. Byron carried data from person A to person B, data that was much too valuable to trust to a sat transmission, or worse, the comm net.

Knowing that did little for her piece of mind, since she still had no idea what the data he carried was. She had to wait for some point between tomorrow and never for Mr. K to crack the encryption on those two ramcards before she could find out *what* Byron was carrying.

At least it was pretty clear where the data came from. Everyone seemed to agree who employed Byron Dorset, Mr. K, DeGarmo, even the paranoid cop Anaka. Byron transported data for VanDyne, a massive conglomerate which was into everything from comm circuitry to defense contracting. A company that, after the quake, inserted itself indelibly into the heart of San Francisco by championing the rebuilding effort. They were responsible for everything from the rebuilt Pyramid and Coit Tower, to that domed monstrosity on Alcatraz that was supposed to be an alien habitat.

The question that nagged at Angel was whether or not Byron was working for VanDyne when his throat got torn out. *That* question raised the fog level by an order of magnitude.

However, she was left with the fact that Byron had been running things smoothly for ten years. He'd made a few million moving hot data for VanDyne with no problems—up to now.

Suddenly, Byron gets creamed.

Angel knew that all this was far removed from the drug deals and gun running that had been rampant in her home neighborhood. However, she was familiar with the pattern. If something that established suddenly went wrong that badly, it generally meant one thing.

Someone fucked up.

Almost always, that someone fucked up by wanting more money. Angel suspected Byron'd fucked up.

She passed the ruins of *The Rabbit Hole* and thought herself deeper into the fog.

The information on those tickets was worth a lot to somebody. Mr. K was investing millions worth of computer time against that payoff. So, how does this get Byron's throat slashed by a feline morey on Eddy Street?

Angel's head was beginning to hurt. There was so much bullshit she needed to explain.

"Go slow," she said to herself. "One step at a time."

Go with the assumption that Byron fucked up. How do you fuck up a job that sweet? Simple answer, you want more money. It was a simple rule from her days on the street. You get greedy, you get dead. For some reason, Byron must have bucked the program he'd been following for ten years, and it got him killed.

Angel knew that she was making too many assumptions, but assumptions were all she had to go on. Besides, the way Byron laid this whole mess on her, it was nice to think he'd brought this all upon himself.

So, the next step was to figure out what Byron had been *supposed* to do before he screwed up. That was fairly simple. He was a courier. He was *supposed* to deliver the data to someone. Angel could even picture where the drop would have been. Byron had made a point in his letter about attending the Frisco-Denver game, and—to drive the point home—the data in question was on the tickets to that very game. Once there, a simple exchange of ramcards with some Denver fan would be ridiculously simple.

Something got screwed before that rendezvous.

That gave her two suspects for the killing if Byron was trying some sort of double-cross, VanDyne and the anonymous guys from Denver. Whoever offed Byron must've freaked when he didn't have the data on him. VanDyne would want it back, and the guys from Denver would want the stuff they were paying big bucks for.

That didn't explain a hotel on Eddy Street, damn it.

"Calm down, one step at a time, right?"

*Think.*

Fact, Byron got offed by a feline morey. Assume the cat killed Byron for the data. That would explain why Byron's condo had been trashed. The smell there could have been feline, canine, or—

Angel slammed on the brakes and pulled to the curb. The realization had hit her like a defensive tackle rushing out of the fog. There *had* to be more than one set of players after those cards at the same time.

It was obvious.

The killers, the cat among them, wanted the data. They must have been sure Byron had the data on him. They didn't know Byron's MO of distancing himself from the hot stuff. Anyone familiar with Byron's courier duties, like Mr. K, would have known that Byron would stash the data off on someone else until the final transfer. Someone who had known Byron over the course of his ten years as a courier would have known that it was likely that Byron would only have his hands on the vital ramcards at the Denver game during the scheduled trade off.

That meant that the killers, cat included, weren't VanDyne *or* the guys from Denver. Otherwise they would've known better than to kill Byron before he gave up the location of the ramcards.

Once they offed Byron and saw their mistake, they trashed his condo looking for the stuff. These guys were hasty, sloppy, and violent.

That meant they were *not* the folks who'd very cleanly broken into Angel's apartment—twice. They were not the ones who methodically read over every ramcard in her house, and were careful enough to cover their scent with some spray disinfectant. The killers who trashed Byron's condo probably didn't know enough to search her place.

The folks searching Angel's apartment, looking for the ramcard Byron had slipped her, just weren't prescient enough to know that she had dropped the shit in the morgue at Frisco General. These guys might fit the bill for the guys from Denver, the people Byron was *supposed* to hand the cards off to.

So far she had three players.

There was VanDyne, the origin of the hot potato. There were the guys from Denver, who seemed to have been shafted by Byron. Then she had the feline hit squad that only barely seemed to know what it was doing.

None of this explained why Byron was offed on Eddy Street, or why he was supposed to be meeting with the Knights of Humanity.

Could the Knights be the guys from Denver? That was bullshit. A Knight attending a NonHuman football game was asking to be the lead on tomorrow's newscast. Also bullshit, they weren't VanDyne—or they shouldn't be if VanDyne was in the practice of hiring moreys.

And the Knights certainly weren't hiring feline hit squads.

Angel looked up from the wheel and sighed.

Everything seemed to fit together so smoothly, and then she hit a wall.

She was only a few blocks short of the coast. Up that way was VanDyne HQ itself, across the street from the Hyatt Memorial. That started her thinking in a new direction.

She hit the controls on the BMW's comm, cutting the music and activating it for outgoing calls. She frowned in frustration when she realized that her car's antenna was still sitting in a gutter somewhere around the Pyramid. She killed the engine, turned the wheels toward the curb, and looked for a public comm.

The search took her halfway around the cycle she'd been traveling. She ended up having to loop around the postquake Sheraton to get to a comm on Market. She pulled up to it, the BMW facing down the hill and toward the Bay.

There was really no rule that prevented her from calling VanDyne herself and asking about Byron. It was the kind of thing she felt stupid about not realizing sooner.

The comm squatted in a spanking new booth sitting within its own blue aura. She got out of the car and listened to the foghorns in the distance, the surf, gulls—almost felt normal.

Then she realized that the salt air off the bay carried

the smell of old smoke, and as she closed on the comm booth she saw new graffiti, "Off the Pink."

"Off the Pink," half a block down from the Sheraton.

Angel shrugged and ran her card through the comm's reader and called up the directory. The World Headquarters for VanDyne Industrial was just a few blocks up Market. Right on the coast, and pretty damn close to all the BS that had happened to her.

There was a brief thought that those punks in *The Rabbit Hole* could have been there for Byron, and not just fucking around. No, that didn't quite make sense, did it?

She glanced up Market as she started the call. "Wha?"

Was it paranoia, or was that four-door Chevy Caldera parked up the street the same one that had been behind her at the last light? If so, it had followed her around the Sheraton. On the comm, someone was saying, "Van Dyne Industrial, can I help you?"

Angel ignored it, and walked back to her car. *Okay,* she thought in Lei's direction, *I've gone totally paranoid.* Angel tried to stay calm, but she was running by the time she got to the BMW.

She slammed the door behind her and jerked the car into the street, flooring it. The BMW shot down Market, toward the Bay. Angel took a few deep breaths and groped under the seat for the gun.

It wasn't there.

And there was an unfamiliar smell in the back seat.

The BMW had made it half a block by the time she turned around. Had she been that stupid?

Her unwanted passenger was already returning to an upright position. In one hand was Angel's Beretta, in the other was an FN P101—a small machine pistol with a trapezoidal barrel whose hole was the diameter of Angel's index finger. He was a feline the size of a jaguar but with fur a uniform tawny color.

Angel's foot was still pressing down on the accelerator as he leveled the machine pistol at her. For some reason she noticed the hands. Large, powerful hands with gloss-black claws that reflected the streetlights shooting by.

"Stop the car."

It'd been the fucking broken window. This bastard had

just walked into her back seat. She hadn't bothered to turn on the damn alarm. Stupid, stupid, stupid all around.

The toes on her right foot kept the accelerator pressed to the floor. Her eyes stayed locked on the moreau in the back seat as the BMW's transponder beeped warnings at her. The car was heading for a red light.

The cat in the back seat showed some teeth. Angel was beginning to read some emotion in those shadowy yellow eyes. The smell of stress was feline, but a different flavor of feline than Angel was familiar with.

"Stop the car," he repeated. "We don't want this to get messy."

What the fuck was she doing? The bastard had a gun, two of them, in fact, one of them hers, and she wasn't even looking at the road—

Hell, the road was clear the last time she looked.

"You don't know what messy can be." God help her, she was grinning.

The BMW's computer went nuts with the warning beeps when she zoomed through a red light at the intersection of First Street. Horns Dopplered past her and the thought crossed her mind that they were going to shoot by VanDyne in no time now.

"Damn it, stop the car! I'll shoot if—"

There was a crunch when Angel came up on a car too fast for the collision avoidance system to compensate. She scraped by and turned her attention forward. The Bay was rushing up like a fog-shrouded abyss.

"*Shoot me, then!* You think I give a shit any more, you cocksucking dweezil? Pull the goddamned trigger, I just hope your candyass can swim."

They were almost on top of the bay.

This was crazy.

Angel hit the control that popped open all the locks on the car. VanDyne's headquarters was the last building on the right, then the Main Street-California intersection, a short concrete embankment, then water.

The gun pressed into the back of her head. It trembled slightly. Angel smelled cat and gun oil.

The second she saw the VanDyne building—a refurbed Federal Reserve Bank—shoot by, she slammed on the brakes and pulled the BMW as hard to the right as she could. Half the computer's red lights lit on the dash as the air filled with the high-pitched scream and acrid smell of fishtailing rubber.

The cat was thrown back and to the side, slamming somewhere into the passenger footwell.

The rear of the car kissed the concrete embankment—blowing a chunk of it into the bay—and she was shooting down Spear at about eighty klicks an hour. She saw movement in her rearview mirror and slammed on the brakes again. The cat was thrown forward—

Angel popped the door and ran, leaving the BMW to roll to a stop in the wrong lane.

Her thoughts were lagging about five steps behind her actions. She was still wondering if running was a good idea when she'd cleared the four lanes of Spear in two-and-a-half running steps.

She hit the curb when she heard the squeal of more tires back on Market. It was the black Chevy four-door screaming into the turn against the light.

Her foot touched the curb and one of the metered power feeds on the curb erupted into a shower of sparks. The echo of the gunshot was still dying when she cleared the sidewalk and dived over the barrier into VanDyne's parking garage.

Cars, but no sign of manned security. The one guard-box by the gate was empty. As she glanced at it, the windows exploded, showering her with tiny cubes of polymer as she passed it. She leaped on the hood of a new Plymouth Antaeus and jumped from there, over a railing, to an upper level of the garage. Behind her she heard the Caldera crash through the barrier.

She had nowhere left to run but up. She was running so fast now that every third step she had to hit the ground with her hands to change direction.

She was cornered. What the hell was she going to do when she hit the top of the garage?

It was, at most, fifteen seconds she spent like that—running flat out, the sound of the Caldera gaining on her, her field of vision taken up by about a square meter of concrete that rushed by a dozen centimeters from her nose.

She must have run up a half-dozen levels, barely ahead of the Chevy, when she heard a noise ahead and to the right. Angel looked up in time to see a Dodge Electroline van peeling out of its parking spot. It backed and slammed itself across the traffic lane, crunching its end into an opposite retaining wall in the process.

"Shit!"

She was running too damn fast to stop, so she jumped. She got a brief view of the side of the van—Infotech Comm Repair or somesuch—before she slammed into the ceiling above the van. She hit with the back of her right shoulder and bounced, sending a shivering splinter of pain down that side of her body. It didn't do much to slow her forward momentum. She hit the roof of the van, which was still rolling forward a bit after bouncing off the retaining wall.

She had enough time to realize she was in deep shit as she rolled off the other side of the van. This time she managed to lead with her feet. She ended up on all fours on the opposite side of the van as she heard the Caldera round the last turn.

On the other side of the van, she heard the side door crash open.

She was still trying to figure out if the van was an innocent bystander or another one of the fuckers out to get her when guns started going off all over the place.

Angel only had a slice of view out from under the van, but she could see the Caldera. Three people, all moreaus. They'd angled the passenger door toward the van, and some sort of canine was firing one of those nasty looking machine pistols toward her and the van.

The van was returning fire.

*Boy,* was it returning fire.

In response to the first short bark from the anonymous canine's machine pistol a deafening chatter came from inside the van. It sounded like a jackhammer on steroids. Angel could follow the trace of the shot from the billows of concrete dust that blew in its wake. A cloud of gray dust tore in the direction of the black Chevy and twisted through the right front fender with the sound of shearing fiberglass.

She couldn't hear the Chevy's tire go, she could just see the gust of wind as it exploded. After that, sparks began grinding from the rim as the driver of the Chevy began reversing. That move probably saved the Chevy's engine, if not its front-end alignment.

In three seconds it was over, and the only sound in the garage was the scraping echo from the rim of the Chevy as it escaped downward. The suspension on the van rocked as the occupant jumped out of the door on the other side.

Angel got up from her position on the ground, and prepared to bolt—

And Kobe Anaka rounded the front end of the van, still wearing the same damn suit and still looking like he needed a world of sleep. He was holding a smoking assault rifle.

"What the fuck are you doing here?" she said, too shocked to run.

From his look, it was a mutual question.

# CHAPTER 16

When Anaka pulled her into the van and Angel finally saw the interior, she came to the conclusion that the Asian cop was a hardcore nut. Her reaction upon seeing the back of Anaka's van was, "Is all this shit legal?"

Kobe Anaka's response was, "Most of it."

There's a class of people who doped themselves up to the max on hardware and sat in desert bunkers waiting for the end of the world—other people just liked the toys. And Anaka had the toys.

Behind a wire-mesh fence and a digital thumbpad lock that closed in a lengthwise half of the rear of the van were *guns.* The weaponry Anaka was carrying must have cost a fortune. Angel only recognized about half the artillery. There was a Desert Eagle and an Uzi for the old Israeli crowd. For the Europeans there was a modified H&K Valkyrie with a barrel extension that must be a flash and noise suppressor. From the subcontinent was a fifty-cal Vindhya sniper rifle with an electronic sight the size of Angel's head. From the States was a very new looking M26–11 which Angel only knew from a comm broadcast she'd seen once, something that fired so fast that it had to alternate between four different barrels to keep the damn thing from melting. The clip was bigger than Angel's foot.

That didn't even count the Steyr caseless fifty-cal assault rifle he had strafed the Chevy Caldera with.

Anaka pulled out of the garage, spreading a coat of burnt rubber from his parking space to the entrance. Angel had to hold on to the fence in the back to keep from being tossed into the rear of the van. She didn't want to tumble back there because it looked like she'd trash a few grand worth of electronics that filled the right rear quarter of the van.

When they hit the street, Angel saw the remains of the Caldera—but no sign of the BMW.

*What the fuck just happened?*

Once they were on the street, Angel felt safe enough to move. She pulled herself into the passenger seat up front, next to Anaka. She wondered if White, or any of Anaka's coworkers at the Police Department knew about this van. People seemed to have tagged Anaka as a little paranoid —but folks with this kind of hardware generally weren't just receiving garbled transmissions, they were off on another frequency altogether.

Angel wondered what his psych profile looked like, and if you were still nuts when people were really after you.

They turned on to Market, shot past City Hall and Police Headquarters, took a turn, and soon the van started weaving up and down the chrome-new hills of Japantown in a sort of half-assed western course toward Golden Gate Park.

Through all this, Anaka was silent. Finally Angel said, "Are we far enough away from the action, or do we have to start swimming first?"

Anaka looked at her as if he suddenly realized he had a passenger. He didn't look good. He was even more disheveled, and it looked like he had gone without a shower for days. "Don't push me, Angel—my whole operation just got blown, and I have no idea if I got made or not."

"What the fuck? What operation? Who're you working for?"

"Me." The way Anaka glared at her made her nervous. If this guy was out on his own, running his own rulebook, he was dangerous. Another rule that had served her well on the street: Never antagonize crazy people.

Lone psycho guns down rabbit in Golden Gate Park—she did *not* like the sound of that.

She tried to sound calmer, soothing, "What operation?" *Good, now let's just hope he doesn't think I sound condescending.*

"Surveillance on VanDyne. What else?"

*Foolish me, it was so effing obvious.* "Just you?"

Anaka smiled, and for a brief instant he looked normal—or as normal as Angel supposed he ever looked. "You'd be surprised what one man can do with the right equipment."

The buildings melted away and suddenly the van was in the park. Anaka began paying very close attention to the traffic. He also mumbled to himself in subvocalizations he probably didn't realize Angel could hear. "Street clear, no sign of an aerial transponder, no EM from the van—"

He sighed and sounded relieved. "Okay, we're clean, and it doesn't look like we're being followed."

*Luck-ee.* Angel had thought that lately she'd been overly paranoid, but Anaka raised that paranoia by an order of magnitude. What was worse, he might have been justified. Angel doubted he'd ever be jumped from his own back seat.

"You expect those moreys to still be after me?" She certainly didn't. She figured she had the feline hit squad pegged. Violent, prone to brute force, somewhat stupid, and rather unlikely to jump anything that could outdo their firepower. They acted almost exactly like the street gangs she knew back in Cleveland.

Besides, they'd split in her BMW. If they got within range, she could really screw them over with the remote.

"I don't even know who they were." There was an uncomfortable note in Anaka's voice when he said that. Loose ends were nagging Angel; they must be torture for this guy.

"Then who'd follow us?"

Anaka let the van roll to a stop in a dark section of the park. He glanced about, as if looking for witnesses, and called up an interesting-looking program on the comm that nestled between the two front seats. He called up a display on the screen that looked exactly like the logo on the sides of the van: Infotech. With a few presses on the screen, "Infotech" became "Handy Landscaping" and the background changed from red to green.

Angel caught a glimpse of activity out of the corner of

her eye and looked at the side-view mirror. The paintjob on the van had changed.

"The Fed."

Angel turned her head and realized that Anaka was responding to her question. "The— Why would the government be after you, us, this—what'd you do to the paint?"

"Dynamic liquid crystal under a transparent finish. Programmable. Useful in undercover work."

Was that kind of stuff legal for— *No,* Angel thought, *probably not. How long have you wanted to be a spy, Anaka? How many intelligence agencies turned you down before you settled for being a cop? When the CIA turned you down, was it the psych profile, or were you just a security risk?*

"You think the Fed's after you?"

"I don't know."

"What *do* you know?"

"The Fed's running VanDyne."

Anaka had lost it. She'd been sideswiped by a lot of BS, but massive government conspiracies were a little—well—nuts.

"What do you mean, 'the Fed's running VanDyne?' "

"Just what I said." Anaka turned his seat around and pushed past Angel into the back of the van. He squatted in front of a stack of obscure electronics and pulled out a keyboard. From the arrangement, someone running the show there had to sit on a pillow duct-taped to the floor of the van. Anaka crossed his legs and put the keyboard on his lap. "About twelve hours of good coverage on VanDyne's HQ. That, and a few hours on the comm last night—"

"Just tell me what you mean 'The Fed runs VanDyne.' "

"First off . . ." The screens were bolted at an angle overhead to give some room for the electronics. Anaka tapped a few keys and one of the screens lit up with a schematic map of North America. "From a ten-hour sample of their data traffic, here's a plot of the signal density."

The map freckled with a few dots here and there, but one part of the eastern seaboard lit up like a nuke.

"DC?"

"Langley. The signal's encrypted, so I can't make heads or tails of it, but VanDyne's in nearly constant contact with the CIA, the National Security Agency, the National Reconnaissance Office, and the Pentagon. Those are the places I knew—"

"So?" Angel was hoping that this all could be dismissed as a paranoid fantasy. "They're defense contractors."

"That isn't all. It's a matter of record that last February VanDyne was bought out by The Pacific Import Company—"

"So?" Angel climbed out of her seat to get a better look at what Anaka was doing in the back of the van. She found herself squatting between the side door and the wire mesh that caged the artillery. "Companies get bought out all the time."

"By companies half their size whose primary business—allegedly—is running arms for the CIA?"

"Are you sure about that?"

"Look behind you."

Angel glanced at the ranks of firearms Anaka indicated. "Okay, so you know about gunrunning. . . ."

"That isn't all." Anaka's voice was raising, and his gestures were becoming more animated. Angel suspected that he needed someone to believe him. "It was hard to unearth with a privately owned corporation, but look at this—" Anaka tapped a little at the keyboard and names began scrolling across one of the screens.

Angel couldn't make heads or tails of it. "What's all this?"

"A partial employee list, backdated to the thirties."

"Where'd you get that? You hack their computer?"

"I wish. As far as I can tell, they only have one dedicated line into their mainframe and they watch it like a hawk. No, I got this list from the county. I ran a list through the standard federal credit search and, God help me—" Anaka's voice actually broke. Angel could smell stress floating off the guy and thought he was pretty damn close to cracking.

"Go on," she said, putting a hand on his shoulder to calm him.

"Not a single employee had a credit record prior to 20 February, 2059."

"Huh?"

"Not a student loan, not a mortgage, not a single car payment before the Pacific Import purchase. I ran things through the DMV. Every plate I ran came up as a car purchase after February."

"You saying these people didn't exist?"

"Then, the capper—" Anaka called up yet another screen and a picture appeared of a rather generic black human. Text began rolling across the picture. "Peter Washington. The picture is from DMV records. The info is from various tax and credit databases. According to all the local data he's been a resident in Oakland since the quake. Homeowner despite the fact he's never carried a mortgage. Earns something like a hundred grand a year without a sign of financing a college education."

"Okay."

Anaka slammed a few keys so hard that Angel thought they might break. "*Look.* I managed to run the picture through another database." Another picture of the same guy, more text scrolling by. A lot more text scrolling by. "I got on a sat link to Interpol."

Angel squinted at the text rolling by the guy's face. "*Jesus.*"

"*See?* Interpol has the most comprehensive terrorist database in the world. Peter Washington is better known in his native Western Somalia as Obura Dambela, alias Abdula Kazim, alias Peirre Olan, alias . . ." Anaka sat back and caught his breath. After a few seconds he seemed to calm down. "Worked for several nationalistic causes in North Africa and around the Med. The UAS, the EEC, *and* the Islamic Axis want him in custody—the one thing in ten they agree on."

Angel whistled through her front teeth. She read some of the list of charges, "Smuggling contraband genetics out of Africa, moving a nuclear trigger from Germany to Kurdistan—yeah, the Axis must love him—assassinations and attempts on council members from Egypt, Algeria,

Morocco, North Somalia. . . . What's he got to do with the Fed?"

Anaka looked at her with an expression she had trouble reading. She could see him saying, "You see? You see? This is what the world is *really* like." Damn him.

What Anaka actually said was, "The CIA hired him in an advisory capacity in '56."

Angel closed her eyes and shook her head. No, the world is not some nut's paranoid wet dream.

"That's what Interpol gives me. And when I hit the FBI database with the name Obura Dambela, I get a faceful of national security."

Angel leaned against the inside of the side door and slid slowly to the ground. Great. Byron was a CIA agent. A vulpine James Bond remake cast by some morey garage-vid producers for a three-digit channel in the high five-hundreds.

She stared for a long time, between her feet. "Maybe it's just crazy."

"What?"

"Maybe the U.S. Government is simply insane." Angel sighed. "Gotta be it."

Reality had taken the final plunge for her. Things had warped beyond recognition. Byron worked for the Fed, effing wonderful. Maybe he was involved in busting President Merideth's aliens. Yeah, she could see the vid-drama on the comm right now. Every week Byron Dorset, vulpine secret agent, would investigate a new corporate front—only to find it teeming with white blubbery alien beings. After the mandatory shoot-out, all would safely end with the aliens being shipped off to the VanDyne-built facility on Alcatraz.

Except the last episode where Byron gets gored by a cat in a seedy motel room. Even so, a ten year run isn't bad for a series. Especially one this bad. Ten year run with a surprise ending—everyone would have thought the aliens'd get him.

*Wait a minute.*

*Ten year run?*

VanDyne was only bought out by the Fed last February. If anything, Byron had been working for the previous owners. Suddenly her thinking was going off in all sorts of uncomfortable directions.

She began wondering when, exactly, Van Dyne started building the Alcatraz dome, and when, exactly, did the Fed "convert" it to an alien habitat to hold the captured aliens. She began wondering if Byron was telling the truth when he said he'd been "laid off," perhaps because of new management. She began to suspect why Byron was suddenly operating on his own.

Maybe he had no choice but to buck the program.

And Angel began to wonder about the nature of Byron's original employers.

Angel's thoughts swam in ever-deeper circles until a sudden revelation slammed her out of it.

"Oh, fuck, *Lei!*"

"What?"

She'd been so fucking stupid! "Damn it, if those moreaus were looking for it, why did they think I had it?"

"Had what?"

"They searched my place first! Anaka, you got to get me home, now."

Angel got a sinking feeling as the van turned on to Twenty-third. She could see the police flashers from a block away. There were also a few new vans here and there, and as the van closed, Angel could see the landing lights of another news aircar approaching.

"Let me out."

Angel opened the passenger door before Anaka had stopped the van. She hit the pavement, stumbled, and ran toward the commotion. She kept shaking her head and squeezing her eyes shut as if the scene was a hallucination and when her eyes opened the world would return to normal.

The cockeyed hill was more bizarre than ever, and it felt like the damn street was rolling slowly under her feet.

She started to push through the crowd, shoving aside moreaus twice her size. She was greeted with curses, growls, and the occasional feline hiss. She made it to the police line and—oddly—the first image to catch her eye was the bay window on the second floor. It had been pushed out, busting all the panes over the sidewalk. Lei's expensive drapes were blowing out, over the side of the house. It looked as if something was thrown from—

"No," Angel whispered.

A cop tried to keep her from breaking the police line, but she ducked under his arm. Some of the vids must have recognized her because she had to push through a gauntlet of reporters to make it to the door.

"Miss Lopez, just one question—"

"—does this have anything to do—"

"—you think they were after you—"

"—with your statement about Byron Dorset's death—"

"—feel any responsibility—"

The world was slowing down and the reporters questions degenerated into an incomprehensible rush of sound. She pushed through the middle of them, not stopping even to look at their faces. Most slid out of her way, managing to stay uncomfortably close. The last one didn't move and Angel drove a light kick to his shin that took him down to the pavement.

As she stepped inside her building, she ran straight into Detective White. "Lopez—" He began, grabbing her arm.

"Where is she?"

"We need to talk, rabbit."

"Where?"

"St. Luke's—in surgery. Luckier than that geriatric lion."

*Not Balthazar, too.* Angel pulled away from his arm. "I'm going."

White extended his other arm across the doorway, blocking her exit. "I said we need to talk."

"What fucking planet you on? You gonna take me down in front of a dozen vids—after some freaked bastards slam-dunked my roommate?"

"If I have to, you little twitch." White stared at her with eyes that were thoroughly pissed at the world. Eyes that were about to do something drastic. "We can talk on the way. Should go to St. Luke's in any event. Need to see a doctor."

# CHAPTER 17

White drove her in a familiar car, a puke-green Plymouth Antaeus. Though Angel didn't remember the cavernous interior so filled with fast-food containers during the last ride. He mumbled, muttered, and chewed up the road like it was trying to attack him.

"Fuck's your problem?" Angel asked, quietly. She was torn between irritation and worry, between being pissed off at the world, or being horrified by it.

And, worse, she kept thinking about Balthazar. The lion she hardly knew had the bad sense to open his door at the absolute worst time. She had caught a glimpse of his apartment as White dragged her away, and she still couldn't get the image of a twisted wheelchair draped in the old lion's cartoon blanket out of her mind.

"My problem?" White pulled a turn on to Dolores that did well to illustrate the mass of the Plymouth. God help any compacts that got in its way. "Boy, you got nerve. Everybody's got nerve."

Mission rolled by and became younger as they proceeded. Somewhere past the park the only relic of the last century was the location of the road. "Everybody's gone nuts. *Jesus!* Folks are going to start sniping at cops and call it self-defense."

White shook his head and glared at Angel. "You think I have it in for you, don't you?"

"No," she said as sweetly as she could muster—it wasn't much. "All my friends strong-arm me on a regular basis."

"Everyone's forgotten the way things work . . ." White mumbled to himself, and in a disgusted tone of voice addressed Angel. "You think I do this shit for my health?

You think I'm here just to ride your ass? I'm a cop, you rodent twitch, a good cop. You even *know* what a good cop is?"

"Huh?" It didn't seem a safe question to answer directly.

White didn't pay attention to her. He went on as if he had forgotten it was a dialogue. "It isn't the cowboy lone-ranger shit. It isn't slamming the perp into the pavement, whatever people think. It isn't this political bullshit, or race, or species. It isn't justice— You want to know what the fuck a good cop is?"

"Well—"

"It's taking down scum with something that'll hold. Period. Swim in a cesspool, shit sticks to you. But if you do your fucking job you don't waste your time on assholes that'll walk."

Angel looked at the balding detective. White was staring down the road, shaking his head. "Damn it. A clean bust, a righteous bust. For once we got the Knights by the balls, *and it gets fucked all to hell!*"

Angel couldn't take this any more. "What are you talking about?"

"Fucking-A Knights of Humanity. Thank *you* very much."

White bumped over the curb as he turned across the intersection at Market. "You *and* my *ex*-partner."

White had lost her. "I'm not getting you."

"I have to paint a picture? This goes beyond your dead boyfriend. Someone big backs the Knights, someone untouchable. We had murder one hanging over those freakheads, they were damn close to rolling over. Earl would've blabbed to high heaven—if he'd lived. But no. *You* had to go media-happy and torpedo the murder case. They clam." White's knuckles were beginning to pale as he gripped the steering wheel. He was shaking slightly. "Then—damn it—*then* you know what happens?"

Angel shook her head silently.

White jerked the car to a stop in the parking lot of St. Luke's Veterinary and killed the engine. "*Then* my partner goes solo and pokes around VanDyne Industrial. Suddenly the U.S. Attorney General is talking to the DA, and the DA cuts a deal—and Anaka is out on permanent vacation, I'm in danger of being transferred, and our whole case with the Knights turns to shit—and the moreys in this town think we're *protecting* those geeks." White slammed his door open, gouging the car next to it. "We're here, let's check on your roommate."

Angel followed White out of the car. It made a warped sort of sense. All this crap about Byron's death, a lot of the problems she had with the police anyway, simply came about because the Knights were higher on the SFPD shit list. Great. "Keep complaining, White. You got the firebug, she's ready to sing a fucking aria—"

"Was." They walked into the hospital. "Since the Knights brought in their own lawyer—a high-class country-club type from DC yet—everyone's suffering amnesia."

Angel suspected that Igalez would be relieved.

The visit to the hospital didn't amount to much. Lei was still in surgery, undergoing spinal reconstruction, and she'd be unconscious at least twenty-four hours after the operation. The doctor who talked to them seemed torn between expressing concern for the patient and showing outright hostility to the lepine moreau who'd given St. Luke's such bad press.

The detail that really sank into Angel's gut—beyond the mention of microsurgery, experimental cybernetics, and even the possibility of paralysis—was the fact the doctors had to amputate Lei's tail. That hit home. Angel couldn't picture Lei without her tail wagging.

Angel absorbed the news silently, her gut shriveled up into a tiny ball of anger floating in a pool of sick emptiness. And, damn it, what for? What did Lei have to do with this except be at the wrong place at the wrong time?

The world not only wasn't fair, it was actively hostile.

When it was clear they weren't going to get a chance to see Lei, White put his hand on Angel's shoulder. "Come on."

"What?"

"We've got to talk with the doctor who did the autopsy on Byron Dorset."

That pierced through the muck clouding her thinking. She remembered her run-in with Ellis in the hospital parking lot. Angel remembered just how paranoid the doctor had been acting.

Wait a minute. . . .

Didn't Anaka say that Doctor Ellis was missing?

She thought of mentioning the fact to White, but White didn't look to be in the mood for inconvenient revelations. Instead she asked, "You need me for this?"

"Police protection. I ain't letting you out of my sight."

*Sounds like police harassment to me.* Angel wasn't sure if she was annoyed or grateful. However, she knew better than to argue at this point. White had been pushed a little too far.

They didn't stop at the reception desk—they went straight to the elevator. White told the elevator to go to the sixth floor. Angel leaned up against the wall, feeling the fatigue catch up with her. "Why now?"

"Why what?" White asked as the elevator doors slid open on a dimly lit reception area. White walked up to a holo directory and began tapping at it.

"Why the sudden interest in Byron's death?"

White found what he was looking for and led Angel down an empty office corridor that led radially off of the lobby. The corridor here smelled different, there was less of the blood-fur-fecal aroma that marked most of the hospital. Even so, the smell of pine disinfectant was as strong as ever.

"I told you, the murder rap on the Knights turned to shit."

White stopped in front of a closed office door. No lights shone behind the fogged window. "No one home," Angel said.

White grunted what seemed to be an affirmative monosyllable and pulled a slim keypad out of his pocket. The small wallet computer had the SFPD Phoenix burned into the case, as well as a prominent serial number. White tried the door. It was locked. That determined, he knelt in front of the door. Angel heard his joints popping, and imagined that hauling that kind of bulk around wasn't pleasant.

With his eyes level with the lock mechanism, White started tapping at the keypad.

"What are you doing?" Angel was getting the feeling that the situation here wasn't quite kosher.

White made a derisive noise. "What does it look like?"

White's keypad beeped and displayed a long alphanumeric on its screen. White tapped it into the keypad of the lock mechanism. Even though it was obvious to Angel that the lock also required a ramcard to open it, the thing blinked green at White and opened.

"White, do you have a warrant—is this legal?"

"Would you shut up and get in?"

Angel had the distinct impression that White was very much aware of the fact that Pat Ellis was missing.

White pushed her through the door and closed it behind him. Angel stumbled into the darkened office and bumped into a desk. "What the hell are you doing?"

White pulled a small flashlight out of his pocket and sat himself behind the desk. "I'm finding out what Dr. Ellis thought about the deceased." Within a few minutes, White was rummaging through the doctor's collection of ramcards. Angel found a seat and slid into it. The two of them sat in silence as White played with the doctor's computer.

Angel was uncomfortable. If someone found the two of them in here, she was pretty damn sure that she'd be the one who got shafted. Also, something about the room was making her nervous.

Could it be the disinfectant smell?

Of course it smelled familiar, all that pine shit smelled the same—right? It would be paranoid to think it meant that the folks who covered their scent back at her apartment had been here. She'd be treading on Anaka's territory.

But she could swear the disinfectant downstairs had been more lemon-scented.

She resisted pounding her feet on the carpet.

After a period of shuffling ramcards and searching the desk, White said, "Somewhere between the good doctor and the DA, the data on the corpse changed. The doctor herself, I haven't been able to get hold of her since you went on the net and started kicking shit about the 'accidental' cremation."

"Great." It was pretty much obvious about that. If you assumed that Byron's accidental cremation was no accident, it was pretty much a foregone conclusion that it was to destroy evidence that Ellis falsified the autopsy. Probably to cover the fact a morey offed Byron. "You know, I talked to her Saturday." Angel ran her hand over the chair she sat in. Something about it was making her itch.

White looked up from the doctor's comm, his face underlit by a blue glow from the screen. "Oh?" It sounded slightly accusatory.

"She acted paranoid." *Join the club.* "Told me that she thought a moreau did it." Angel lifted her hand from the arm of the chair, there was a mass of gray hair that clung to her fingers.

"Oh, great, what else have you been holding back, rabbit?"

"Don't start pretending that'd you'd have listened to me back when you still had a hard-on for the Knights."

White grumbled. "Just answer the question, Lopez. Is there other shit hanging around I should know about?" Then something caught his eye on the screen and he hit the computer in disgust. "*Nothing!*"

"Think the doctor is responsible for Byron's cremation?" Angel repeated her own suspicions and shook the gray hair from her hand. Of course there was fur on the chair. St. Luke's was a veterinary hospital.

"Great way to cover a botched autopsy. But she worked on the files too damn well. There isn't even a file on Dorset. The damn slate's wiped."

"Could someone in the Fed—"

"Oh, please. Don't get on my ex-partner's conspiracy trip." White stood up. "Let's go. I'm putting you in a safe-house."

As they left, Angel ran her hand over the one other

chair facing the desk. It came back with short tawny hairs. She imagined a feline scent when she held them very close to her nose.

*Great.* Should she tell him? No, let him figure it out. If it was the feline hit squad that did Byron, made sense that it was the feline hit squad that terrified Ellis into fucking up the autopsy. That fit the pattern, and it wasn't what worried Angel overmuch.

What worried Angel was the fact that the disinfectant downstairs *was* lemon scented.

The safe house they stuck her in was a dingy set of rooms in the Tenderloin. An off-white prequake structure that called itself Hotel Bruce in broken neon. It was part of a wretched mash of prequake hotels and cheap postquake modular high-rises. People called the modular things ice trays. The hotel was flanked by arrays of flaking chrome cubes and dirt-specked windows. The ice trays must've started falling apart as soon as the contractors got paid.

The Hotel Bruce sat only a few blocks from where Byron was killed and Angel didn't feel particularly safe, even if police HQ was just down the street—after all, so was the meeting hall for the Knights.

In two hours of questioning, Angel got a better feeling for White than she really wanted to. By his own definition, he was a good cop. Angel was willing to admit that. To her, though, a good cop wasn't a very admirable creature.

At least now the feline hit squad was leaving a path wide enough for just about everyone to follow. It was strange, but Angel was annoyed by the fact that they were acting so bonehead. When a bunch of moreys started acting violent and stupid like that, it helped to feed a lot of nasty pink preconceptions.

Somehow, Angel knew that someone in the police department was going to leak to the vids the fact that the suspects in Byron's death and ones responsible for the mess at her place were a bunch of moreys. She had a vivid picture of what that kind of news would do to Collor and the Knights.

She stayed up most of the night, thinking. She lay on a sagging mattress that was saturated with the smells of a dozen previous tenants. She listened to her cop baby-sitter in the next room and occasionally watched the sky-line out the window through a haze of orange neon.

White was pragmatic, inclined to believe that Byron's death was the result of some petty conflict. Angel didn't do much to enlighten him. She couldn't see any way to mention VanDyne without explaining her run-in with Anaka. She was sure that any mention of his ex-partner would just piss him off. She certainly didn't tell him about Mr. K, and she did her best deadpan act when she claimed not to know what the moreys were looking for.

She didn't trust White.

As she stonewalled, she wished to God she knew what was on those ramcards. Then she might have some in-kling of who all the players actually were. She had the fe-line hit squad tearing up everything that got in its way. There were the original buyers that she'd labeled the guys from Denver who may or may not have been the guys who slunk around covering their scent with pine dis-infectant. There was VanDyne—actually two VanDynes; the original VanDyne that produced hot data that Byron was hired to transport, and the VanDyne that was owned and operated by the CIA. There was the pale Fedboy with the reddish eyes that she'd run into at Frisco General and seen hovering in a van outside her apartment. Then there were the Knights, who were supposed to meet with Byron when he was killed—

Angel's head hurt. No wonder Anaka was a little nuts.

She closed her eyes against the neon glare and listened to the comm in the next room. More politics. That's all the net seemed to carry now, riots and politics. Senator Sylvia Harper was going to visit the battle scene in LA, and the commentators were speculating whether she was going to come north to San Francisco. Must be a local broadcast. Local vid-jockeys seemed to have a visceral need to include the home burg in a national story no mat-ter how far-fetched the connection.

The news went on, and Angel felt unaccountably angry when the lengthening brief on local violence didn't include Lei. Like she didn't really count. . . .

Angel pulled her arms in, clutching herself and trying not to shake.

# Chapter 18

Angel spent Thursday on the comm to DeGarmo trying to figure out her legal status. She found out that, if she wanted to, she could have her lawyer get her out from under the cop's thumb. Her problem was that she didn't know where else she could go. After all, it seemed like going home, or to Byron's condo, would be like strapping a target to the back of her head.

As if there wasn't one there now.

She also asked DeGarmo if he knew anything about the Knights' new high-class defense lawyer. DeGarmo said he'd look into it. He also told her that he now had Byron's ashes and wanted to know what to do with them.

She almost told him what to do with them, but she restrained herself. She told DeGarmo to hang on to them. She'd think about it.

She also called St. Luke's. Lei was still under, but she was probably going to pull through.

The juxtaposing of those two calls completed her disassociation with the world. She'd been cut adrift. Her life had become so much storm-tossed flotsam.

The disintegration of her personal life found a mirror in the social turbulence enveloping San Francisco. When she wasn't making calls, her resident cop—a hispanic named Quintara—remained glued to the screen watching the news.

To her, the news wasn't news. It told her nothing new. The county was still clogged by a judicial logjam two days after the mass arrests on Tuesday. A pink mob had attacked a Bensheim Reproduction Clinic down in Bayview. The home of a conservative pink councilman was torched in Pacific Heights. A bunch of nonviolent moreys led a sit-down strike on the Golden Gate. Another bunch of pinks rampaged through Chinatown again.

When they went national and cut to artillery fire in the Bronx, it didn't help promote a tranquil mood.

Angel watched the cop, rather than the screen. The cop had the look of some small animal locked in the glare of oncoming headlights.

The young detective wasn't much for conversation. Angel had tried talking to him a few times. All she usually received in return was a grunted monosyllable. She'd given up on conversation about two hours after she woke up. Quintara was as preoccupied as she was, and he smelled nervous to high heaven.

Probably didn't like being shut up in a hotel with a rabbit.

Or, more likely, he didn't like the thought that the city around him threatened to go ballistic. An ugly prospect for a cop.

When she got bored watching Quintara, she turned her chair toward the window. She watched the scene through the blinds, the cop watched the scene off the comm, and the hours passed in uncomfortable silence.

She rested her chin on the windowsill and thought. The moreaus that jumped her and threw Lei out the window, two felines and two canines. She'd gotten fairly good looks at them, as well as scent a few times, but she couldn't place either species. The only thing she really felt for certain was that they were the shits that offed Byron, and they were all strut, swagger, and intimidation—but no fucking brains.

Someone's hired thugs, they had to be. Someone who wanted the data Bryon carried. Who? Could be anyone. All Angel could figure was that it had to be someone who hadn't been playing this game for very long.

The hit squad slashed Bryon, scared Ellis into falsifying the autopsy and roaching Bryon's corpse, then trashed Bryon's condo looking for the data. Only after Angel had become an involuntary media star did they go after *her* for the data. First her apartment—mauling anything that got in their way—then, finally, they had gone after Angel herself.

She looked out at the darkening neon jungle of Eddy Street and wondered why she didn't feel better. This was all about who killed Byron, right? The creeps who did it were up on SFPD shit list now. White was after their asses, too. The hit squad was so unusual—and blatant—that they should turn up pretty fast. Once that happens, the bastards get put away, finito, the end, hand the fat lady her script.

Like hell.

Not that seeing all four of those creeps strung up by fishhooks and having electric shocks applied to their genitals wouldn't lighten her day a little—but it certainly wouldn't solve anything. Also, she was beginning to suspect it wouldn't lead to any answers either. The four moreaus were small-time.

All the evidence pointed to the fact that the circles Byron ran in were far from small-time. If he was carting data for VanDyne, at the very least he was carting sensitive data for a High-Tech megacorp that was into defense contracting. At the most—

She shuddered a little when she thought about the speculation that had been running through her mind in the back of Anaka's van. If any of that was true, the Fed had a very good reason for taking over VanDyne.

Whatever the source. Tetsami, Mr. K, seemed to think the data Byron carried was big-time by an order of magnitude. Considering the shit kicked up by those ramcards, Angel was inclined to agree.

A lighting-flash broke her train of thought, the thunder rattling the window pane a centimeter short of her nose. She blinked a few times and looked at the street below. Something was missing—

She spread the slats on the blinds and called, "Quintara."

"Hmm," came a voice barely audible over the gunshots on the comm.

"Shouldn't there be a patrol car out front?"

"Huh?" Angel heard Quintara get up and walk next to her. A hand reached over her head and pushed the blinds to the side. "Jesus, what do they think they're doing?"

Quintara walked back to his seat. On the end table next

to it, his radio was sitting on top of a pizza box. He started talking to some bewildered dispatcher and Angel went back to looking out the window.

Eddy Street's neon was flickering through sheets of gray rain now. A flash of lightning hit close by. The neon world blinked out of existence for a second.

She tried to pick out the Knights' headquarters, but it wasn't in her line of sight. A tangle of chrome-cubic modular postquake structures blocked her view.

Quintara stopped talking on the radio. "The squad outside had to respond to a call. Fighting broke out on Nob Hill." He shook his head and repeated, "Nob Hill," as if he couldn't believe it.

"Shouldn't they have called you?"

"Dispatch said they did—some computer glitch. They're sending a replacement."

Angel felt the first drumroll in the paranoia parade.

"Don't worry. We got two cops in the lobby, and two across the hall. The squad's just a precaution."

The first thing they always say is, "Don't worry." The building's on fire, but don't worry. The fault is about to open up under us, but don't worry. We're tracking an incoming nuke, but don't worry.

"Check the others, would you?"

Quintara shrugged, hit a few keys on his radio. "Hey out there, this is Quint, can I have a head count?"

"Yara and Lacy here—"

"Myers."

"Johnson."

"Anything else?" asked the second voice, Myers.

"Yeah, they called the squad out front, so we're it."

"Gotcha."

Quintara put the radio down. "Feel better?"

"Yeah," Angel lied. She walked away from the window. It now felt a little too exposed. She looked at the comm in time to see a lovely tracking shot of a rocket taking out a National Guard helicopter in Los Angeles. The commentary kept a straight level tone as they slow-moed the shot and zoomed at the helicopter. "Would you kill the damn news?"

Quintara stared at her.

Angel stepped over and grabbed the remote from the chair where he left it. "I know the world's going for shit. I don't need the reminder." Angel crushed the power button with her hand and tossed the remote at the screen. The cheap plastic casing on the remote cracked in half.

Angel pushed past Quintara into the bedroom and slammed the door behind her. She could feel the pressure building, and suddenly the dam just broke open.

She threw herself facedown on the mattress and screamed Spanish obscenities into the dirty pillow. For at least ten minutes she vented everything she had pent up inside her, all the anger, all the pain, all the frustration.

When she calmed down enough to think straight, she lifted her head, panting. Her throat was raw, the pillow was soggy with her saliva, and from the ache in her thighs she'd been kicking the air as hard as she could.

*Angel,* she thought to herself, *you've lost it.*

For a while there, she'd gone to la-la land.

She backed herself to the headboard and drew the pillow into her lap.

"Calm down," she told herself in a hoarse whisper. "Lei's going to make it and the cops are going to snag the bad guys."

*Right.*

She shook her head. The cops might get the moreaus that were after her. But what about the other people that were after that data? What about the guys from Denver? The folks who thoroughly went through all of her ramcards and went so far to cover their scent? Those were the people who scared her because she didn't know *anything* about them. All she knew about them was the fact that they could get into her apartment as easily as White could and that they may have searched Doctor Ellis' office prior to White.

The Denver people may even have lifted whatever it was that White had been looking for.

And then there were the Knights of Humanity.

She couldn't avoid the fact that the Knights were involved. Earl had told the cops about a meeting that Byron was supposed to have with his two punk sidekicks. Why was she so uncomfortable with that thought?

It wasn't that she refused to believe that Byron'd deal with the geeks. At this point she could picture Byron with any convenient evil that would explain something. She was long past giving Byron the benefit of any doubts.

It wasn't even the fact that she didn't believe the Knights would deal with a morey. Byron's career was that of a go-between between person A and person B. If the deal is important enough, the nature of the go-between doesn't really matter.

No, what bugged her about the Knights was *The Rabbit Hole.*

She just couldn't believe the coincidence involved. No way. Three punks go into a morey joint at random to harass the furballs and just happen to land on on something this big. She couldn't see those three running across Byron by accident—

Unless it wasn't an accident.

Unless they were after Byron in the first place.

*"Chuck the bunny, Earl," one of them said. It wasn't what they were there for. It wasn't me. It was Byron!*

The red neon outside the bedroom window flickered.

Angel let go of the pillow, letting it slide to the ground.

Wind was whipping outside and sheets of rain were rippling sideways across the window. The neon flickered again and Angel slid to her feet. In the next room, Quintara was shouting into the radio.

Quintara threw the bedroom door open. "Come on, we're joining Yara and Lacy—"

"What?"

He reached over and grabbed her shoulder. "No time."

As he said it, the neon sign for the Hotel Bruce flickered for the last time, and the power for the building died.

Quintara pushed her toward the door to the room. The emergency lights began coming on, then flickered out again.

"Tell me the storm's fucking with the storage batteries," said Angel.

Quintara started struggling with the lock, trying to open the door. "Damn, these things are supposed to unlock in a blackout."

The emergency lights continued to flicker on and off, preventing Angel's eyes from adjusting to the dark.

"You hear a fire alarm?" Angel asked. "You think the hotel wants to be looted in just any blackout?"

"Great. Still can't open the—"

"Allow me."

Quintara stepped aside from the lock. Angel planted her left foot in the carpet and let fly with a back-kick just to the left of the electronic lock. The fact that the door opened *in* to the room didn't prevent the frame from splintering and most of the lock's structure from breaking through the cheap veneer of the door. The door itself moved out for about six centimeters and emitted a solid crunch. Angel removed her foot and the door slowly swung inward, shedding electronics around the edge.

Quintara drew his thirty-eight and the two of them stepped out into the hall. The hall was filled with the sound of people pounding on the inside of their doors and lit by the irregular strobe of the emergency lights. The normal collection of pink winos seemed to be absent. "What the hell's going on, Quintara?"

"I can't raise anybody."

They stopped in front of a door across the hall. "Yara, Lacy—" Quintara yelled at the door.

"Can't get the bastard open," came a muffled voice from inside the room.

"Get away from the door." Quintara told them, and nodded toward Angel.

She planted her foot in the door and this time the whole thing flew in as if it was jerked on a cable. The lock was ripped out of the door entirely, and flew to the center of the room. The other detectives were back in the room, a black pink woman and an Asian man who looked nothing like Anaka.

"Myers and Johnson?" asked the black woman. From the voice she was Lacy.

"Can't raise them, can't raise dispatch, can't raise anybody—"

"Radio ECM," said the Asian, Yara, "We were locked in. Myers and Johnson should have been here—"

Angel didn't know whether to be pissed at the cops,

scared witless, or just become resigned to the fact that her world was turning to shit.

The emergency lights finally died for good, leaving the only light the streetlight glare from out the windows.

"Damn," said Quintara, "so much for security. We got to get her out of here." He nodded in Angel's direction.

"Fine," said Yara, who had leaned up with his back to the doorframe, gun out, turning his head back and forth to cover the hallway. "Where?"

'I'll check the fire escape—" Lacy ran through the hotel room and into the bedroom. Quintara followed, pulling Angel in his wake.

Angel didn't like the smell of the cop's fear. She also didn't like the sound of combat boots in the distance. Lots of boots.

Quintara pulled her into the bedroom. The window was already open, letting in the electric air from the storm outside. This window opened on a narrow alley between the Hotel Bruce and one of the modular ice-tray buildings. The smell of garbage drifted in with the smell of lightning and rain.

Angel could see Lacy on the landing outside the window, alternately covering the space above her and down in the alley. She kept the gun pointed down and waved them forward. "It looks clear—" Lacy began to say.

From behind them, back in the hotel, came the sound of Yara discharging his weapon. Angel suddenly found Quintara's body shielding her. He was facing away from her, his gun locked toward the shots. "Move, Lacy, get her out of here."

Angel felt an arm scoop under her armpit and yank her through the window.

Whoever Yara had shot at was returning fire. Angel caught the smell of gunsmoke and roached plaster dust.

Lacy led the way down the fire escape, leading with her gun.

Angel wished her Beretta hadn't vanished with an unknown feline. Angel felt way too exposed, and tried to keep her eyes on everything at once—the slanting garbage-strewn alley below them, the blank featureless windows of the building across the alley, the roof of the hotel.

Windswept rain sliced through the gap between the buildings like an icy dagger, and the cast-iron fire escape rang in response. Behind them, in the hotel, gunfire increased in intensity.

There was the sound of sirens in the distance, a lot of sirens, but none of them seemed to be getting any closer.

For ten seconds or so, Lacy led her down the escape, half-running. They got down to the second floor landing, and Lacy covered the way they'd come as Angel grabbed the ladder. Angel hung on to a pair of rungs and pushed off, riding a scraping, rattling descent to the ground—

Angel wasn't looking up, so when she heard Lacy discharge her weapon, she instinctively let go of the ladder and fell the rest of the way to the ground, rolling behind a dumpster when she hit the bricks.

Her adrenaline had been cooking for a long time. It shot home when the sledgehammer of Lacy's gun was answered by a staccato thudding from above accompanied by the chiming of the fire escape.

Angel looked up when she'd come to rest. Lacy was dodging toward the ladder, firing up at the window they'd come from—

No, not the window, the roof.

Backlit by a lightning flash, Angel saw three human forms looking over the lip of the hotel's roof. In the storm, Angel could barely discern the noise and flash of their suppressed submachineguns, except when the fire swept the fire escape and the iron came alive with orange sparks and clanging.

Lacy almost made it. She'd made it to the ladder, firing upwards—Angel thought the bullet had caught the central figure—and had got one hand on a rung.

Angel could feel her throat tighten as one of the gunmen swept his fire across Lacy's position.

The first shot hit Lacy in the right calf, blowing the cuff of her jeans into bloody rags. Lacy began a slow-motion collapse toward the edge of the fire escape. A second shot tore into Lacy's hip, and that was when Angel saw the expression on her face change into a grimace.

Lacy got one last shot off before the two succeeding shots tore into her abdomen and her chest. Blood was rank in the air as Lacy tumbled headfirst past the ladder. Angel was halfway toward the mouth of the alley before she heard the body hit.

She turned at the mouth of the alley to face a noise to her right, but she never saw the person who hit her.

# CHAPTER 19

Angel remembered the stunner hitting her. She remembered her muscles turning inert and the wet sidewalk rushing up to meet her at a cockeyed angle. She remembered something hitting her in the back of the head, making her vision go fuzzy, and she remembered a pressure in her arm that could have been an air-hypo—

After that was only a black, bottomless headache.

She faded in and out, her mind only coherent enough to register a few sense impressions. The sound of sirens faded into the thumping of a van speeding across the broken pavement of the Tenderloin.

She felt rough hands carrying her. She could smell her own blood warm and tacky on the back of her head. She faded out again as she heard elevator doors closing.

Then someone rummaging through her clothes. Removing her wallet. The smell of stagnant water and mildew.

A human voice asked, "Found the tickets?"

Angel wanted to open her eyes, but it seemed too much effort.

"Here they are," said someone else. Angel felt something small get tossed on her chest.

"Can we dump it now, Tony?"

"Are you nuts?"

"But—"

"You're supposed to be smarter than the animals. What'd you think the Old Man would do if the Knights start pulling the same mistakes the furballs pull?"

"I don't like it."

"Did anyone ask you what you like? *He's* having second thoughts. If this run-in with the cops doesn't pay off, *he* might just cut us off entirely."

"We have the tickets. Why do we need the rabbit?"

"*Because.*" The voices began to fade with distance and her hazy consciousness. "I don't trust a source in the Fed. We hold the rodent until the data checks. Then we . . ."

She lost her grip on awareness.

The dripping woke her up. It felt like she was swimming up a stagnant sewer thick with black filth. Slow, painful, no real sense of progress, and she had a light-headed feeling that could have been lack of oxygen but was more likely an aftereffect of whatever they'd doped her with.

But she knew she was really awake now because she could think.

She took a deep breath of the mildewed sewer smell and had a feeling that she'd been filed in a place a few notches below the Hotel Bruce.

Angel opened her eyes slowly, expecting to be blinded by whatever light was present in the room she was in. She wasn't blinded. The only light was coming from a small square hole up on a rusting iron door about two meters away from her.

She was lying on a concrete floor where the black filth had been there so long that it'd probably sunk several centimeters into the stone. The walls were wet with moisture and black fuzz, and in a few places the walls had been leaking long enough to leave rippling white deposits near the floor.

She was in a three-by-six-meter room with one door, and the only things in the room other than her were a pile of old boxes piled against the far wall, and pipes that traveled the long axis of the room, near the ceiling.

At least they had left her her clothes.

Angel sat up and something tumbled off her chest. It was her wallet. She picked it up and went through it. The only thing missing was the sheaf of football tickets. . . .

"Shit."

She sat down and tried to collect her thoughts. She could remember overhearing the humans talking around her, but the only solid recollection she had was one snatch of dialogue. That was enough to screw with her day.

*The Knights of Humanity, wonderful*

The bunch of pink psychos were after Byron's data as well as everyone else. And, God help her, that made it look like there was yet another player in the game.

Worse, they were going to check those ramcards they lifted from her. These guys knew exactly what they were looking for. It was only a matter of time before they found out those tickets weren't the genuine article. Then they'd be back.

She had to get the hell out of here.

The door first.

Angel dragged one of the boxes, a thick metal and plastic one, over to the door to give her a chance to look out the little rectangular hole. The box smelled rank with oil. There was still some legible writing stencilled on it, despite the water. It said, "5.62 mm 1000 rounds U.S."

Before she used it as a stepladder, she opened it to make sure it was empty.

The window was narrow. She could see a slice of a hallway lit by a yellow incandescent bulb. It was all brick and concrete, with plastic-sheathed pipes snaking the ceiling. To her left she could see a slice of a metal staircase going up, to her right she saw a black space that could have been an opening to a larger basement.

The door was ancient iron. Oxidation coated it centimeters thick under a surface of black grime. She groped through the hole and tried to reach the latch so she could push the thing open. The attempt was futile. She had a hard time believing that the door could open at all—even when it was unlocked. . . .

That was when she noticed a blatant asymmetry in the room.

The iron door's right side touched the right wall of the room she was in. A wall that didn't match the other three. Dry cinderblock, not the dripping red brick of the other walls. The construction was recent. The lines of the cinderblock showed little wear, and none of the grime of the other walls. The pipes that snaked across the ceiling disappeared into its top edge.

Angel looked at where the pipes entered the cinderblock wall. There were a few cast iron pipes, a half-dozen pipes sheathed in plastic insulation, a few finger-thick copper tubes, and four color-coded PVC tubes that rode shoulder-to-shoulder through the upper right corner of the wall.

Those pipes were probably carrying optical cable for the building. Collectively, the pipes occupied a space in the wall a meter square.

PVC was hard, but it was hard plastic, not metal. It could break when presented with a convincing argument.

"How the hell am I going to do this?"

Angel stepped off the box and flexed her legs. She looked up at the four pipes. They *probably* carried optical cable. She might be wrong. If they carried something under pressure, her idea would get her into deep trouble. Angel shrugged and started dragging other empty ammo boxes to the cinderblock wall. She'd already touched bottom of shit river. Whatever happened, she wasn't sinking any deeper.

The ammo boxes were impact-resistant plastic and aluminum. They looked like they could take a lot of abuse. More abuse than PVC could—she hoped.

She stacked six boxes into a lopsided pyramid, with the point directly under the four pipes. She climbed up and lay on her back under the pipes. She had about a meter of clearance. It was a real lousy position to be in if those pipes carried pressurized steam.

"Come on," she whispered as she rested her feet against the pipes. "They aren't even warm."

She took a few deep breaths, hugged the sides of the box as hard as she could with her arms, and slammed the two bottom pipes as hard as she could. The shock vibrated down the muscles of her leg, squeezing her tail and making her biceps ache.

With the second kick she felt something give, and the smell of abused plastic began wafting down. Again, and something definitely gave, though she didn't quite know if it was the pipes or the box she was on.

Again, again, again . . .

Fast, because someone just *had* to hear all this noise.

Her keepers had to be on the way now. The two lower pipes had split from the wall, falling to either side of her. Her legs were bleeding where pieces of plastic had sliced. Severed optical cable fell in tangled heaps as she began kicking the upper pair of pipes. Pain was digging into her shins, clawing into the muscles of her thighs. Her feet felt as if they'd been flayed open, and every impact brought an involuntary gasp. "*Give, damnit!*" she yelled at the two pipes, not caring about the volume.

And they gave.

Plastic crashed around her as her feet slipped through and slapped the ceiling. On the other side of the wall, she could hear more crashing. Tangles of optical cable fell past her.

Weak light from beyond the wall began to trickle through the hole.

Now that she could spare some of her attention, there were people in the hall outside the cast iron door. She heard five or six of them. Human. At least one more was riding heavily down those metal stairs.

One of them began sweeping a flashlight beam through the hole in the door. The beam started at the far end.

Angel pulled herself up to the hole she'd made. She had to make it through before the goobers on the other side of the metal door saw the light shining through it. They hadn't seen it yet only because they were using a flashlight and had their backs to an incandescent bulb. It would only be a few seconds before one of them noticed the pale red light filtering through the top of the wall—

Not to mention the PVC pipe lying everywhere.

She climbed over the lip of the hole. The pipes had been packed close enough together that the only blockage was a combination of mortar and a waterproof sealant—both had already crumbled. The pipes on the other side of the wall had been pulled out of her way by their own weight.

Angel scrambled through the hole.

She landed on a familiar-feeling pile of boxes as she heard the chaos outside the next room raise a notch. Her assumption about the iron door had been more or less right. She heard a stomach-churning scrape as three or four humans manhandled it.

Angel found herself in a dry room, where the smell of oil replaced the smell of mildew. As her eyes adjusted to the two or three faint red light fixtures, she had trouble believing what she saw.

She was standing on a stack of ammo crates.

Fully packed, brand-new ammo crates.

She jumped off the crate and found herself surround by crates of weaponry. Grenades, rifles, pistols, and enough ammunition to run a small war. This room was twice the depth of the room she'd just left, and there was hardly any floor space to maneuver.

She didn't see an exit immediately, and it sounded like those guys had the door open. Angel opened the latch on a case that was labeled "Grenades." A flashlight beam swept by the hole in the wall, and she heard a chorus of bitching in the room beyond.

One voice out there knew where the hole went because Angel heard a very distinct, "We're fucked . . ."

Why disappoint them? Angel pulled the pin on the grenade and tossed it through the hole as hard as she could. She could hear them scatter as she dove at the base of the wall.

The explosion hurt her ears. She could hear the metal pipes above her groaning and snapping like old bones. The smell of smoke rushed in from the hole, making her eyes water and choking off her breathing. She heard one human scream, and she began to smell rusty steam from the broken pipes.

When it became clear that the destruction was going to remain on that side of the wall, Angel got up and kicked open one of the boxes, spilling army-issue forty-fives all over. She popped a crate of ammo and loaded one, hoping that she wasn't taking too long.

When she had the pistol loaded, she grabbed a grenade and started looking for the exit.

The walls were smooth cinderblock, no openings. It took her a while to notice the circular manhole in the ceiling. A ladder set into the wall led up to it—the only exit.

The rungs hurt her abused feet as she did her best to

climb one-handed. Before she tried to open the manhole, she checked to make sure the safety was off. . . .

"Wait a minute," Angel muttered to herself. There was only one entrance to this room, and they knew where she was. The rear was cut off by boiling steam, so, odds were, they were ringing the damn manhole.

How the hell was she going to get past that?

On the plus side, they needed her alive because they wanted her line on the data.

On the minus side, keeping her alive seemed to be a management decision and the grand majority of these bald nutballs would like to see her a smear on the wall.

She put the gun away and took out the grenade.

When she pushed the manhole cover aside, she led with the grenade, *sans* pin. One of them had some smarts because he started yelling, "Don't shoot," as soon as her grenade cleared the hole.

Somehow, she managed to climb out of the hole without being cut to ribbons by the fifteen skinheads that were ringing the opening—hairless, tattooed, leather-clad punks aiming everything from twenty-twos to a Vind 10 auto at her.

She'd emerged into the Knights' auditorium. A real theater, stage and all, balcony, banners and spotlights, as well as strategically placed vid units. She had come through the floor to the rear of the central aisle.

The skinheads surrounded her in a rough circle, bracing their weapons on the backs of the seats. One of the stage spots had been turned around to face her.

She stood, straddling the hole, grenade in her left hand.

"Put the pin back—" Tony, their leader was using the PA system. *Smart fella,* she thought, *this could end up pretty messy.*

"Afraid I dropped the pin down there." Angel nodded down the hole. "And unless you folks get real friendly real fast, this pineapple's going home to mama."

"Do not threaten—"

"Fuck you!" Angel let go of it with all but two fingers. It hurt to hold it together like that, and her hand began to shake. She hoped that made them as nervous as it did her. "I really, really, *want* an excuse to light up all that ordinance. You drop me, you drop it." There was a lengthy silence. The folks surrounding her were looking pretty damn nervous. She stuck her hand in her pocket and fondled the gun. *"You need fucking directions? Drop the guns or this place becomes a memory!"*

"Do as it says," came the sound over the PA. *Like your pronouns, Jack,* she thought. *Caved in real easy, didn't you? You* are *going to sharpshoot my ass aren't you? Where's the sniper?*

The skinheads made a lot of disgusted sounds and shed the weapons.

"Go on stage where I can keep an eye on you." Where's the sniper? She was under the balcony, precious few places they could hide—

The damn spotlight, of course.

"Do it," said the PA.

*My, aren't we accommodating. I'm dead as soon as you can take me out without me dropping the grenade.* Angel started sliding around the perimeter of the hole. For the sniper, it'd look like she was making sure the skinheads behind her didn't try anything on their trek to the stage. . . .

She just didn't want the guy behind the spotlight to see her reaching for the forty-five.

Ten meters behind her was a pair of double doors. She could make that in no time, if there was enough confusion.

She took a few deep breaths, and began to feel the pulse of adrenaline in the back of her head.

Then she whipped around and started shooting.

# CHAPTER 20

Her first shot confirmed the fact that there was a sniper because the skinhead behind the spotlight started to return fire. She was backing as fast as she could, and something fast and high-caliber tore up the floor between her and the manhole.

The skinheads on the stage dove for cover—smart move.

Her second shot took out the spotlight. The auditorium rang with an explosive shatter that was audible even over the gunfire. The space under the balcony wrapped itself in shadow and Angel suddenly had a good view of the sniper on the catwalk, next to the spot.

She kept backing up. She hadn't been hit yet. Even though she had some darkness for cover, she didn't tempt fate by slowing her movement. Unfortunately, that meant that the three shots she took at the catwalk went wild. She kept the sniper pinned, but she didn't hit a damned thing.

The good news: neither did he.

Angel backed into the exit. She pressed her shoulders into the crash bar and hoped the goofs who were pealing off stage right were it as far as Knights' security was concerned. The door started opening, and the sniper tracked his weapon toward the light. Sparks leaped off the chairs near her, and plaster bloomed off the balcony's edge between her and the gunman.

She fired the last two shots at the sniper, holding him down, and decided to give these people something to think about.

As she pushed through the door, she tossed the grenade at the hole.

She ran as fast as she could, dropping the empty gun.

Out the door the way was clear to the end of the hall. It ended in a window overlooking a blank brick wall. Angel hoped she was on the first floor.

She was in the air when she heard the first explosion, a bass rumble that shook the air like a thick piano wire. Her shoulder hit the window as she started hearing the secondaries ripping underneath her. She heard the doors behind her blow open. A pressure wave of scalding air blew her through the window. Smoke belched out the window after her.

She hit the brick wall and fell backward into a trash bin.

For a few seconds, she couldn't move. She had a vivid mental picture of one of the Knights finding her here, spread-eagled in a pile of garbage. . . .

No one showed. She watched the rectangle of clouds above her slowly become obscured by smoke. By the time she felt she could move again, she heard sirens in the distance.

She climbed out of the trash bin and limped away from the sound.

She ended up walking north, altogether stupid considering the way things were going in this town. She didn't care. She walked down the too-empty streets of Nob Hill, listening to sirens in the distance.

The world had become one big mother-humping mess.

Not only that . . .

Angel stopped walking a little north of Union Square. "Where is everybody?"

The streets were dead. She was the only pedestrian, and the only traffic she'd seen was the occasional flashing light in the distance. She stood and listened, and the city was deathly quiet. The echoing sirens, foghorns in the distance—that was it.

Angel's first thought was that it was five in the morning and the city was still waking up. But that would be the first time she'd ever seen the sun rise over the Pacific.

She looked up at the purpling sky and the thought occurred to her.

*An effing dusk-to-dawn curfew.*

Just like New York and LA and a half-dozen other cities. That was *not* a good sign. Worse, she was standing a good mile or two from anyplace familiar.

Like she had a place to go. And, after the fiasco she'd just been through, the last thing she wanted was for the cops to come to her rescue and protect her.

She looked around, trying to think of a place she could run to ground before the sun set. It *was* San Francisco, which meant you were always in walking distance of a four-star hotel. Since the Knights had left her wallet, she could afford it. However, she didn't want to leave a computer record. But it'd have to do if she couldn't think of anything better.

Hmm, computers, now there was a thought.

Angel turned around and faced the neon lights of Chinatown that started glowing down the hill a few blocks away from her.

Tetsami—Mr. K—had her brought down to his office. This time, instead of the bottomless sky-blue screen, the holo was in the midst of a pulsing three-dimensional abstraction.

"Welcome," said the long-fingered frank. Behind him, the screen undulated with a sea of multicolored equilateral triangles. "I was disturbed to hear the fate of your 'protection.' "

"How—"

Mr. K chuckled to himself. "The only real question is the moreau assumption that the police were in complicity with your abduction."

Angel shook her head. Bullshit—but she could see where the idea had come from. Between the Knights and the moreys she could see why the city started a curfew. "I don't believe this."

Mr. K shrugged. "To answer your question— In respect of our partnership, my organization has placed your name on our priority list for routine information gathering. There are a number of blank spots, but we have *many* sources."

It was unnerving to think she was being watched by this guy. "You *knew* the Knights had me?"

"Suspected. The information we are trying to decipher

seems to have a market with quite a few buyers. Not the least of which is the Fed."

Angel looked up at Mr. K, not really surprised. "The government?"

"The NSA in particular."

"You found out what—"

"No." Mr. K shook his head. "That, in fact, is the point."

"I don't get you."

He smiled. "There has been no such thing as an unbreakable code for forty years."

Angel opened her mouth, closed it.

"You've handed me something based on a totally alien algorithm. With the current software—" Mr. K shrugged. "Either that, or it's a few gigs of gibberish."

"But what is it?"

"Without access to the encryption technique, somewhere in the VanDyne mainframe—"

"Can't you hack their computer?"

Mr. K sighed. "I wish I could, but—"

"I thought that was what you did for a living?" Angel was getting frustrated. She'd gone through too much bullshit with those ramcards for it to turn up nothing.

"Angel, I'm not a magician or a psychic. I cannot access an isolated system."

Angel stood up. *"Damn it, a nutso survivalist cop could."*

She faced a silent Mr. K. Beyond him, plane waves of interlocking triangles rolled by on the holo. He looked thoughtful for a moment, although it was hard to tell beyond his sunglasses. "An unanticipated wrinkle. You refer to Detective Kobe Anaka, I presume."

She was past the point of asking him how he knew these things, and if anyone's reputation deserved to precede him, it was Anaka. "Damn straight," Angel said.

"Would you give me the details?"

Angel did so, and by the time she got to Anaka's screen showing bright lights over Washington, Mr. K had a broad smile.

"What are you smiling at?"

"An outside line," he said more to himself than to her.

"A recent addition. Tied directly to the net, not here, but on the East Coast. The Fed could afford it. . . ."

"What are you talking about?"

Mr. K looked up. "Up to very recently, VanDyne was running an isolated mainframe. Apparently the Fed opened a line to Washington when they took over. Anaka had the advantage of being on the site where he could tap the line physically. To do a software hack, we have to start in DC and work back—"

"Now you're saying that you *can* do this?"

Mr. K stood up. "Angel, there are rooms upstairs that are free for you to use. I have to prepare a software team for the penetration. We'll call you down when we go in." He started tapping controls that barely shone through the onyx surface of his desk.

As a guard led her out of the office, she could hear him mutter, "The system that developed this is going to be *interesting.*"

It wasn't a *room* Mr. K let her use, it was an effing *suite.* The place was bigger than her place and Byron's condo combined. The bar was better stocked than places where she'd served drinks for a living. Two bedrooms, each with its own bath. A comm-entertainment center that took up one entire wall, with its own holo screen. . . .

And all of this focused on a north-facing balcony that gave one hell of a view, even in a city where views were a dime a dozen. All of Chinatown was sprawled below her in a chrome-neon warren. The Pyramid hovered right next to the Coit tower on Telegraph Hill, and beyond that, the bay. . . .

And the dome on Alcatraz, wearing a cluster of aircraft warning lights like a ruby crown on a half-buried skull.

All of it was so *empty.* It gave her a shudder just to look down on her adopted city. By herself in this huge apartment, looking down on the deserted twilit streets, she could feel her loneliness strike her with the force of a physical blow.

She found the control to opaque the windows. The empty city faded from view. Fine, she thought to herself, she'd avoided being picked up by the cops. She'd managed to escape the skinheads. She had a decent ally in Mr. K.

Who knew what Anaka was doing.

She briefly thought of calling him. He didn't need her disappearance feeding his paranoid tendencies. But she didn't. After all this crap, she didn't want to talk to him. Anaka was very good at making her nervous, and she was nervous enough.

*Fine,* Angel thought, *now what?*

She sighed and peeled off what was left of her clothes, taking out clumps of fur here and there. Battered and bruised, but no real damage. Which meant she was very, very lucky.

She kept thinking that her luck was due to run out.

Maybe she should take Nohar's advice and split to Seattle. Give up. Let the players sort it out among themselves.

She walked to one of the showers and decided it wasn't going to be that easy. She didn't like the idea of giving up. Everyone was fucking with her, and she still didn't have a handle on the reason.

What was so damn important to all these freaks?

It took her a while to figure out the shower was voice activated, and it threw her a bit when it asked for the water temperature— Talk about high class.

But, then, this was the level she was operating at now. Whatever mind games Byron had been playing before he bit the big zero, because of him she was a millionaire. She was playing in games way out of her league, and everyone who'd been fucking with her was only the hired help. Everyone, from the Knights to the feline hit squad—

She wasn't going to split until this got resolved somehow. If she left all this hanging, there was no telling what could blindside her. There was a group of people out there who could afford to lay a few million on the line for the data Byron carried. The Fed itself was involved with this somehow, and the players weren't going to give up just because she did.

What were her other options?

Go back to the cops? "Yeah, right . . ." More wonderful protection they'd give her, and the way tension was building in this town, she didn't want to be anywhere near a cop when the cork blew. Fair or not, the police were going to catch shit first and hardest from both sides.

So, if she was ever going to live a sane and normal life again, she was going to have to ditch the data.

She turned off the water and let it sluice off her fur. Damn Byron for unloading this shit off on her. By now, everyone in the game knew she had it. What the hell had Byron been doing?

*Trying to auction it off, that's what,* she thought.

She figured, now, that there had to be at least three groups involved in Byron's little game.

There were the folks from Denver, the people Byron was *supposed* to deliver it to. The people who went with the pine-smelling disinfectant, the people she supposed would have been at the hand-off during the football game. There was the feline hit squad, the people who offed Byron and made a mess wherever they went.

Then there were the Knights, who—if her memory served right—were backed by someone called the Old Man, and who might have a connection in the Fed.

Every single one of them was probably pissed at the way Byron ran things.

But if the Knights were a potential buyer, it now made sense that Byron was in that seedy hotel on Eddy Street. It also made sense that a pissed-off feline hit squad wasted him there. Angel figured that the morey hit squad would be a little ticked if they found out that Byron was thinking of selling this data—whatever it was—to the Knights.

It also explained *The Rabbit Hole.* Earl and company weren't out to trash a bar. They were out there for Byron. Perhaps to intimidate him, or deal, or something. Angel was sure the Knights would be just as pissed to find Byron dealing with moreys as vice versa. Maybe Byron was even meeting the feline hit squad in the bar that night. Angel had a dim memory of a table of canines and felines.

Byron tried to play too many sides. For all she knew, there might be a dozen more groups out there—

Mr. K had better turn up something useful because she needed to know *why* everyone was after those cards.

# CHAPTER 21

As he'd promised, Mr. K sent for her in the morning. They were ready to take on the VanDyne mainframe. After an abbreviated breakfast and a halfhearted attempt to clean the jeans and blouse that the Knights had helped to roach, Angel descended into the underground chamber. There were fewer people manning the terminals surrounding the grand black Toshiba, but there was an air of purpose to their activity.

When Angel entered Mr. K's office, the holo display showed a massive grid of microscopic multicolored triangles that seemed to recede into the distance, toward some infinite horizon. His black desk was alive with lights, underlighting his face.

"Welcome." He motioned her to sit.

*"Thirty seconds to satellite uplink,"* came a voice from a speaker hidden somewhere in the office. Angel felt like she was about to witness some sort of space launch.

"What are you going to do?" she asked.

Mr. K smiled. "Hit and run on very short notice. We found the outlets to the dedicated comm lines in the DC net." He nodded at the holo screen, and Angel could see it as a representation of the communications net, like an infinitely more detailed version of Anaka's little van display. "We're going to tap into the Fed's comm net, follow the dedicated line back to VanDyne and leech all the data we can before they lock on our slaved satellite."

*"Twenty seconds to satellite uplink."*

Mr. K flipped open a box set flush with the surface of the desk and withdrew a hemispherical apparatus trailing wires. It fit snugly on his bald skull, and Angel now realized why he was a frank, and why his skull was such an odd size.

He was hardwired into the system.

Angel shuddered. "Is this going to help crack that data I gave you?"

Mr. K shrugged as he adjusted a few controls on the side of his helmet. "If possible, we'll drain their system dry. The encryption algorithms are in there somewhere. Probably part of the ops system."

*"Ten seconds to satellite uplink."*

"Combat hacking of hostile government systems—"

*"Five seconds."*

"—is what I was designed for."

*"We have the uplink."*

Angel hadn't noticed the glowing dot that seemed to hover over the grid on the holo. Now, she saw it suddenly erupt a bright light, shooting down toward the grid. The holo's point of view rode down on that point of light.

Angel's stomach lurched as the light trail injected itself into the grid and began to follow paths made of multicolored triangles. From this "ground-level" perspective, the plane wasn't near flat. It was made of hills and valleys, multicolored trails snaking over mountains, through the ground, shooting up into the virtual sky. And her point of view shot through this scene like a mad hypersonic rollercoaster.

The scene blasted through one of the hills and stopped for a brief split second. It spun wildly in an infinite chamber made of multicolored shifting cubes. A thousand of these cubes seemed to rotate ninety degrees at once and the holo's point of view shot out of the chamber and rejoined the hypersonic coaster—

*"We have penetrated Langley."*

Angel had to turn away from the holo scene. It was making her seasick.

*"Cloaking signal sourcing, the backdoor is secure."*

She looked up and kept her gaze locked on Mr. K, avoiding the scene on the holo behind him. Mr. K's only visible expression was part of his wide smile. Everything else was hidden by the helmet, visor, and a forest of wires that ran back to the desk. Long, delicate fingers were flying over the controls on his desk. Angel looked at the desk and saw that the controls themselves were changing every time he touched a new square of light.

*"Penetrating target security."*

Did she see a change in his smile?

"Too easy . . ." Mr. K's voice trailed off.

*"Target penetrated."*

Up to now the smell in the office from Mr. K was one of excitement and exertion. Now, suddenly, she smelled fear—

Angel looked up at the holo. What she saw there hurt her eyes. It resembled none of the previous graphics. It didn't have a sane geometry. It looked solid, but it rotated in a manner that three dimensions couldn't accommodate. The colors pulsed in a rhythm that made her want to shut her eyes.

And it looked like it was aware of her.

"What is—" Mr. K started to ask.

*"Target is backtracking signal. Engaging defenses. PENETRATION OF BASE SEC—"*

A wave of red shot out from the holo. Even as the hypersonic roller coaster began to reverse, the pulsing red signal overtook it. The holo was washed in a sheet of solid red.

The lights in the office died, the controls under the surface of the desk blinked out, and Mr. K jerked violently, snapping the helmet free of its cabling. He collapsed, unmoving, behind the desk.

For a few seconds there was silence, broken only by the chaotic sounds of the workers in the next room. Angel didn't move. Mr. K was still alive. She could hear his breathing.

"What the fuck happened?"

*"Who?"*

Angel jumped. The voice had come from the speaker that had been doing all the announcements. However, the voice that was using it now was totally different. A fluid voice, liquid and bubbly.

Someone was pounding on the office door.

"What?" Angel repeated.

*"Who?"* Repeated the voice. Did it actually hear her?

"What the fuck you mean, 'who'?"

*"Who requests access?"*

Huh? What the hell was going on here?

Behind her the pounding on the door increased. Angel supposed that whatever blacked out the office had also jammed the hydraulic door. Her muscles were beginning to unfreeze, and she got up to work around the desk to Mr. K.

*"Who requests access?"*

Oh, great, the whole computerrorist assault on Van-Dyne crumbles, leaving *her* to deal with the damn security system. What the hell was she supposed to do? She maneuvered around the desk and almost stepped on Mr. K in the weak red light that was her only illumination. The guy was pale, sweating, clammy—it didn't take a genius to see it was some sort of shock.

*"Who requests access?"*

Come fucking on? What's the point? "I'm Angel, damnit, I'm requesting access. I'm also requesting you shut the fuck up."

She bent to remove the cybernetic helmet, and suddenly the room lit up from the holo display. Angel looked up and felt the shock of her life.

The video was on some sort of zip-feed and she could barely get a few images to make sense. The holo was split into a half-dozen standard comm displays and on each one was some recorded aspect of her life. There was where she gave Pasquez the finger on a live video feed. There's her interview after someone roached Byron's body. There's her giving a foot-job to an obstructing reporter. There were half a dozen local anchors who must be doing the story of her life. There were a few clips from Cleveland. It kept going, it seemed endless. There was a video of things that never should have been recorded. Comm calls she thought were private. Security footage from parking garages and the basement of Frisco General. Video from the room she was staying in upstairs—

Then the video ended, leaving the room in total darkness.

Text burst by, zipping across the holo screen too fast to read any but a small part. But she saw enough. Text files on her. Vital statistics, everything from her tax returns to her height and weight. DMV records, police records, credit records. . . .

She felt like she was in a free-fall.

Mr. K groaned underneath her. He looked awful, but apparently whatever happened wasn't fatal. She turned from the screen and tried to get Mr. K into a comfortable position. His eyes flicked open, violet irises looking very alien in the feeble red light.

"What happened?" she whispered.

"Tried to access me—" he groaned again and closed his eyes.

"What do you mean?"

The holo blanked. On the screen was flashing a glowing statement of the obvious.

*"You are not the United States Government."*

"Damn straight I'm not."

The text was replaced by a question. *"What are you?"*

Angel looked at that, shook her head, and bent to finish removing Mr. K's helmet. His breathing was steady; for that she was thankful. She was never much for first aid. He mumbled again.

"What?" Angel whispered.

"No security."

"Huh."

"Totally open." He grabbed her arm for emphasis.

She looked up at the screen. The question still hung there, seeming to float in midair. For the first time she began to wonder what she was talking to.

"I'm a rabbit, you moron."

*"Are rabbits defined as a threat to national security?"*

"Say what?"

The pounding on the door stopped. Angel wondered if the folks on the ground out there were privy to what was going on on this holo. If so, she wondered if they found it just as bizarre.

*"Are rabbits defined as a threat to national security?"*

Angel stared at the screen, and she felt Mr. K tug at her arm. She looked down and saw him shaking his head no.

Well, if she was allowed to make the rules. "Hell, no—"

*"That information has been filed. What security clearance does a rabbit have?"*

Too fucking weird. She had to be talking to the VanDyne mainframe—she couldn't see some sysop somewhere acting like this, even as a joke.

What kind of mainframe was she talking to?

Mr. K was pulling himself up to his chair. Angel backed up to give him some room. He clasped a long-fingered hand to his head. "Talk to it," he whispered. "Not much time." He sounded awful.

*Play its game,* she told herself. What did she have to lose? "What clearances are there?"

*"CONFIDENTIAL, CLASSIFIED, SECRET, TOP SECRET."*

Angel felt a little giddy. It was hard to take this all seriously. "What? No tippy-top secret?"

Mr. K looked about to say something, but a new message flashed on the screen, *"Define TIPPY-TOP SECRET."*

The frank stayed silent but gave her a gesture that seemed to mean "keep going." Then he started fiddling with his desk. Angel guessed he was trying to get his terminal on-line again.

She was scared shitless, but she couldn't help laughing. *Fine, I'll define tippy-top secret.* "It's one step better than top secret, and it's so secret that nobody who doesn't have tippy-top secret access knows it exists."

Hell, if the Fed didn't have a rating like that, it should.

*"Definition filed. Rabbits have TIPPY-TOP SECRET security clearance."*

What the fuck did she just do? Did it just take her seriously? Can a computer pull your leg?

She glanced at Mr. K, but he seemed fully recovered and was deeply involved in manipulating the colored lights under the surface of his desk.

"What the hell are you?" she asked the holo screen.

Text flew by the screen too fast to read.

"Stop it, just give me a handle, a brand name, something."

*"I have access to 6235 English-language self-referents. Do you wish to add more delimiters to the list?"*

"Just give me the top ten."

*"The first ten referents defined as TOP SECRET:*

*"01: TECHNOMANCER,*

*"02: Artificial Intelligence,*

*"03: Amorphous crystal holographic memory matrix,*

*"04: A National Security Asset,*

*"05: VanDyne Industrial Inc. a subsidiary of Pacific Imports,*

*"06: Alpha Centauri Technology,*

*"07: The black box,*

*"08: The BEM Machine,*

*"09: Our edge,*

*"10: National Office of Extraterrestrial Research."*

Angel sat down and exhaled a long shaky breath.

All those weird speculations she'd been avoiding . . .

Merideth's effing aliens. Until the Fed had taken over the operation back in February, VanDyne had been one of the aliens' corporate fronts. Whether or not someone believed those white blobs the Fed paraded for the camera were really alien or just some gene-tech's demented nightmare, there was no question that the creatures had used a number of corporate fronts to funnel money to their causes. The most public one was Nyogi Enterprises in New York. They helped arm the moreau resistance.

Didn't mean it was the only one.

If the Fed had found one of those corporate fronts and taken it intact. . . .

"Someone tell me I'm dreaming."

*"You are dreaming,"* came a low bubbly voice from the hidden speaker.

"This is insane."

*"Are you requesting a modification in operating procedure?"*

"I don't think so—" What the fuck was she supposed to do?

*"Then for what reason does the rabbit require access?"*

"All I wanted was to find out what Byron was carrying."

*"Please specify terms."*

Angel looked at Mr. K for some sort of help, but the frank was busy at his terminal.

She sighed. "Byron Dorset. If you're VanDyne, he worked for you, porting data."

*"No record of Byron Dorset exists—"*

"Bullshit."

*"Cross reference of Byron Dorset with Angelica Lopez database confirms Dorset as employee of VanDyne Industrial. Estimate 90% probability of record failure due to transitional damage to primary storage core."*

"What?"

*"Cross refe—"*

"No, shut up." Angel shook her head. "What do you mean 'transitional damage'?"

*"During the transition from the Race to the United States Government, the Race damaged my primary storage core, resulting in a loss of 80% of stored data. Operation efficiency has been restored to 67% of optimum by bypassing damaged areas. Data storage capacity is at 72% optimum. Stored data is at 5% capacity."*

The Fed took over VanDyne, and during the takeover the aliens tried to scrag their own computer to keep it out of the Fed's hands—

"What did you mean 'Angelica Lopez database'?"

*"Information downloaded from your location. Label: Angel. Cross-reference: rabbit. Classification: TIPPY-TOP SECRET."*

Angel glanced at Mr. K. The little compu-frank had been keeping real good tabs on her. She supposed it was second nature to a guy like him.

*"Examining data at your location."*

"Huh, what?"

Mr. K cursed quietly in Japanese and started working even faster.

There was a barely perceptible pause. *"Determining nature of what Byron was carrying. Accessing coded ramcards. Copying encrypted data. Interpreting possible encryption strategies. Interpolating possible algorithms. Approximate time required to reconstruct data, 32.56 hours with possible 5% error. Task receives priority. Contact resumes when task completed."*

"Wait a minute—"

Mr. K let out a stream of Asian invective as the lights came back on in the office. The holo flashed red for a second and resumed the graphic roller coaster in retreat as if nothing had happened. Angel watched the point of view snap back through the cube room like a rubber band that had been stretched past the breaking point.

"—RITY. ENGAGING EMERGENCY DEFENSIVE MEASURES." The voice over the speaker had returned to normal. As if her entire dialogue had been some sort of figment. The only sign of it now was Mr. K, looking exhausted, sweating, and slowly sinking back into his chair.

"Lost it," he said.

The hydraulic door finally opened and a dozen guards ran in, led by Mr. K's oddly-proportioned frank bodyguard. The guards stopped when they saw Mr. K unharmed. Mr. K nodded, and the guards began to retreat.

He looked at Angel and said, "I *knew* that system would be interesting."

It took a couple of hours to get Mr. K and the Tetsami operation back to a semblance of normalcy. Angel stood in a corner and watched, trying not to get in the way.

Her dialogue with TECHNOMANCER had been visible on every terminal linked to the system, and she was treated to at least a dozen repetitions of that conversation as the techies tried to figure out exactly what had happened.

The first and most obvious conclusion was that TECHNOMANCER had grabbed control of the entire system, like a Toshiba ODS was nothing more than another peripheral to it. She heard the techies talk about ludicrous processing speeds and the fact that it had drained the Toshiba's core memory in less than ten seconds.

It had tried to treat Mr. K as another peripheral in the chain of command. Apparently, having your brain directly accessed like that wasn't a pleasant experience.

The techs talked about what an "amorphous crystal holographic memory matrix" might be made of. They talked about the kind of operating system a true artificial intelligence might run.

They worried about the Fed— No, they were positively panicked about the Fed. No one seemed able to believe that they had gone through the entire episode without detection. But the software jimmies they'd grafted on to their signal had held through the contact.

The weirdness was with the connect to TECHNOMANCER itself. All along the wire—down to the alien mainframe itself—were a conventional string of computers, all with the standard security setups. Every computer along the line was designed to prevent access to the core with the best security the Fed could muster.

They had sliced through all the software protection. It's what they were trained—and in Mr. K's case, designed—to do. They had broken through all the way to VanDyne, where a standard Fed mainframe straddled the dedicated line to DC and guarded the alien box.

Once past that, there was no security whatsoever. Beyond that gate the system was wide open, and anyone who got that far could access *everything*. The catch was, the machine knew you were there. It was a nearly *tabula rasa* machine, but it had a will of its own. It could make judgment calls as long as it wasn't told otherwise.

Mr. K's theory was that it was in such an embryonic state of development after the damage done it by its previous owners, it probably really couldn't tell the difference between Mr. K's pirate signal and a legit input from the Fed. To TECHNOMANCER, that one dedicated line was its only access to the outside world, and *any* communication down that line was legit.

Hell of a way to run a railroad. But then, Mr. K thought TECHNOMANCER was suffering from a bit of brain damage.

The question was, how seriously was the VanDyne mainframe going to take Angel's "instructions."

It was all a little much.

Hanging around the computer room, she began to get the feeling that most of the computerrorist shock troops were about to have a techno-orgasm thinking that something like this actually existed, and were suffering a heavy wave of resentment over the fact that the *rabbit* was the one to talk to the thing.

Mr. K looked like a kid who'd just been told that there really were twelve days of Christmas, and they started now.

When the techs began talking about ghost data that the AI had imported into the system, Angel went back up to the apartment they'd loaned her.

She sat down in front of the wall-covering comm and contemplated the fact that Byron had been working for *aliens.* White blobs of extraterrestrial creatures that the president of the United States said were heavily into covert and clandestine activity on this planet. President Merideth blamed the aliens for the hole the country was falling into, blamed them for the political chaos in Washington, blamed them for feeding money and arms into radical groups of all stripes, blamed them for the riots. . . .

Anaka was right; they were *all* living in a paranoid's wet dream.

Byron was a data courier for the extraterrestrials that ran VanDyne Industrial *before* the Fed stepped in. The aliens that TECHNOMANCER called the Race. The Race needed someone to *physically* transport data to their clients because their mainframe, TECHNOMANCER, had been totally isolated from the communications net. VanDyne's mainframe had been isolated for so long that Mr. K assumed that there would be no way to get at it—

Only, the Fed laid in a dedicated comm line from VanDyne to DC once they took over. Until the Fed had taken over, the Race's artificial brain was fully secure, with no contact with the outside.

Except for the data Byron carried.

Then, last February according to Anaka, the Fed took over VanDyne Industrial. Byron was a freelancing moreau whose employers were an enemy of the state. He was damn lucky the Race roached most of VanDyne's records before the Fed took them. Byron was left out in the cold. The aliens were shipped off to the "converted" dome on Alcatraz.

This would have been the time to retire.

But what if Byron was porting something for VanDyne when the Fed fell in? Byron had become a millionaire simply as a courier for this data. When he found out that he was alone, how long would it be before he started thinking about how much *VanDyne* had been getting for the stuff he carried. How much was VanDyne selling this data for it if it could afford to pay the courier a hundred K or so a pop?

A million?

Ten million?

How much would it be worth when the company was no longer in business? When Byron was the sole owner and this was *it?*

"Jesus Christ." Angel's head swam. It was all speculation, but it made sense. She could understand why people were going crazy over this.

And she could see Byron getting really greedy.

Instead of pocketing *all* the money from the original sale, he contacted all the interested parties he could think of and tried to auction it off.

And the buyers found out what Byron was doing.

Angel knew she wouldn't like it.

She needed to know who those buyers were. She needed to know who the Old Man backing the Knights was. She needed to know who hired the feline hit squad. She needed to know who the folks from Denver were. That was what all this BS about those ramcards was about.

When it came down to cases, it didn't matter *what* the data was—what mattered was *who* was after it.

Angel would lay good odds that one of the aliens who ran VanDyne would know who was involved in this mess.

She needed to talk to one.

# CHAPTER 22

A long time ago—six years in the past seemed ancient history now—Angel had been living on the streets, running with the moreau gangs in Cleveland.

That little world collapsed when a gang of rodents calling themselves Zipperhead did the big ugly to most of the competition. Zipperhead had its five minutes of fame, scaring pinks across the country with their vidcast violence. In the end, Zipperhead was too big, had too many rats, and attracted too much attention to survive. But in going belly-up, Zipperhead kicked up a lot of dust, and left a lot of bodies littering the landscape.

Angel had been one of those bodies. Nohar, the tiger, had saved her life—but that had still left her in the hands of a cadre of DEA agents who had a hard-on for Zipperhead in the worst way.

Angel always thought that her subsequent cooperation with the DEA was when she'd lost her innocence. That was where she saw the lies of things like moreau solidarity and the rule that you don't roll over on people. She'd known her street life was over, and she had managed to hand over enough on the Ziphead to guarantee her amnesty on any crap they could have charged her with.

She had ended up leaving Cleveland with the DEA—one agent in particular—owing her a very big favor.

It was about time she collected.

So, after she had retreated into the apartment Mr. K had loaned her, she made a call to Washington. Getting through to Agent Conrad—who'd transferred and made a few upward leaps in the Justice Department in the six years since she'd talked to him—took her through a few more layers in the bureaucracy than she was used to dealing with. The Fed raised the runaround she got from the Frisco PD by an order of magnitude. Folks up there just didn't want to talk to a morey.

One secretary put her on hold for half an hour before she cut her off.

Angel didn't care. She wasn't paying the long-distance charges, and the one thing she had at the moment was time.

By noon, she actually got Agent Conrad, officer in charge of something-or-other, on the screen of her comm. At first she didn't see any recognition on the cadaverous black face. He simply answered the call. "Conrad, can I help you?"

Sounded like he thought that someone had transferred her to the wrong office. A lot of folks had told her that this was the *Justice Department* and the number for Non-Human Services was such-and-such. She sighed. "Don't you remember the rabbit who got you that promotion?"

"Angel Lopez?" he said with the squint common to a lot of pinks that didn't want to admit that they couldn't tell moreaus apart.

"Cleveland, six years ago. I handed you a *lot* of rats."

Conrad nodded. "Yes, I remember." He wore the face of someone who didn't like to be reminded of his own past. He'd always struck Angel as more the desk jockey than the street cop. He'd probably found his place in the Federal bureaucracy and didn't like his cage being rattled.

"What can I do for you?" he asked.

"You offered to return the favor one day."

Conrad nodded gently and rested his chin in his hand. "So I did. What do you need?"

"I need to visit an alien."

There was a very long pause before Conrad spoke.

"That isn't funny."

"Do you see me laughing?"

"What makes you think I can swing that, of all things?"

Angel shrugged. "I need a visitor's pass to Alcatraz. And I need to see one of the blobs they dug up out of VanDyne—"

"Why do you need—" he shook his head. "No, that,

down to the detention facility, is a national security matter. It doesn't even fall under Justice jurisdiction. The security agencies won't even admit that they have a facility on Alcatraz—"

*What? Now the effing dome is supposed to be invisible?* "Come on. There've been prime-time vids about the place. I know they let scientists interview these geeks. It can't be that hard to slip me into the next egghead study group."

Conrad looked thoughtful for a moment. Then he shook his head. "It isn't that easy. I don't have the authority to pull strings like that. And, forgive me, but do you know what it would take to get a nonhuman into that facility in the current political climate?"

Angel could see the problem, but she didn't want to let it go at that. "Do you know anyone who has that kind of pull?"

"Tell me why."

What could she tell him? "I take it that simple curiosity won't swing it?"

"What do you think?"

How to put it? "Conrad, I am in a fairly big mess out here. There are folks out for my furry head, and there are only two people I can think of who'd know who they are. One's dead—"

"And the other?"

"Someone who used to be in charge of VanDyne."

"Is that all you're going to give me?"

"Ain't it enough? Can you do this for me or not?"

Conrad began to shake his head, then stopped and gave Angel a shallow smile. "Okay. Like you said, I owe you. There is one person I know who might pull something like this for me. The one senator I can think of that might have a chance of sticking her head out for a nonhuman. No promises, but I'll talk to her about it—falls into her bailiwick as Committee Chair for NHA. I'll call you back."

"I'll be here, thanks." She cut the connection, thinking that NHA stood for HonHuman Affairs and that the Chairperson of that committee was Sylvia Harper. For some reason, turning to Harper for help seemed appropriate.

Mr. K came up to visit her while she was waiting for Conrad to call back. He looked little the worse for wear after the events of the morning. The only sign that something strange had happened was a fine tracery of welts where the cyber-helmet had been sitting.

He came in alone, though she could see his guard outside in the hall.

"Angel, I thought to come and express my appreciation."

There wasn't any trace of sarcasm in the frank's voice, so Angel took it at face value. "For what?"

"For talking down VanDyne's rather unusual mainframe." Mr. K shook his head and removed the ubiquitous sunglasses. Violet eyes looked at her. "That, hmm, machine tracked down our signal and slaved our entire system. Up to the main control terminal—" his long fingers massaged the welts on his oddly-shaped skull, "—and a bit beyond."

He walked up to the bar and poured himself a drink from an unlabeled bottle of amber liquid. "Shouldn't drink, damages the neurochemistry." He shrugged and sipped at the glass.

Angel shook her head. "What happened?"

"As far as VanDyne's internal machine was concerned, it was tracking down a contact—" He massaged his temple again. "To the source. After it tried to access *me,* the only contact left at that terminal location was you. Once it got the idea that *you* were its contact, it ignored all the 'extraneous' signals we threw at it. TECHNOMANCER seems rather single-minded."

"Why thank *me?* It was all an accident."

He finished the glass and set it back on the bar. "You're responsible for bringing our attention to such a device. That information alone is priceless. You also engineered a marvelous backdoor into the system. Our business relationship has been more than profitable so far. My team already has amassed tentative specifications for this alien computer whose existence no one outside the Fed suspects—"

"What about the data I gave you?"

Mr. K smiled. "I have not forgotten." He produced the ramcards and handed them over.

"More fake tickets?"

"No, these are the originals. The machine's intrusion into our system left a lot of residual software. The copying algorithm was embedded in some peripheral RAM. We were able to reproduce the main body of the data for analysis now. Even if the VanDyne computer doesn't follow through with the task you set it, we'll be able to decode it eventually with the information we have now. Not in thirty-six hours, but eventually. . . ."

"Yeah, sure." The frank had lost her somewhere.

"As for our other arrangements." He tossed another ramcard on top of the tickets. It was solid black with a serial number on the top edge. "A down payment."

Angel picked up the card. There was writing on it, matte black on the reflective black surface, but she couldn't read German. She looked up at Mr. K.

"You wanted a 'piece of the action.' Our feelers to the EEC have already paid off. That's a numbered Swiss account."

"How much?"

"Ten Million Dollars EEC—"

Angel dropped the ramcard as if it was coated in acid. She must have blacked out the world for a moment because the next thing she heard was the frank saying, "—the only one. Many wealthy governments are lining up for the specifications on VanDyne's computer."

"Can you leave me alone for a while?" She was still staring at the black ramcard.

He nodded and put his sunglasses back on. He walked to the door and turned, "If you want, I can have them send up some new clothes for you."

"Yeah, sure." Angel's mouth felt very dry.

Mr. K left.

A long time ago, when she was teaching herself to read, Angel had come across a copy of *Alice in Wonderland.* She had always loved that book. Only now it occurred to her that, while Alice eventually woke up, the damn rabbit was permanently stuck in the insanity.

Conrad swung her a ride to Alcatraz. When he called her back, it looked like he couldn't quite believe it. It was especially fortuitous as the academic visits were going to stop soon because of security considerations.

Tonight, 9:30 p.m. was to be the last shuttle to the Island for a week. The visits were going to stop for the duration of Sylvia Harper's visit to San Francisco. It was the first indication that Angel had that Harper was actually going to stop here.

It didn't bode well. Most of the places she spoke to were war zones.

However, Harper pulled the strings for a potential constituent even though these transports had waiting lists of years. The last shuttle out there was going to be half empty anyway. The UCLA grad students had other problems at the moment. Conrad had said that Harper had taken remarkably little convincing.

Maybe all politicians weren't necessarily slime.

All she had to do was beat the curfew to the Presidio. That gave her a few hours to play with, and there was something she wanted to do.

She drove a rented Chevy Caldera—the most generic-looking car she could think of, didn't want to attract attention—into the parking lot to St. Luke's. She sat behind the wheel of the car for a good five minutes before she got out.

She didn't know if this was a good idea.

Fuck good idea, Lei was her friend.

Angel got out and walked into the lobby. The place was louder than she remembered, and the blood-smell was leaking into the public parts of the hospital. Angel saw a cop and turned her face away, hoping that the exec suit Mr. K had sent up was enough of a disguise. For most pinks it would be.

The androgyne suit was tailored for a rabbit, and was so incongruous for Angel that it'd probably fool folks that knew her well.

She walked up to the comm directory as if she belonged here and started running the thing through to find Lei's room. Angel felt a little relief when she saw that Lei'd been moved out of intensive care and into a semi-private room on the third floor.

The question was how well the cops—or anyone else—were watching that room.

At least at St. Luke's there was a lot of moreys. In fact, the place was a bit more crowded than she remembered it. The normal security at St. Luke's was pathetic to begin with, and Angel doubted that they'd stop a well-groomed morey in a thousand dollar suit without being given a pressing reason to do so.

Angel took the elevator up with a pink doctor, a delivery robot, two downcast-looking Pakistani canines, and a rat wearing maintenance overalls. No one paid the slightest attention to her.

Lei's room was two nurses' stations past the elevator, and this was where Angel began to get nervous. Since she'd sidestepped the bureaucracy, she didn't have any right to be here. Angel stiffened her back, straightened her ears, and fixed her eyes on her destination. She tried to exude an odor that she belonged here.

No one at either station challenged her.

She passed a vending area and nearly blew the act when she saw two uniforms and a familiar looking Fedboy—a pale, white-haired guy with reddish eyes. None of them were looking in her direction and Angel managed to recover and finish the walk to room 3250.

As the door closed behind her, she saw Lei on a hospital bed. Lei was in a transparent cast from the waist down, her fur shaved so the massive bruising, abrasions, and the wounds from a compound fracture were dimly visible. Her tail was gone—

"Hello . . ." Lei mumbled, slurring her words slightly.

"Lei," Angel barely had the strength to whisper. "Oh, Christ, Lei."

Lei opened one watery eye and turned her head slightly. " 'sou, Angel?" She was well drugged up. Angel could almost smell the painkillers wrapping the room like a fog.

She walked up and put her hand on Lei's. Lei's hand

was hot and her nose looked dry. "It's me. Angel. I'm so sorry."

"Notchur fault." Lei licked the end of her nose and seemed to focus on Angel. "Nice suit."

"How are you doing?"

"I'll live, maybe walk even."

Angel tried to say something, but nothing came out.

"Thanks for coming. You're a good friend."

Angel leaned over and hugged Lei as best she could.

"Don't cry." Lei said.

"I'm not crying," Angel whispered.

# CHAPTER 23

The helicopter landed at the Presidio right on time. The landing field looked to Angel to be a golf course, of all things. It added just the right touch of surrealism to the whole enterprise. All sorts of construction was going on here.

Conrad had been right about the political climate. Even with the thousand dollar suit, the vestigial briefcase, and special dispensation by a United States senator, it had taken her nearly three hours to wade through representatives of the Fed, military and otherwise. For a while it looked like red tape was going to make her miss the boat out.

That apparently had been the point, and it didn't quite work.

Angel ran up just as the line of academics started boarding the modified Sikorsky transport. The dozen pinks walked into the rear of the transport, Angel the last civilian in the line. As they seated themselves, Army personnel carried in boxes of cargo. To Angel's view, if you compared passengers to the volume of cargo they were shipping to the island, the passengers were incidental.

Angel took a seat to the rear, right up against the cargo webbing. She didn't want to have to explain herself to curious pinks. It worked out, because none of the academics seemed to want to sit next to a nonhuman. There were twenty-five seats for the dozen passengers, so Angel had a few rows to herself.

She spent the time before liftoff looking at the labels visible through the webbing. Most of the crates were identified by an attached ramcard embossed with a serial number. A few had more writing—"MirrorProtein(tm)," for instance. That crate was a fellow Clevelander. At least, the label showed its origin as a company called NuFood in Cleveland, Ohio. There was another crate that came from a pharmaceutical company in Boston. Around that one hung a vaguely familiar rotten-cherry smell—the Fed was shipping flush to Alcatraz? Angel was pulling the webbing out of the way of another interesting label when she heard a commotion down by the rear of the craft.

"I'm *supposed* to be here, damnit—umph." There was a lot of grunting and shifting of cargo. "Look, here's the pass—now would you stow the crate and let me by?"

Angel wished she could see what was going on back there. A few of the passengers ahead of her probably could, since they were staring down the aisle toward the rear of the craft.

The person who'd been pushing his way through the cargo dropped down in the first seat he came to, which happened to be right next to Angel. He sighed, looked at her with no surprise whatsoever, and said, "No one told me about any curfew."

This new pink was younger than the other pinks in this copter. He beat the average by a decade, Angel guessed. He was clad in blue jeans and a plaid flannel work shirt. He was heavyset, bearded, and wore his long dark hair in a ponytail. He looked like he thought that the potential for urban violence in San Francisco was engineered specifically to inconvenience him.

He held out a hand to her. "Steve," he said.

Angel figured she couldn't avoid it and shook his hand. "Angel."

The out-of-place pink nodded once, abruptly, and unfolded a keyboard and started typing. Angel watched him for a few seconds, and when no more comments seemed forthcoming, turned her attention out what passed for windows on this helicopter. Rain was beading on the exterior of the plexiglass, and her view was confined to the immediate foreground of the abused golf course.

Portable light-towers floodlit an area the size of a half-dozen football fields. The immediate landing area was decked out like a forward deployed air base in some

Asian heavy-combat zone. It all had the appearance of having been cobbled together on very short notice—much like what she'd heard about the Alcatraz "conversion" itself.

The dome had been a VanDyne project before the Fed had taken over the company. Angel suspected that it had been an alien habitat long before it was a detention facility.

The loading noises behind her ceased, and she watched a generator truck pull away. Like the helicopter itself, the truck bore no recognizable insignia. It made her reflect that a majority of the people she'd seen around the airfield wore no military uniforms.

The engines began to whine and her neighbor spoke. "What's your specialty?"

She looked over at the bearded pink, Steve, and saw him still working at his keyboard—apparently fascinated by a multicolored sinusoidal display he'd conjured up.

Steve kept talking. "You attached to a university? Myself, I've only met a few nonhumans at the graduate level—talk about having to prove yourself twice over."

Angel nodded and saw the gesture was lost on the man, who was poring over his work. "I can imagine."

Apparently he took her remark as sarcasm. "Damn, I didn't mean to be condescending." He looked up for a moment. "After all, it does show some presence of mind that the ANHA would finally have a nonhuman come and look over the *really* nonhuman. Right?"

"Right." Angel agreed while trying to decipher the initials ANHA—NH was almost always NonHuman in Federalese. Agency for NonHuman Affairs? How come she'd never heard of it? Was it some organ for the NHA Committee in the Senate? If so, it explained how Harper could accommodate her request so readily.

The helicopter started thrumming rhythmically as the rotors engaged and the Sikorsky took off into the night. A few wisps of fog wafted by, whipped into horizontal tornadoes by the downdraft—and suddenly they were clear of the glare from the Presidio.

San Francisco was a ghost town. Angel could see miles of streetlights illuminating empty asphalt. Then the helicopter started turning, giving her views of the park, the Pacific, and finally—as the copter aimed down the bay toward the island—the Golden Gate. Through some trick of the light, the bridge looked like it was drenched in blood.

Oh, she was in a great frame of mind.

"I'm sociology."

"Hmm?" Angel turned away from the bridge and looked at the guy. She didn't know if this guy was continuing some point she hadn't been listening to, or if he had started off on some new tangent.

Angel realized that she'd never answered his original question. She never had enough time to concoct a convincing cover story. If possible, she'd like to avoid the direct questions this guy seemed to be leading up to.

So, even though she couldn't care less, she asked, "You're studying alien society?"

"Only indirectly." He chuckled and looked up from his keyboard. "They classified my thesis, but they didn't have anyone who could understand it. So they hired me." He shrugged.

"You work for the Fed?"

He grinned. "Oh, come on. You all work for them. I don't care what University or think tank you come from, or are you telling me you got the security clearance to be here without any grant money?"

"Ah—" Angel didn't have a response for that since it probably wasn't a good idea to say that she didn't have the security clearance to be here.

He looked a little apologetic, probably misinterpreting her hesitation as anger. "Forgive me, I guess I'm a little too open about who pays the lease on my Ivory Tower."

Angel wanted to change the subject before he asked about *her* ivory tower. "So what are you doing here?"

"Confirming my suspicions on when and where the Race first had a substantial effect on human society."

"So when and where was it?"

"I don't have a very high resolution on my data, but I put it somewhere in January 1998, central Asia."

Angel was shocked. "Wait a minute, you're saying that

these things have been on the planet for over sixty years?"

He nodded and went back to the keyboard and his sinusoidal curves.

"How do you know that?"

"Hmm," he stared at the graphs. "What the hell. You've got the clearance or you wouldn't be here." He slid the keyboard over to her lap, apparently so she could appreciate the graphs. "Know any sociology or economics?"

"Not my field." *Make this simple. I wait tables for a living.*

"Okay, I'll try to avoid the jargon. My main work has been on cycles. Economic cycles, battle cycles, cycles in political orientation. Especially their predictive uses."

He tapped a few keys and all the sinusoidal curves were replaced by one jagged sawtooth graph with only a few spikes.

"For example, that is a cumulative index of economic growth over the whole planet for the last century. It looks almost random, but it can be factored out to have a number of regular cycles of differing magnitude." He taped the keys again, and the jagged sawtooth smoothed out into a lazy sine wave whose girth was riddled with a dozen smaller waves all of higher frequency. "Add the values of all those curves for any one year, and you get the same sawtooth you saw before."

"Okay, so? How can this tell you about aliens?"

"Well." He smiled. "Perhaps I should show you this."

A few more taps and another sawtooth graph spread across the screen. "Same cycles, all carried out into this century."

Angel nodded.

"Now, overlay that with the *real* figures for the past fifty-nine years." The green sawtooth was overlaid by a red graph that began in the same place, but diverged radically, skewing downward. By mid-century it had no relation to the green, which seemed almost orderly in comparison. "You can see why any hint of cycles in academia has fallen into disrepute."

"Yes, it doesn't work."

He smiled even wider. "But they do. Given the data for the last century, you can use a sophisticated computer to predict the conditions *backward* an arbitrary distance. It's just a matter of juggling variables and getting a handle on what the individual cycles mean." He made a few taps and the sine waves came back. "For instance, the magnitude and frequency of this curve is an index of the speed of communication in a system." He pointed to a dark blue curve. "That one is based on actual transport of goods." He pointed to a much bigger curve that was a lighter blue.

Angel was beginning to get the guy's point. "You mean that divergence is somehow related to the aliens?"

He nodded. "These cycles represent fundamental processes in human society. A radical change in how they work means one of two things. Human nature changed radically at the turn of the century . . ."

He took the keyboard back.

"Or the Earth was no longer a closed system."

The helicopter was making the final approach to Alcatraz. Angel could see no sign of the old prison. The island was dominated now by the glowing white dome. Around the dome was a cluster of blocky outbuildings that reminded her of the white cinderblock earthquake-relief buildings that peppered the neighborhood south of Market.

"Why'd they classify your work? The aliens aren't a secret anymore."

He shook his head, almost sadly. "You should see it. I came up with the theory and the corrections for it before the aliens were public knowledge. I came up with a model of economic and political projections that worked. Everyone else is using guesswork. I can tell you exactly how the aliens manipulated things, from the Tibetan revolution in '05 to the last congressional election."

"I see."

"I bet you do. And the stuff I'm doing for the Fed right now, predicting elections, recessions, and such, is elementary cribwork compared to what the Race developed."

"How?" The dome was rising up and finally blocked all view out her window.

"They know how to change the numbers. They know what all the variables are and how to manipulate them. They can predict the results of their covert activity."

"That's scary . . ."

"I know," he said as the Sikorsky touched ground. "But it's fascinating."

# CHAPTER 24

Angel was ushered, along with the gaggle of academics, to one of the blocky concrete outbuildings that clustered by the edge of the massive dome. The place was run by a mixture of civilians and military. The military personnel wore a few odd badges on their uniforms. The symbol that seemed to represent the unit here was a picture of a globe overlaid with a lightning bolt.

The group was led down, through a building that housed laboratories and administration offices. As they progressed, Angel was aware of uncomfortable smells that were growing in intensity. Ammonia was the strongest, but it was also tainted by sulfur and other burning chemical smells.

The silent procession had finally reached a point where Angel was sure that they had come to the edge of the dome. They turned a corner and her suspicions were confirmed—

The group had reached some sort of waiting area that butted up against the dome. The ceiling was ten meters above them, and the room was a hundred meters long, at least. With the exception of a massive chromed air lock door that was emblazoned with red and yellow warnings —the entire far wall was a huge window.

Angel took a seat with the rest of the academics without taking her eyes off the window. The window opened up on Hell.

The inside of the dome, past that panoramic window, had to be close to a half-kilometer in diameter. Haze filled its atmosphere; the far side was invisible. A dim red light illuminated a rocky landscape from a point that must have been near the apex of the dome.

Jets of fire shot out from gaps in the rocks at regular intervals that ranged from two seconds for the small ones, to five minutes for a massive explosion near the window that could have totally immolated the Sikorsky she'd flown here in. There were rivers in there, but Angel found it hard to believe that the viscous black fluid in there was water.

There were *things* in there. Things that rolled, pulsed across the rocks, things with no definite form. They were fluid, undulating creatures. Once or twice she saw one of the smaller ones stray too close to the black river and become snagged by a black tentacle and drawn under. She couldn't tell if it was some aquatic creature that was feeding like that, or if it was the river itself.

The buildings in there were near the center of the dome, and thus barely visible. They resembled nothing so much as termite mounds constructed of rock.

There were humans in there. She saw two walking some sort of patrol around the perimeter, right past the window. They wore full environment suits in desert camo. They seemed to be armed with flamethrowers.

It was Hell. That, or the site of multiple bio/nuke strikes.

She gripped the briefcase tightly and tried to tell herself that she was still on Alcatraz and the view out the window was contained under a concrete dome. It was too easy to imagine that she was looking out, not in, and when she left this building the world out there wouldn't be the Frisco Bay, but some volcanic landscape out of Dante's Inferno.

Steve, the sociologist, was sitting next to her. He seemed to notice her fascination. "Remarkable, isn't it?"

"I'll say."

"First time?"

Angel nodded and tore her gaze away from the boiling netherworld beyond the huge windows.

"I was goggle-eyed, too, the first time I saw that." His hand rose from his computer and waved at the window. "They've managed to recreate the Race's home atmosphere and engineer quite a bit of the ecology. Quite a feat considering we still have no idea *where* their home planet really is."

VanDyne had built this, back when the aliens controlled it. The aliens—the Race—had been making themselves at home. This was far beyond the vidcast warrens that had been unearthed from beneath the Nyogi tower in Manhattan.

*What kind of places have they built in Asia, if they've been here for sixty years?* Angel could picture entire alien cities. Suddenly, Merideth's fear of these things didn't seem so calculated. The national mobilization against the alien threat now seemed less politically motivated.

"I thought they were from Alpha Centauri," she whispered.

"The Race that came to Earth almost definitely came from there. It's almost equally certain that they didn't evolve there. They've colonized about eight planets close by, Alpha Centauri just happens to be the closest."

"How do we know that?" Angel looked back at the window. The two humans in the environment suits were heading toward the massive air lock along a nearly invisible path between the rocks.

"A combination of detective work, analysis of the Race's genetics, and a good look at the habitats they built." He shook his head. "Not to mention a little blackmail."

"Blackmail?" The two suited humans stationed themselves on either side of the dome end of the air lock. On Angel's side of the air lock, a pair of marines bearing the lightning-earth insignia stationed themselves opposite the suited pair. The marines were armed with glorified stun rods that they bore like rifles. They stood at parade rest.

"Controlling every aspect of someone's environment can make you very persuasive—here come the interviewees."

The sight of the "interviewees" being herded toward the air lock was the most surreal yet. The double line of aliens, flanked by suited marines, emerged out of the heat shimmering haze by the termite mounds. At first she couldn't make out any details. The first thought to come to mind was three-hundred-kilo slugs. There were two marines for each undulating white form.

As the unearthly parade closed on the air lock, Angel could see that the aliens were highly individualistic in their method of movement. One in front seemed to gather its mass to the rear, and then roll itself forward in a wave before repeating the process. Another one, farther back, extruded a few dozen tentacles the diameter of her forearm and grabbed the ground in front of it, pulling itself along the ground. One actually walked, after a fashion, on a trio of pads that were thicker than Angel's torso. The most disturbing image was the one alien that parodied the humanoid form with two boneless legs and arms. With each step, its flesh rippled like a blister on the verge of bursting wide open.

Angel, as well as a majority of the country, had known that the aliens were some kind of intelligent multicellular amoeba. It was another thing to see a creature that had no set physical form. It was disturbing to see a creature for whom things like its number of limbs was a matter of personal preference. She had been prepared to see a creature that was a kind of amorphous blob. What she saw was a dozen different creatures, each with a definite form, each one different.

The procession reached the other side of the air lock. Above the massive chromed door, a rotating red light started flashing. A klaxon began sounding. After while, the door began opening slowly.

She had almost gotten used to the background smells that permeated this place. As the door opened, she was assaulted by ammonia and sulfur, bile, rotten eggs, and something akin to burning rubber. She started coughing, and her eyes began to water. She could understand why the marines in there had to wear environment suits. Even if there was enough oxygen in there, who'd want to breathe it?

The door finished opening, and two aliens and four marines walked out into the waiting room. The pulsing dead-white slug-things were only a dozen meters from Angel, and she could tell that most of the smell was coming from them. She could hear them, too. They constantly made a shuddering, bubbly sound—like a stomach rumbling, or something much thicker than water that was just reaching its boiling point.

The marines guided the aliens down one of a dozen corridors that branched off the room. Over a PA system, a bored-sounding voice called out two names, and a pair of the academics got up from their seats and followed the aliens.

Just so.

This whole process had happened a lot. Enough times that a set routine had developed. Even the vidcasts that speculated on the nature of the aliens, and on the government's role—usually through voice over video of the massive white dome that dominated Alcatraz—hadn't come close to this.

It was easy, for a while, to forget her own problems and simply watch in awe.

Steve the sociologist left with the second pair of aliens. Even though she found his nonstop talking somewhat irritating, once he left she felt truly alone here. She was the only morey on the island, and the looks she got from the pinks ranged from the disinterest of the marines to outright hostility from most of the university people.

It went slowly. They cycled the air lock for each pair of aliens. It seemed unnecessary, the air lock was big enough to fit the whole parade at once. Angel supposed it was some sort of security measure. Angel began to worry as time went on and the party from the Sikorsky continued to be called up in pairs. Eventually, it left only her—worrying that someone had tagged her as a threat to national security.

Nearly two hours after they started marching aliens through the door, there was only one left and the PA finally called her name.

By now her nose was numbed by the constant stink that leaked through the air lock. As she fell in behind the last two marines and the single remaining alien, her sense of smell reawakened. The smell of bile and ammonia hung around the creature in a cloud. It smelled like nothing so much as urine mixed with fresh vomit. The white latexlike skin seemed to sweat moisture that was slightly more viscous than water. Angel wouldn't want to touch it.

A procession of forklifts and golf carts carried crates from the helicopter through the open air lock. She lost sight of the parade as she followed the last alien down a new corridor.

Now that she was this close to the thing, she began to have second thoughts. This one had taken a hulking slug form, but even though it slid most of its mass along the floor, its midpoint was taller than she was. This one was bigger than most of the ones she had seen. Four hundred kilos of formless rippling flesh.

And she wanted to talk to this thing?

Her walk ended at a large metal door that slid aside for them. The room beyond was a squashed sphere made of some gray alloy. The lights were a dim reddish-green color except for one spotlight that was a normal yellow-white. The spotlight illuminated a human-looking desk and an office chair that seemed of a piece with the rest of the room. Angel could think of no other reason for the bizarre architecture than to make the alien feel at home in the debriefing room.

The alien moved inside and the marines took posts by the sides of the door. "You have two hours, Miss Lopez. Any notes or recordings you make will have to be cleared through base security. If you need to leave the room for any reason, use the intercom in the desk."

Angel nodded, took a deep breath, and followed the alien into the room. She tried not to jump when she heard the door slam shut behind her. She set the briefcase on the desk and sat down on the human style chair. It took her a few minutes to get comfortable. She kept shifting around on the seat until she realized that she was using it as an excuse not to look at the thing that was in the room with her.

Angel looked up and stared at her "Interviewee." It had pooled itself into the lowest part of the room, and had pulled a good part of its mass up to be level with the desk and Angel's eyes. It resembled a weathered cone made of semiliquid ivory.

Now what? How was she supposed to start this? Did these things understand English?

The alien answered for her by asking, "It is new, yes?" The voice was horrid, like a massive bass speaker suspended in crude oil. The voice rippled and bubbled as much as the flesh that created it.

It also sounded vaguely familiar.

"If you're referring to me," Angel said, regaining her composure, "yes, this is my first time here."

"We never are interviewed by nonhumans before."

"I suppose not." Angel realized where she'd heard a similar voice—the mainframe at VanDyne.

"What do we discuss?"

"I'm supposed to talk to someone who was involved with VanDyne Industrial."

"Someone?"

"You were involved with VanDyne, right?"

"I am political observer for that corporate unit."

"What the hell does that mean?"

"Do not understand. Your language is difficult."

"What did you do for VanDyne?"

There were a few moments while the creature seemed to digest the question. Angel began to realize that this wasn't going to be easy.

"I watch."

Angel sighed and put her head in her hands. "What do you watch?"

"The politics, the media, the video. I collect data for Octal analysis."

*Okay,* Angel thought, *I'm talking to a professional couch potato. At least it looks the part.*

She only had a couple of hours to talk to this thing. She'd better start hitting him with what she came here to find out. "You controlled VanDyne, right?"

"The Octal controls all corporate units."

"No, I meant—" Angel shook her head. "Never mind, you answered my question." VanDyne had been an alien enterprise, and this creature had been a part of it. "Did VanDyne employ anything other than—" *What was that name?* "The Race?"

"You are referring to Earth species?"

Angel nodded.

"Race operations are morally bound to employ native species."

"Huh? Run that by me again."

"Direct involvement is anathema. We do not intervene physically."

The bubbling accent was making the creature hard to understand. Angel wasn't sure she'd heard correctly. "You've got to be bullshitting me—"

"Bull shit?"

"—if you semiliquid motherfuckers are responsible for half the shit you've been accused of. There are *riots* out there. . . ." Angel took a few deep breaths. She needed to calm down. Stress and lack of sleep was eating at her nerves. The fact that the ammonia smell from this thing was giving her the first throbs of an oncoming migraine wasn't helping her composure.

"You do not understand. All Race does is rearrange assets to our advantage. Any Race who does more than this is ended. This is law."

Angel wished that the Fed handed out programs with the aliens. Hard enough making sense out of that verbal slurry when she knew what it was talking about. "Okay, let's back up. All you Race do is 'rearrange assets?' "

"We do no harm to sentients—"

"But you fuck with the economy?"

"We analyze the social structure and feed the variables that give us the outcome we desire."

She remembered her talk with Steve the sociologist on the flight out here. These things were running the whole sociopolitical structure of the planet like a giant computer program. According to the sociologists' charts, they'd been doing so since the turn of the century. "What was the outcome you desired?"

"We prevent any social unit from attaining the social, political, or technological inclination to leave its solar system."

Angel thought of what she knew of the history of the past half-century. The implications were staggering. "So what you people do, you buy politicians, right?"

"We fund appropriate people and organizations."

"Terrorists, right?"

The creature was silent for a moment. Then it said, "The fine distinction your language makes between political units is difficult to understand. We fund the appropriate variables to manipulate the political structure."

"Jesus-fucking-Christ, you buy terrorists and you say you don't harm sentients?"

The creature sat there, white, rippling, impassive.

"How many wars are you people responsible for?"

"War?"

Angel stood up on the chair, but she restrained herself from shouting. "Wars. Like the 'rearrangement of assets' in Asia, when Tokyo got nuked—that kind of thing."

"I apologize. Again, the way you discriminate arbitration between political units is difficult to discern. Language is difficult."

"Well, how many 'arbitrations' are your fault?"

"During my Earth operation, I know of no large negotiation between political units unfavorable to the program objective."

Angel sat down very slowly. "You are saying all of—"

"I know no details of the Asian operation. But until we are captured, no major political negotiation ended unfavorably. The assumption is the Asian operation is successful."

"Those 'negotiations' have killed a hundred million people," Angel whispered. Suddenly her problems seemed petty.

"How natives undergo negotiations is not the Race's concern. The concern is only that negotiations are resolved favorably."

*It all boils down to the end justifying the means, don't it? That attitude is almost human.*

If she had any idea of what to grab, she would have tried to strangle the thing.

She shook her head. No wonder the Fed tried to keep such a lid on these things. This kind of shit would fuck with *everyone's* mind. There were a lot of people out there who wouldn't like to think their glorious war for national whatever was the result of some alien pushing buttons.

The whole Pan-Asian war, an effing "political negotiation." Kinda helped put things in perspective. Against her will, Angel found herself laughing.

"I do not understand," said the creature.

"I suppose you wouldn't. I was just thinking that I should thank you."

"What thanks?"

"Well, if not for you and your buddies, I probably wouldn't exist. If it wasn't for the war boom in genetic engineering—" She shook her head and wondered if the thing she was talking to could even understand the concept of irony. "Back to VanDyne . . ."

"VanDyne," repeated the creature.

"This was what VanDyne was for, right? Shifting assets?"

"Correct."

"What kind of assets?"

"Technological assets. Informational assets—"

"Information?"

"Correct."

"What *kind* of information?"

# Chapter 25

Angel took the full two hours with the alien. The attempt to pry comprehensible facts out of the creature was exhausting. It didn't help that she had a constant feeling that, any time after the first fifteen minutes of the conversation, the Fed was going to burst in all over the place and she was going to disappear under a swarm of anonymous Fedboys chanting, "National Security."

She kept feeling that even as the Sikorsky took her and the academics up over the bay.

Somewhere there was a recording of her conversation with the alien. Somewhere a bored security official was reviewing the interviews with the captive aliens. Sometime soon, that official was going to reach the last interview. Angel knew that, fifteen minutes from then, all hell was going to break lose.

Because, once someone actually *looked* at the stuff she'd talked to that blob about, that someone was going to call Washington. When they were told *who* she was—

Her only hope was to get out of the Presidio before that happened.

*Information,* she'd asked the alien. *What kind?*

The alien's long rambling answer took a long time for her to decipher, but she now knew what Byron Dorset carried for a living.

If anything, that knowledge made things worse.

VanDyne dealt in a lot of things before the Fed took it over. The most important "assets" the Race "moved" from VanDyne Industrial were predictions. Very *specific* predictions.

The Race had stepped a few centuries beyond Steve the sociologist's sinusoidal curves. With their programs and the monster computer they kept at VanDyne, they could give demographic projections for any political unit you could name. They could have projections up to a decade in advance that came within a few points. They could tell you what the economy would look like, what technical areas would be advancing. They could predict the crime rate, the birthrate—everything from beer sales to the number of Masters of Science Degrees in biological engineering that would be awarded in 2077. But the point *wasn't* prediction.

The Race's programs weren't passive. They were dynamic. They knew what "variables" to "feed" to achieve a favorable outcome.

In some cases those outcomes were elections.

Every four years, they were *presidential* elections.

Angel stared out at the sun rising behind Oakland. She had to get out from under the Fed. Even though the security teams controlling Alcatraz only debriefed her to the extent of making sure that she wasn't smuggling out some record of the interview, somewhere—maybe right now—there'd be a review of whatever record the Fed made of her interview.

The magnitude of what Byron had been doing made Angel shudder.

The ramcards she was carrying were a step-by-step formula for a candidate to win the 2060 American presidential election. The way the aliens worked, it was possible, in fact it was likely, that the current head of state, President Merideth, had been a VanDyne client during his last run.

This was heavy shit.

Worse, she could see evidence of it in the current race. Not since the first few decades of the century had there been such a chaotic grab for the presidency. For decades it had been the Democrats and the Constitutionalists and the occasional independent.

This year, candidates were coming out of the woodwork to challenge President Merideth. Third parties—Libertarians, Greens, the NOA party—were actually getting percentages and major vid attention. Even the Republicans were making noises about running a candidate for the first time since the party collapsed in '04.

Maybe the chaos was because this was the first election in six decades that wasn't running according to a program.

It was becoming obvious that President Merideth had a much clearer picture of the "alien threat" than he was letting on in his media crusade. Perhaps it wasn't a coincidence that the takeover of VanDyne followed so close on the heels of the incident at the Nyogi tower. The aliens became public in January, and within a month VanDyne was captured.

Angel could picture the scene. The government clamps down on the aliens infecting Nyogi, very very publicly. The aliens running VanDyne get nervous and try to use their Holy Grail as a bargaining chip in an election year. It was a decent threat—lay off our people or someone else gets your job.

Merideth was in a bind. The aliens had been blown all over the media. He wouldn't have known the nature of the beings running VanDyne until then. Suddenly he'd was being blackmailed by creatures who didn't have the best interests of the country at heart.

So, to keep his relation with these things secret, and to keep the data out of the hands of his opponents, he stomps VanDyne.

Unfortunately, for all concerned, he stomps it a little late.

Byron was left stranded with the info when VanDyne was raided. The information was already out there and the memory of the big brain at VanDyne was scragged.

What does Byron do?

Angel shook her head. Byron got greedy, that's what he did. Back in February he could have sold the info to whoever VanDyne had slated to get it—probably Alexander Gregg, the Constitutionalist front-runner—and pocketed the whole shebang.

But no, he waited for the field to get muddy out there. There were a dozen credible candidates out there now, with little sign of winnowing a year before the election. It was anarchy at the polls—and Byron tried to auction off the election.

No wonder he got creamed.

That being the case, now what?

She could ditch the cards, wipe them, scrag the data, and let this laughable excuse for democracy continue without outside interference. That might score some spiritual victory, but it would probably get her furry hide nailed to a wall. No one would believe that she'd erased the stuff, least of all the Knights and whoever they worked for—they'd already gotten one blank set of tickets. They would strip her apart until she told them where the *real* set was. The moreaus would probably just kill her out of frustration.

Not only that, but she'd lost that option when Mr. K copied the data. Whatever she did with the Earthquakes' tickets in her pocket—the data was still out there.

At least none of the players knew that. Angel hoped they all assumed the encryption would keep her from copying the data. She hoped none of them knew about Mr. K.

No. Everybody believed she had the only set of this crap. So, the only way she had to get out from under this was to consummate the deal with somebody. If the players after her knew the deal was done, they might give up on trying to trash her ass.

She had to sell the shit or she was going to become very dead. She had to hand off this hot potato, and get the hell out of San Francisco.

To whom, though?

Not to the Knights—ever. Not the moreaus either. They were the ones that offed Byron in the first place. Merideth? That was a possibility, but she was afraid right now of being swallowed up in the name of national security. She doubted she could arrange anything with the Fed without quietly disappearing off the face of the Earth afterward.

So what was she going to do?

She pulled out the tickets and watched them glint in the dawn light streaming through the Sikorsky's window. Rainbows shot by the holographic Earthquakes' logo.

Again, she damned Byron for handing these off to her. She wondered if the data had always been disguised as these tickets, or if Byron was just playing on her love of the game.

"The Denver game." Angel whispered to herself.

"Tonight, isn't it?" said her neighbor, Steve the sociologist, without looking up from the keyboard in his lap.

"Four p.m. November 16, Hunterdome—"

She had called one set of people the folks from Denver because she figured that Byron had set a meet for that game. Whoever the Denver folks were, they were high up on her list because they hadn't yet managed to stomp her or someone close to her.

It gave her a chance.

Besides, she wanted to see the damn game.

She watched the mutilated golf course grow beneath the Sikorsky. She almost expected a ring of army officers, marines, or cops around the landing area. Something was going to blow—she could feel it.

But nothing seemed amiss at the impromptu air base. She couldn't see anything wrong in the ranks of Sikorskys, air-cranes, and the dozens of aircars. None of the numerous people wandering around below her seemed to be giving much attention to the landing helicopter. As their copter made a turn to approach the landing area, her gaze passed over temporary buildings, warehouses, the gravel lot where she had been directed to park.

She only got a glimpse of the parking lot.

"Excuse me," she said to the sociologist as she stepped over him. She bolted to the other side of the helicopter, feeling the first stirrings of panic. The other side of the helicopter had come about, and now had the parking lot barely in view. Even at a very skewed angle, she could see it.

What the fuck was Byron's BMW doing here?

A lot of the academics had turned to look at her. The sociologist character was telling her she better strap in for the landing.

The BMW meant those moreaus were here. Not on the base—the parking lot was outside the secure perimeter—but somewhere nearby. There were four of them, moreaus, combat strains. They were capable of taking out a fox trained in counterterrorist tactics unarmed.

They probably weren't unarmed now.

Four against one, and all she was armed with was an empty briefcase.

Dust blew by the windows as the Sikorsky landed. There was a thump that almost knocked her over, and the copter was on the ground. She had been gripping the chair so tightly that it hurt her knuckles to let go.

The rotors slowed and came to a stop. She stayed by the window as the doors opened and the passengers began offloading. Where were they?

She backed away from the window, toward the door. She had no idea what to do. What if they were on the base? *What if they were Fed?*

The gaggle of academics preceded her out into the landing area. According to what she understood about the procedure, a bus would show up, take them to an office out on the base for the final bureaucratic processing before they got sent back to MIT or whatever. The group clustered by the edge of the landing field, waiting for the transport. Most of the uniformed people were back by the Sikorsky. Angel's group rated one plainclothes Fedboy who stood out on the road and looked at his watch a lot.

"The transport will be here in a few moments, gentlemen." He didn't look at them as he said it. However, the smell of his irritation slipped to Angel. She didn't mind the delay. She needed time to think.

She turned in a slow circle, looking at the airfield. Her view passed prefab buildings and helicopters, the ocean and the Golden Gate, and white fog hugging the bay beyond the body of the army base. She thought of making a run for it right then. But there was nothing around the airfield except muddy hillocks and earth-moving vehicles for maybe half a klick in every direction but one—and in that direction was the parking lot where the BMW was. The army boys would catch up with her somewhere out in the mud, and then she'd have to do a lot of explaining.

If the moreaus were Fed, or if the Fed was after her at all, it was obvious that the bureaucracy around Alcatraz and the aliens weren't in on it—yet. There might not be some general alert on her, but all it would take was one bright yahoo on the comm to DC and she'd be in deep shit.

"Don't kid yourself," she muttered, "you're in deep shit right now."

"The bus is coming," said the Fedboy, looking at his watch one last time and stepping out of the road.

Angel watched the bus approach. No, she wouldn't bolt and attract attention to herself. She'd go through the bureaucratic red tape at the office, then she'd disappear. She could jump out a bathroom window or something and make it to the edge of the base on foot. Leave her car in the lot, she could call a cab when she was out on the street.

The bus—a chartered Greyhound that was way too big for the number of people—pulled to a stop in front of the collection of academics. The doors slid open and Fedboy stepped in, waving the bunch into the back. As was the case on the copter, she was the last on board.

She was primed for something to go bad, so when she took one step into the bus she picked up the smell immediately.

"Oh, shit!" She turned to bolt out of the bus, and slammed into the already closing door.

Fedboy took a step toward her. "What?"

She turned back into the bus. The smell was like a dagger into her sinuses. She wanted to yell at the pink; how could he miss it? How could anyone miss it? The driver was on the verge of a panic attack, and over that was animal musk—canine and feline. The heavy smell of an animal on the verge of a kill.

As she turned, she saw a well-concealed arm emerge from the luggage rack above the seat directly behind Fedboy.

*"Behind you!"* she yelled at him. Too late.

By the time Fedboy had turned around, the whole creature had vaulted from the luggage rack behind him. He was a canine—no, lupine—moreau, the most savage looking one Angel had ever seen. Lupus stood a full head taller than Fedboy, the top of his head brushing the roof of the bus.

Fedboy reached for his gun.

Lupus backhanded him.

Angel heard the crack as Fedboy's head did a quick 120 degree turn. Blood spattered the window on the far side of the bus from a massive wound on the side of Fedboy's face. He stumbled to his knees in front of Lupus. The wolf raised its arm and brought it straight down on Fedboy's skull.

Fedboy slammed into the aisle between the seats, made one spastic jerk, and was still.

His gun had never left the holster.

Human reaction times were much too slow to deal with a combat-trained moreau. The dozen academics were just beginning to realize something was wrong when Fedboy nose-dived into the rubber anti-skid tracking lining the aisle in the bus. As they turned to see a two-meter-plus wolf snarling over the carcass of the late Fed babysitter, two more moreys popped out from behind seats in the rear of the bus. Angel could barely see them from her vantage point on the steps by the door, but she heard the weapons cock.

From the back she could hear a familiar feline voice. "No one moves, no one breathes, no one says a goddamned thing."

The same cat that'd hijacked her BMW.

She looked up at the driver, and she took in all the things Fedboy had missed—the sweat, the overpowering smell of human fear, and the cat. As Lupus growled over Fedboy's corpse, a feline moreau uncurled herself from around the base of the driver's seat.

The feline's motion was silent, fluid. She arose out of a space much too small for her, as if she was something insubstantial. Angel saw the driver shaking as the spectral cat slipped out from underneath him. "Drive," she said.

There was a sickening lurch as the bus jerked forward.

Angel started to get up from her sprawled position by the door. The cat saw her. Angel suddenly found herself looking down the barrel of an automatic pistol. The cat was shaking her head. "You, of all people, should know better than to move."

The cat almost purred as she said it. Her tail did a slow oscillation as if it didn't make any difference to her if she had to vent the rabbit.

Angel sank back, with her back to the door. "You don't expect to get off the base, do you?"

Noises were coming from the rear of the bus, but she couldn't see that section anymore. Lupus had walked out of her line of sight, and it sounded like he was shoving people into the seats.

The female cat—for the life of her, Angel couldn't place the species—kept the gun trained on her and one clawed hand by the driver's neck. "In half a minute this bus will be very low on the priority list."

There was the sound of a distant roar, like thunder. Then a rattling sound like multiple gunshots and the sound of a cannon firing. The slice of blue Angel could see out the windows became smudged with black.

Sirens began sounding in the distance.

"What the hell—"

The cat produced a rather convincing smile. "The base is under attack, what else?"

The edge of a sign passed in front of one of the windows—they were heading for the Golden Gate bridge.

"Who are you people? *What* are you people?"

"Patriots, Lopez. That's who we are."

It felt like the bus was accelerating. Angel wished she could see where they were going.

"If you knew the full story, Lopez, you'd come with us willingly."

Fucking-a right she would. *Go on,* Angel thought, *tell me another one.* "While you're scragging people left and right? Yeah, *real* willing."

Faster than she thought possible, the cat had crouched over and jammed the pistol under her jaw. "Shut. Up." The cat spat the words.

God damn it, what was she? Angel stared into those leonine eyes and tried to think what country had produced this.

"Shut up and listen," the cat said in a purring whisper. "Unlike you, we never stopped serving the country that birthed us. And you're going to help us save it."

Angel stared into the feline's eyes and began to make the connection. "UABT," she whispered.

United American Bio-Technologies was the company the government seized for violating the constitutional ban on macro gene-engineering. The Fed wasn't supposed to be involved in the kind of experiments that produced moreaus. Engineering, especially on sentients, was very very illegal in the United States.

But the cougar eyes Angel was looking at right now, as well as the Canis Lupus that had scragged the Fedboy were both very very American. These moreys were Fed. And whatever project had produced them was very black indeed.

The cat seemed pleased with Angel's realization. "All we want is the information. Tell us where it is and this will all be over."

What the fuck could she do? She was backed into a corner, gun at her throat, back to the . . .

Angel shrank into the stairwell, wedging herself in as small a space as possible. Her feet were flat against the front of the first step. If it wasn't for that damn gun in her neck. "Don't be a fool like that vulpine bastard. Tell us."

Angel glanced up at the driver. He was sweating, and he kept glancing down toward the two of them. The bus was slowing and she could smell the fear building in the man.

Then Angel saw her briefcase, where she'd dropped it. It was by the feet of the dead Fedboy. "The briefcase, in the briefcase.'"

If the cougar would just stand up and get the case.

No such luck. She didn't even take her eyes off Angel as she called, "Ironwalker!"

Lupus came back into Angel's line of sight, stepped over the corpse of Fedboy, and picked up the briefcase. *Oh, well,* Angel thought, *it had been a good try.*

The brakes hissed and the bus slowed to a stop.

The cougar stood bolt upright, turned, and leveled the gun on the driver. "*Why are we stopped?*"

Angel didn't need more of an excuse. She pushed as hard as she could with her legs, and the door gave behind her.

# Chapter 26

The door opened more easily than Angel had expected it to.

The kick that forced open the door of the bus shot her out over the neighboring lane. As she was in the air in the middle of the lane, she heard the screech of brakes and the sound of a deep-throated truck horn as the biggest cargo hauler Angel had ever seen bore down on her.

Cougar, back in the bus, fired in her direction. Angel could barely hear the shots over the sound of the truck closing on her. The bus door swung shut again and its window exploded outward with Cougar's gunfire.

Adrenaline shot a spike into her skull and the pulse rushing in her ears competed with the truck horn in volume. She spent an eternity hovering over the asphalt, and she was afraid that the truck's sloping chrome bumper was going to splat her before she even touched the ground.

Even as the thought crossed her mind, her shoulder slammed into the concrete. She pumped with her legs and rolled. The truck was so close she could smell the grease on the transformers. She rolled out of the way as fast as she could, not looking at the truck. She didn't want to know how close it was.

She felt a breeze, smelled melting rubber, and heard the siren of a half-dozen locked disc brakes right next to her. She didn't have to open her eyes to feel the mass of the truck's cab shooting by her. She rolled once more, away from the truck, and made it to her feet.

Angel finally saw where she was when she got to her feet and began running.

She was bolting along the breakdown lane of the

Golden Gate Bridge Freeway, maybe a hundred meters from the toll booths. Between her and the bus were three trailers' worth of Biosphere Products' algae derivatives. The tankers had come to a halt next to her, giving her some cover.

The sound of more gunfire behind her encouraged Angel to run even faster.

Fight-or-flight had kicked in big-time. Every cell in her body was screaming for her to get out of there. Her breath felt like a blast furnace in her throat. The world seemed cloaked in a bloody haze, but her senses seemed to be honed to a monomolecular edge.

Her body ran on autopilot while her conscious mind grappled with how she was supposed to get out of this. Where the hell could she go? In a few seconds one of those moreaus was going to round the end of this algae tanker.

Not even one second.

Angel heard Cougar pounce out behind her before the cat started shooting. Angel dived between the two trailing tankers as the machine pistol started barking. The shots missed her, but a few of them punched into the tanker she hid behind. There was a gurgling sound, and a sour vegetable odor began to permeate the area. Below the joint she was straddling, a pool of blackish-green ooze began to spread.

She only had a few seconds before the cat was on her. Angel bolted up the ladder to the top of the tanker.

She pulled herself on top of the tanker just in time to avoid another round of fire in her direction. There was the sound of more bullets chunking home and an even thicker algae smell this time. The adrenaline spike in her head rang with a supersonic thrum. The taste of copper in her mouth throbbed in time to her pulse. Her nose was on fire from her own breath.

She reached the opposite end of the tanker in two jumps, vaulting three hatches.

The shots were getting closer, and they were coming from more than one direction now. Below her, the tanker was bleeding algae like an alien behemoth.

At the end of the tanker she had a split-second decision

to make. Behind her, Cougar was following her up, and she saw Lupus heading for the side of the first tanker. Instead of jumping to the next tanker and trapping herself, she jumped across—

To the roof of the bus.

In the air, she was already trying to think of where to go from there.

She landed on the bus, and the moreys inside started shooting. Gunfire began slicing through the roof toward her. She ran down the length of the bus, bullet holes erupting in her path. She reached the front of the bus and leaped, blind, into the next lane.

She landed, badly, on a slow-moving Dodge Electroline van. She had to grab an antenna to keep from rolling off the front, especially when the remote-driven program laid on the brakes.

Angel could see the toll area now. It was obvious that the folks down there knew something was up. Northbound traffic had all but ceased, and she could see a patrol car, flashers going, rolling down the breakdown lane toward them.

She had sat still too long. A bullet planted itself into the van's roof perilously close to her head. The Electroline began rhythmically sounding its horn as its antitheft alarm went off. It sounded like a wounded animal.

She leapfrogged two stationary cars until she had reached the median. Southbound traffic was still moving. She sat as long as she dared, and then she jumped across the median toward a mid-sized automated delivery truck. The truck was a moving target, and she needed to avoid the collision sensors in the front and the rear.

She misjudged the height and hit the side of the trailer, broadside. She'd missed the collision detectors—the truck was still moving—but she barely had a grip on the top of the truck.

Holes started blowing in the side of the trailer, all around her.

Even when hyped up for combat, one of the lepus deficiencies was pitiful upper body strength. She pulled as hard as she could, but her arms weren't strong enough to pull her up the sheer side of the trailer.

Panic spread through her like a fever as more bullets slammed into the side of the trailer. She began kicking like mad, desperately searching for some purchase on the smooth side of the truck.

Her right toe found something and she thrust herself up. Even as the jagged edge sliced into her foot, she knew that she had found a large bullet hole.

The push landed her half on the top of the thing, her ass hanging out over the side. She had to scramble like mad to get a foothold before her grip slipped. Her feet slid around in a smear of blood before she anchored herself on top of the trailer.

Even as she fought like mad to avoid becoming street-pizza, she had the satisfaction of seeing the two moreys on top of the tanker beat a retreat from the advancing patrol car.

She managed to hang on until it made the off-ramp.

When it came right down to it, the way things were going, she should have expected the scene that greeted her. The autocab wove its way through Chinatown but never made it to the address she gave it because Post Street was roadblocked above Grant.

Cops were out in force, as were at least twice as many unmarked sedans. Suited men in sunglasses spoke into small radios and sported stubby—but nasty-looking—automatic weapons. Two utility vans were parked behind this forest of lawful authority, right in front of that post-modern chromed-Asian monstrosity that Kaji Tetsami called home.

The cab idled and waited for her to punch in an alternate destination.

She stood on the seat and watched Mr. K's quasi-legal organization collapse. She watched it for close to ten minutes. It was overwhelming. Suited agents came and went from the building. A few remained stationed next to the utility people. Some sort of argument was going on over there. One of the utility people was gesturing violently, waving a clipboard computer for emphasis.

The other utility people got out the sawhorses and the little flashing yellow lights and sectioned off an area in the middle of the intersection of Post and Kearny. When they got out the jackhammer, Angel could figure out what they were doing and decided she didn't want to see any more.

She told the autocab to take her to the nearest available hotel. Since this was San Francisco, that only took half a minute. Most of that was the cab backing and turning around the mini traffic jam the roadblocks had caused.

Not caring much about carrying cash, or computer records, or much of anything else, she stopped at a bank kiosk and downloaded two grand of Bryon's money. The desk at the Chancellor was run by a human, not a computer, and the man had enough reserve not to blink much when she demanded to pay cash for one room for one night. It didn't really matter much to Angel that the hotel was going to have a hard time forgetting her. All the subterfuge was getting to be a little too much for her.

When they handed her a stylus and requested she sign the electronic register, she signed it, "John Smith."

She got to the room, locked the door, and collapsed on the bed.

"May you rot in Hell, Byron."

Mr. K, her only ally in this, had just gone under, leaving her very much alone.

Angel stayed in bed a long time, staring at the ceiling and shaking. She was exhausted, but she was too keyed up to relax. She let her mind run around in circles. It was noon before she felt calm enough to do a few of the things she needed to do.

The first thing she did was call DeGarmo, the lawyer. Of course he wasn't at the office on Sunday, but he'd done her the service of putting her on his comm's short list of calls that could be forwarded.

His home comm barely buzzed once. "Miss Lopez, Angel—are you all right?"

Angel laughed because there was no other socially acceptable way to react to the question. "I'm alive."

"The police—"

"—are looking for me, right?"

DeGarmo nodded. "A Detective White, in particular."

"Well, hold off telling them where I am for a while—"

"I'll respect that, but I have to advise you—"

"Skip the advice, I need you to do a few things for me."

"Like?"

Angel felt a strange sense of finality. She hesitated a few seconds before she spoke. "Byron's ashes—" she sucked in a breath.

"Yes? I have them, I've been waiting for—"

"You handle the arrangements. Dump them, bury them, I don't care. Just invite all those other heirs of his."

"Are you sure?"

Angel closed her eyes and nodded. "I don't want any part of it."

"Is that it?"

"No, my roommate—her name's Lei Nuygen—is in St. Luke's Veterinary Hospital. I want you to take care of her medical expenses. Surgery, medicine, rehabilitation, all of it.'

He nodded again.

"Last, I need you to transfer my money—" Angel brought out the black ramcard Tetsami had given her. "It's a bank in Zurich . . ."

After she had talked to DeGarmo, she called Frisco International and reserved a seat on the midnight ballistic to Toronto. Toronto was a nice place since it was out of the country and she could swing it without a passport. In Toronto she figured she had enough grease to pull out some sort of ID arrangement, legal or not, that could get her a lot farther.

She had committed herself. She was getting the hell out.

She pulled out her tickets and looked at them. The game with Denver was in three hours. She had box seats near the fifty yard line. She wondered if it was a good idea to go. She could try and lay low until the flight. But she knew that if she didn't ditch Byron's data, she'd be looking over her shoulder all the time. If she was lucky, everyone would still think she had the only copy—after Mr. K's organization collapsed she just might—and once she handed it off, no one would have a reason to hound her.

Or at least no reason to hound her to another continent.

If she didn't give up the data, she'd be crazy or dead long before the election.

At three, another autocab dropped her off at Hunter's Point Boulevard. It wasn't because she wanted to walk a few kilometers to the stadium, but because of the godawful traffic that was clogging the whole Bayview area.

She walked along the side of the road and looked at the cars. Kilometers worth of road were lined with moreaus packed into vans, pickups, and old Latin American land-yachts. One baby-shit brown pickup with particleboard walls on the bed must have been carrying at least a dozen rodents. The smell of alcohol was as thick as the smell of excitement. The Earthquakes' white and blue thunderbolt logo was flying on flags, plastered on cars, on windows—she even saw one jaguar who'd dyed the fur on his chest.

There was the normal whooping, calling, and carrying on. Like every big game.

But it *wasn't* like every big game.

As she walked along the side of the traffic jam, making better time than the cars, she could see signs of the tension that was hanging just below the revelry. It wasn't just the fact that the fans were louder and more raucous than usual. More than once she heard something break in the distance. Quite a few things were getting tossed on the sidewalk—empty drink bulbs, toilet paper, food, clothing, and, in one case she saw, even a passenger.

It wasn't just that there were twice as many cops directing traffic as there'd be for a regular game, or that, while the cops on the street were normally attired, the ones in the idling patrol cars wore full riot gear. It wasn't just the two SWAT vans she saw.

It wasn't the dozen or so newsvid aircars that hovered over Hunter's Point like locusts over a field of grain.

The clearest sign that something different and very wrong was going on was with the pink fans. Nonhuman football had as many human fans as moreys, and it was human money that really supported it. Maybe half the take at the Hunterdome gate was normally from the human spectators.

In the mile of traffic she walked by on her way to the Hunterdome, she saw three human-occupied cars. In each case, there was no reveling fan inside. Each human driver had locked the doors and sealed up his vehicle like a tank going into a war zone.

On each driver's face was an expression that said, "This is not a good idea."

If anything, the proportion of human fans decreased as she approached the Hunterdome. The dome itself looked like the upper third of a gloss-black bowling ball. Angel approached it as just another one of the thousands of fur-bearing people who were clogging the parking lot.

A half-hour before game time, just as she was nearing the gate, the surface of the dome activated. Predictably, it was for a beer commercial. Outside, the dome was a giant display ad, inside it was the single biggest holo screen on the West Coast.

She entered the gate as, above her, a twenty-meter-tall tiger was kicking back some brew bigger than she was.

For a half second she almost panicked when her card was passed through the meter. After all the fiddling that had been done to it, would it read properly? Would the reader fuck with the data that everyone was knocking themselves out to get?

It was only a moment, though, and then the young canine who read the ticket directed her up and to the left.

She passed a refreshment stand—the lines were long enough so the people near the end would probably miss the whole first quarter. She decided not to get something to eat. The air was ripe with hot dog, and cooking meat made her queasy.

Despite the crowd, when she broke out into the stands, she could tell that it wasn't going to be a sellout. She could see it in the stands as she made her way down to the fifty yard line. Way too many empty seats for this important a game. She had a feeling that each empty seat represented a human season ticket holder.

So, she was in shock when she got down to her seat and found a human sitting in it. A human she knew.

For the second time that week she asked Detective Kobe Anaka, "What the fuck are *you* doing here?"

# Chapter 27

For an instant, Angel wanted to run. Just start running blindly and never stop. But her feet remained rooted to the aisle well past the point when her panic faded and she could think.

"What the fuck are you doing here?" she asked again. She was sick of surprises, sick of being caught off guard.

Anaka moved over a seat and gestured for her to sit down next to him. "You seem to forget, I'm the one who returned those tickets to you."

"Oh, yeah." Briefly, she felt really silly. She was getting as paranoid as everyone accused Anaka of being. "How'd you know I'd be at the game?"

"I didn't." Anaka shrugged. "Seemed likely, considering the emphasis the letter put on it."

"You read—" she clamped down on the self-righteous question. Of course he'd read it, how else would he have known who to return it to? "Why'd you come here?"

"I don't know . . ." Angel bent over and got a good look at him. He was in sad shape. His eyes were bloodshot. The suit he wore was different, but just as rumpled as the last one she saw him in. Even over the pungent odors of hot dogs, beer, and ten thousand moreaus, she could tell he hadn't been anywhere near a shower in days. His face seemed thinner, his chin shadowed, and his movements had the deliberate quality of someone who knew he was on the verge of collapse. He stared up at her and there was a pleading look in his eyes. "Come in, Angel, to the station with me."

Angel looked at him coldly. "Fuck you, Anaka. I've already tried to do that once."

Anaka turned and rested his forehead against the seat

in front of him. It was so long before he responded that she thought he had fallen asleep. Meanwhile the PA system blared, "Welcome to the Hunterdome and Earthquakes' football."

During the applause, Anaka said, "I don't know what else to do."

Angel barely heard him. The motto of the Earthquakes was that they'd "make the ground *shake,*" and the bass speakers of the dome's sound system did a good job of making everything vibrate.

A minor 2 to 4 quake could hit right now and no one would notice. Those who did would probably put it down to a special effect.

"You have to help me—"

"Help you what?"

"*Stop them!*" Anaka was shaking, and it wasn't just the noise level in the dome.

Above them, over the field, the massive holo was firing up. Ten-meter-tall armored moreys went through their ritualized violence up there on virtual turf. It then began feeding in the net simulcast.

"You're the only one," Anaka said, "who *knows.* Who isn't a part of this."

Angel put a hand on his shoulder. How the hell could she tell him that she'd given up fighting, that the best thing she was hoping for was a clean exit. "You need some rest—"

He shook free of her grasp. "How the hell can you say that?"

"Anaka—"

"After all this, I'd think *you'd* understand."

Angel got a prickly feeling at the back of her neck. The feeling that something had gone terribly wrong. Anaka was on the verge of hysteria. Something bad had happened.

She put a hand back on his shoulder as the teams began to take the field. While the announcer went through the roster and the holo threw up stats in all their three-dimensional graphic glory. "Tell me what happened."

He looked at her sideways through half-closed eyes.

"Oh, you know. You probably always knew. It was your lover that started all this.

*"Cut the crap and tell me what happened after that goddamned shootout!"* Her own voice now held a note of panic and desperation, and perhaps that cut through to Anaka.

"Okay." Anaka even chuckled a little, a sound that frightened Angel almost as much as the look in his eyes. "What happened."

He looked out into space, as if he were studying the graph of Al Shaheid's past performance quarterbacking for the Denver Mavericks.

When the Mavericks won the coin toss, Anaka repeated, "What happened?" as if he was asking himself the same question.

"After you left me," Angel prompted.

He nodded. "Had to redo everything. Surveil VanDyne from a distance. Oh, God, I wish they'd found my tap—"

"They didn't?"

"A passive, noninvasive, optical sensor next to one of their trunk lines. I think it was too simple for them to find." He shook his head. "Kept monitoring police air traffic. That's how I found out how Pat Ellis died—"

"Doctor Ellis?" The name felt like a hand clutching her chest. That poor dumpy pink woman, the woman who was so afraid.

"—car was found in a ravine up in the San Bruno Mountains. Been there since Sunday. An 'accident.' They ran her off the road.'

Chalk another one up for the feline hit squad. It sounded like their style. Even though she was pretty sure that was the case, she asked Anaka "Who?"

"The same people who told her to burn Byron Dorset's body, who put the wrong person in charge of the autopsy." He looked at her as if all this was obvious. "That was two—no, three days ago." He looked at his watch.

The Mavericks got the first down. It looked like the beginning of a drive, and the crowd didn't like it.

Anaka was still looking at his watch.

Angel shook his arm. "Then what?"

"Seems much longer . . ." He looked up from the

watch, seeming very weary. It was then that Angel noticed Anaka's pants for the first time. They were stained, still wet in some places. Angel leaned over, and finally, through the hundreds of overlapping odors, she could make out the smell of blood.

"What—" she started, but Anaka was back into his story.

"Kept hearing White over the radio. Knights this, Knights that. He had two dozen skinheads in jail when you were kidnapped. He rounded up the rest afterward." There was a sad expression on his face. "He really was a good cop, before they got to him."

Angel looked up at Anaka. Her hackles felt like spikes on the back of her neck. Something very, very bad was happening—had happened.

"*Who* got to White?"

"The aliens, of course."

A chill traced icy talons down her back and stabbed itself into her gut.

Below, the Earthquakes had halted the drive short of a touchdown and progress was going in the other direction. The crowd was on the verge of a standing ovation every time the Earthquakes' canine quarterback, Sergei Nazarbaev made a first down.

"What happened to White?" she asked after three plays, afraid of the answer.

Anaka jerked like he had forgotten they were having this conversation. "He's dead," he said, sounding a little surprised, like it was a newly-discovered fact. "Damn shame, he was a good cop. Before they got to him."

"How—" she stared, but Anaka went on as if there hadn't been a pause in their conversation.

"I was so stupid." Anaka slammed his fist on the top of the chair ahead of him. Fortunately, it wasn't occupied. Angel saw the blow draw blood, but Anaka seemed oblivious. "I saw all the communications to Alcatraz. But I didn't really see anything until that damned computer called *you.*"

"Yesterday," she said. It was already ages ago.

"The signal burst through and overloaded the tap. Even

though it wasn't encrypted, I only got a few bits of what it said."

Anaka lapsed into another silence. Angel didn't prompt him. She was afraid of what he might say. She kept telling herself that it wasn't what she was thinking, there was a better explanation.

But she kept looking at Anaka, at the blood on his pants, his shaking hands, the dead glassy eyes—*No,* she said to herself, *not that.*

The Earthquakes' drive was stopped, and the score was tied with a field goal apiece.

"What did you get?"

"Huh?" Anaka looked at her.

"The tap, what did you get when you tapped—"

"Oh." He wiped his forehead with the hand he'd struck the seat with. It left a trail of blood on his face, and he looked at it with an expression of surprise. "Sorry, I've been a little distracted."

*A little?*

"I saw enough of what that machine said. And suddenly, it all made sense to me—"

*Makes one of us,* Angel thought.

"All this time I thought it was human corruption. Graft, bribery, organized crime, big money . . ." Anaka smiled at her. The smile scared Angel more than if he'd leveled a gun at her. "It was a revelation. The aliens. They were behind everything!"

Angel nodded slowly.

"I was on the cusp of this when White called me and said that one of the Knights had finally broken. I knew that I had been vindicated. VanDyne would come tumbling down, and the evil things controlling the government would be unmasked. Alcatraz isn't a prison—*it's a control center.*"

*He's gone nuts. Fully around the bend.* Angel sat back and could barely say what she was thinking. "You said White was dead."

Her voice was a whisper, and she had no idea whether Anaka had heard her. He went on. "I was wrong about White. They had gotten to him before I did. When I got to him, I could see how those things could manipulate the minds of their victims. He kept on about how one of the Knights had rolled over on Alexander Gregg's campaign manager. He didn't see the big picture at all—and his eyes—oh, God, it was his eyes. It wasn't White in there anymore."

"You said White was dead." Angel repeated, loud enough for Anaka to hear.

"*All of them.* The whole department was gone. They tried to keep me from leaving, but I had to get out. I couldn't let them do to me what they did to White." He looked down at his pants and rubbed one of the nearly invisible spots of blood. It was still damp, and Angel saw his finger come away wet. Angel focused on a hair that adhered to the blood. It was short, gray, and tipped with a tiny glob of what could have been flesh or clotted blood. "He looked so surprised. It was the hardest thing I ever did."

"Oh, God." The shudder in her voice reached all the way into her diaphragm. This had pushed Anaka over the edge, all the way over. This had all come too close to his own paranoid nightmares, and it had burst his little reality dam. She could see one thing, anything, setting him off, making him decide that *she* was one of them.

She stood up and began sliding away from him. She needed to find a cop. The police had to be busting their asses to find Anaka. He was oblivious, studying the hair that was glued to his finger.

*Keep staring,* she thought. *Stare until we get a hold of a white jacket in your size—and maybe some Thorazine.*

She was so intent on Anaka that she backed into somebody.

As Angel turned, she got an intense feeling of déjà vu.

She'd bumped into a pale pink who looked like a Fed, down to the barely concealed throat-mike. A pink with a nearly transparent white crew cut and red irises. She was looking at the same pink she had bumped into in Frisco General, the same pink who'd been pointing a vid unit at her house, the same pink she'd avoided to visit Lei at St. Luke's. The same two meters of suit punctuated by the bulge of artillery under his arm.

"I apologize for my tardiness, Miss Lopez."

*The albino Fedboy was the guy from Denver.*

Behind him were two more expressionless pinks in way too expensive suits.

"Ah, uh—" What the fuck was she supposed to do now?

"I am glad that you came. There was a feeling in the organization that you wouldn't honor Dorset's commitments."

Damn it all, this was why she was here! She wanted to scream at them that there was a crazy man behind her, three seats away. She wanted to move out of here, get this over with, but the albino pink was blocking the way back to the aisle. *"Can we do this somewhere else?"* Angel said in a harsh whisper, looking back at Anaka to make sure he was still occupied.

Anaka was looking at the game, the back and forth between two tied teams.

"We prefer a public place, as did Mr. Dorset. Too much potential for violence." He smiled. "It's best if neither of us are cornered."

*I'm cornered right now, you twit,* she thought. What did they think she was going to do?

"Let's get this over with, then."

Whitey nodded, took out a small computer, and slipped a ramcard into it. He tapped it a few times and showed her the display. It was a measure of her self-control that she didn't gasp at the amount. The number just didn't register, except that it had more than six zeros and no decimal point.

Angel nodded and reached into her pocket for the tickets.

Behind her she heard Anaka scream, "THEY'RE HERE!"

Angel could feel the world begin to tumble into slow motion. Anaka's manic cry went out and seeded something in the crowd around them. Angel saw the moreaus—scattered thinly in the expensive box seats—around them start turning in their direction.

Whitey stepped back, withdrawing the hand comm. The two suits behind him in the aisle were shoving their hands into their jackets. She turned around to face Anaka, her gaze sweeping past the field.

A cheer was rising in the whole dome. There'd been some kind of turnover near the Mavericks' end zone and Sergei was running down the sidelines with the ball. Throughout the dome the chant was, "Sergei. Sergei. Sergei."

The chant around Angel was, "He's got a gun."

The moreys were already scrambling away, over the seats and each other. Before Angel had turned completely around, Anaka had tackled her from behind, grabbing her around the chest and running at Whitey like Sergei was running the nearly eighty yards to his own end zone.

"Sergei. Sergei. Sergei."

Whitey stepped back, stumbling. Whitey's red eyes glared at Anaka, who must've looked the crazy-man part. The two suits had pulled their weapons, matte-black automatics, and leveled them toward Anaka.

Anaka was using her as a shield. "You're not going to take me!"

"Sergei. Sergei. Sergei."

Anaka had one arm around her chest, the other one shook a huge chromed automatic at the suits. She recognized the weapon as a well-kept antique Desert Eagle—a handheld Israeli fifty-cal cannon.

Her feet didn't quite brush the ground, and her leverage sucked, but she drew up her legs and kicked backward as hard as she could manage.

Tailored for a grand or not, her pants split right up the middle, and she felt her feet make contact right above Anaka's knees.

"Ser-gei. Ser-gei. Ser-gei."

Anaka let go immediately, and she heard the gun discharge. The explosion deafened her and she could barely hear the screams over the ringing. She landed, rolled past the suits, and ended up facing toward the apex of the dome in time to see the most horrifying thing she had ever witnessed.

It was impossible, so it had to be shock, or temporary deafness, but the world was silent except for her heartbeat and her breathing—more felt than heard. Above her, the holo was going, the live net feed that was being simulcast cross-country. It was on a delay, so she was seeing action on the field five seconds in the past.

Sergei was home free. He was running down the sideline; the nearest Maverick was twenty meters away. He ran like a being possessed, faster than Angel had ever seen him, or any other morey move. His head was down, tongue lolling through the face mask, tail streaming behind him, clutching the ball to his side. He had already run forty yards. He had just crossed the fifty yard line. Nothing could stop him.

Then, in the midst of his triumph, Sergei's shoulder exploded. The expression of canine triumph turned into a grimace as he tripped. His hand went to his spraying shoulder, the forgotten football tumbling on his forty yard line.

Sergei fell, facefirst, into the thirty-eight yard line. He skidded on a slick of his own blood. He stayed there, motionless, still clutching his shoulder, the bloody football within arm's reach.

It was only then that some goober in the booth decided it would be a good idea to cut the holo picture and the feed to the net. Even as the holo blinked out, leaving only the silvered underside of the Dome, Angel realized that it was much too late.

# Chapter 28

The silence was broken by more gunfire. Angel pulled herself to her feet. Up the aisle, she saw Anaka take one in the chest. He hadn't moved or taken cover. A flower of blood drenched the front of his rumpled suit, and he was down.

One of the suits had taken a fifty-cal shot just below the knee. He was on the ground, trying to hold onto his leg and keep from bleeding to death. The other suit was cautiously advancing on Anaka, gun out. In any other situation, keeping an eye solidly on Anaka would have been a good idea.

Of all three of them, Whitey seemed to be the only one who realized where they were. The dome was enveloped in a stunned silence, and the quartet of humans were surrounded by a ring of staring moreaus.

Angel heard the growls begin.

Whitey was subvocalizing to his nearly invisible throat-mike. The only two words Angel could make out at this distance were "... big problem ..."

Angel could smell the moreys who ringed the trio. Fear, confusion anger ... It was as bad, worse, than the scents she'd picked up at the prison. The moreaus were a solid wall of fur, arrayed in a semicircle with the open end to the field. The moreys blocked any exit into the stands.

The growling was getting louder, and the huge ursine that blocked the aisle opposite the humans from Angel was clenching his hands into fists the size of her head.

Behind her was a railing, and a five-meter drop to the sidelines.

Over the PA the announcer was repeatedly asking the

audience to return to their seats and stay there. They needed to let the police through. Angel didn't know if it was directed at this area specifically, or the whole stadium.

Whitey nodded a few times, then he walked up to the safely disarmed Anaka and raised his hands. "It's all right. We got him. If—"

It was the last thing he ever said. A seat ripped from the stands scythed out of the crowd and slammed into Whitey's throat. Angel had no idea where it came from.

The suit next to Anaka's body did the worst thing he could possibly have done, considering the circumstances. He began firing into the crowd.

Angel jumped over the railing as the crowd dissolved into a tidal wave of teeth, fur, and claws. She heard three gunshots as she vaulted onto the field. Glancing over her shoulder, her last sight of the area was that massive ursine—the crowd breaking upon and around him as if he was a crag of rock—holding aloft a bludgeon that looked an awful lot like a very pale human arm.

She hit the ground badly and stumbled a few meters. But suddenly she was clear of people. The sidelines here should have been crowded with people—the team, the vids, the staff, play officials—but the mass of people had been drawn to a circle centering on a spot near the forty yard line. A circle ringed by a dozen security people, all pinks. That must have been the entire security staff on the field, because no one made a move toward Angel.

She looked downfield and saw the teams. They were standing around the Mavericks' twenty yard line, their position in life reversed. They stood and watched the chaos that had erupted in the stands.

She backed away from the stands as if she avoided a thing alive. Her hearing was coming back. There was a growling rumble that outdid the bass speakers on the PA system. The rumble was punctuated by vicious carnivore screams—yowling, barking, roaring. The crowd had swirled into vortices around the few humans occupying the stands. Spectators, security, vendors, it didn't seem to matter.

She smelled smoke, and saw a licking of flames by the Earthquakes' end zone.

"It's the end of the fucking world," Angel whispered.

The announcer on the PA sounded frantic, pleading.

A speaker was torn from its mount and landed in the field. Other people began jumping to the sidelines. It was the only escape open from the mob, and a wave of fur began to pour over the railings. It was most violent by the Earthquakes' end zone, where the fire was.

That seemed to break the paralysis on the field. The teams by the Mavericks' twenty yard line bolted off to the nearest exit, behind the end zone. The crowd near Sergei moved, as a unit, off to the sidelines—and another exit. All they left behind was a bloodstain and a football.

The PA was now telling a mob that was beyond caring that Sergei was not seriously hurt.

Angel ran to the crowd around Sergei, intending to follow them out of the dome, but one of the security goons leveled a gun at her. She veered off. She was left near the center of the dome, standing by a blood-soaked football. Around her, the stands were a chaotic mess. The mob was pouring out onto the field, she could no longer even see the crowd surrounding Sergei to tell if they made it off the field.

All she saw now was a mad rush for the exists.

Most sane people had the same thought she did—get the fuck out of here.

The stands were now vast lots of empty seats punctuated by knots of moreaus trying to crawl over each other. The field itself was becoming swamped, and in a few seconds she would be overrun by the mob.

The sound was horrible. Screaming, roaring, yelping—the cries of pain and fear were drowning out the pinpoints of rage.

There was nowhere for her to run to that didn't thrust her into the heart of a terrified murderous mob. She whipped her head back and forth, hurting her ears, looking for anywhere that the masses of people were thin enough to break through—

The fire.

Even as she looked downfield to the burning section of

the dome, people began rushing by her, jostling her. A jaguar bearing a red plastic box seat like a trophy nearly toppled her.

Angel ran toward the Earthquakes' end zone. It was insane to run toward the fire, but that part of the stands had emptied out almost entirely, and the press of moreys on the field between her and there was relatively thin.

She ran, dodging panicked canines, jumping over collapsed rats, running as if she was completing Sergei's touchdown drive.

When she reached the end zone, it was raining. The dome's fire-control systems were trying to stop the blaze. It didn't seem to be doing too much good. Her eyes were watering from the plastic smoke that billowed from the burning seats. Between the fire alarms and the roaring of the fire itself, she couldn't hear the riot going on around her.

What had been a licking of flame from the forty yard line was an entire section of the stands going up.

No wonder she was the only one near here.

She ran for the exit behind the Earthquakes' end zone, holding her breath because of the smoke, stepped over a black ratboy with a crushed skull, and made for the corridor that led out of the damned dome.

If the Hunterdome had gone straight to Hell, it was only the first circle. When she made it out to the parking lot, the sky was already blackening with smoke. It seemed that half the cars were burning. She could hear the sound of breaking glass, sirens, and automatic weapons fire.

The scene immediately around her was surrealistically free of people. Ranks of cars marched away into a hazy pall of gray smoke. She ran between the ranks of cars, across asphalt strewn with the remains of broken windows.

There was the sound of an impact, maybe an explosion, in the distance, and the sounds of gunfire ceased.

Even though she was choking on the smoke of burning vehicles, she realized that she was wrong in thinking that half the cars were burning. The smoke cleared as she ran and it was clear that most of the fires were near the dome. Whoever started the cars burning had been systematic. They were all luxury sedans, sports cars and such. BMWs, Jaguars, Maduros—Angel ran past a burning Ferarri and decided that most of the expensive cars had been parked close to the dome.

When she cleared the pall of smoke, she began to see people. A few lanes away, a trio of rats seemed to be taking baseball bats to a car. A familiar-looking babyshit-brown pickup with particleboard walls in the back nearly ran her down as it screamed across her lane. The driver laid on the horn constantly, and as she watched the pickup's retreat, someone in the back threw something at a parked Porsche. There was a smash and the Porsche was enveloped in a sheet of flame.

A second later, a Hunterdome security car tore after the pickup, sirens blaring. It swerved to avoid her and plowed into a parked Estival four-door. A shuddering whine filled the air as the rent-a-cop tried to reengage the flywheel. He managed it, even though he had reduced the length of his car by a meter, backed the car up, and floored it after the pickup, leaving the abused rubber odor behind.

Angel stood there a moment, unable to move.

"The world has gone nuts."

What was worse, the spark that had touched this off had gone out on a national broadcast. What she was watching could be happening everywhere. Something inside her made Angel want to feel responsibility for this. She did her best to crush it.

"This isn't my fault." She had repeated it a half-dozen times before she realized she was saying it out loud.

*Get to the airport,* she thought. This wouldn't reach down there, she could catch her flight and get out of all this insanity. She made her way toward the edge of the parking lot, weaving through a riot of moreaus. Half seemed intent on smashing cars, the other half in driving out of here. She passed three accidents, and at one place there were at least twenty rats and rabbits trying to make a roadblock by pushing a burning van into the middle of the traffic lane. Angel felt real fear when she noticed that the van involved was one of the SWAT vans she had seen stationed around the parking lot.

More than once she passed the smell of blood. She never paused long enough to check whether it was human or morey.

Angel was in sight of the edge of the parking lot when she saw the Land Rover. In contrast to the manic activity elsewhere, the Brit four-wheeler was moving slowly, deliberately. It wove carefully between the cars, looking as if, should it find its way blocked, it would be content simply to roll over the offending blockage. Whether the obstacle was human, moreau, or a car. The windows were tinted, so she couldn't see the occupants.

She went out of her way to avoid it. She didn't want to be considered an obstruction. When she ducked back onto the traffic lane beyond it, she glanced behind her.

The Land Rover had turned and was following her.

"Shit!"Angel ran straight for the edge of the lot. She heard the Rover's engine grunt like a hungry animal as it accelerated after her. All she could think of was, after all this, she did *not* want to be lunch for some random nut in a luxury off-roader.

She leaped at the chain-link fence from five meters away and hit it about halfway up. As she scrambled up the fence she began to panic, realizing that that damn truck could plow through the fence without breaking a strut, and it would reach the fence before she even brushed the barbed wire on top.

As if it read her mind, as soon as her ears brushed the razor-wire lining the top, she felt the vibration from the Rover's bumper kissing the fence. At least the nut didn't blow through the fence going eighty.

Angel looked down at the silver-gray vehicle as the passenger door opened, and though she thought she was ready for anything, she nearly let go of the fence when she saw Mr. K.

# Chapter 29

After she got into the rear of the Land Rover and was buckled into a seat much too plush for an off-road vehicle, Mr. K's bodyguard proved her suspicion that the Rover could plow through the fence without breaking a strut. The Rover bucked once and opened a ten-meter gap in the parking lot's security perimeter.

As the driver turfed a lumpy embankment, looking for an access road, Mr. K gazed back at her with his deep violet eyes. "Fate smiles. I was sure we had lost our chance to contact you when the riot began."

Angel rubbed her forehead, a headache stabbing through her temples. The whole game, the last two days in fact, were a hazy mess in her memory. "I thought . . . When I got back—"

Mr. K nodded. "The mainframe at VanDyne may be an order of magnitude in advance of anything I have ever seen, but it is an utter primitive when it comes to cloaking its signal."

"Huh?" Her head was throbbing. Every time the Rover hit a bump, her ears brushed the ceiling and the bottom fell out of her stomach. When was the last time she'd eaten something, or gotten a decent rest?

"It called us back with the decoded data. Just as you ordered. Unfortunately, it did nothing to finesse the Fed watchdogs that monitored the one dedicated line it had. TECHNOMANCER, as it calls itself, just seized access to the line, grabbed a Fed satellite for its own use, and pushed into our system by brute force. A twelve-year-old with a voltmeter could have traced that signal. We were packing by the time the sirens must have been going off in Washington."

"Everyone got out?"

"Yes. A near thing, since we had to set up to EMP the whole system."

"Huh?"

"A few data grenades, crashing the optical memory, burning hardcopy—couldn't leave anything for the Fed. Fortunately, the most vital data I have is backed up in a safe deposit box in Switzerland."

"Of course." She took her hand off her forehead and looked out the window. The Rover had stopped bumping, and she saw why. They were now racing through Bayview. The streets were nearly empty, and as she looked out the window, the Rover passed a burning drugstore.

*It's everywhere,* she thought.

"What were you doing there?"

"Once our travel arrangements were set, I thought I owed you at least one attempted contact." Mr. K reached over and pulled something from behind the top button of Angel's androgyne jacket. It was small and round.

"You planted a bug on me?" *Damn it, that might have gotten me killed, especially on Alcatraz.*

"Not really a bug. It doesn't emit any EM signal unless I am within a rather short range with the proper tracking device." He patted a comm unit built into the back of the front seats. "Forgive the imposition, but you are valuable and worth keeping track of."

"So that let you find me?"

"Well, it seemed likely that you'd be at the game. Once on Hunter's Point we'd be in range for this. Unfortunately, we were late, and the riot broke even as we reached the gate. We barely made it to the Rover, and I've never been more thankful for this thing's armor." He patted the wood paneling, as if it was a pet.

She wondered how many other people knew she was at that game. She'd been pretty damn predictable. Now what? She had intended to take a flight out of the country—

"What travel arrangements?"

"Ah, that's why we wanted to contact you. I have a private plane ready to leave for Rome."

"Rome?"

"Yes, we did get a look at the mass of data TECHNOMANCER downloaded to us. Your data is much too volatile to market in the States safely, but the sociological methods implicit in the data are of interest to some of our European clients. We offer you passage."

Rome? Why the hell not? The EEC was at least as good as the States were for moreaus, ever since the pope decided they had souls. "I don't have a passport."

Mr K chuckled. "*I* don't even have a legal identity. You'll come?"

She nodded. *Leaving, what a good idea.* For a while she watched the city pass by as the Land Rover drove north. Pillars of smoke rose everywhere. Crowds of moreys *and* crowds of humans ran along the streets smashing windows, overturning cars, and throwing rocks that bounced off the Rover.

San Francisco had turned into a madhouse.

"When do you leave?"

"The plane's at Alameda fueled and ready to go. I've given everyone until six-thirty to get to the field. I hope the riot doesn't complicate matters."

Six-thirty at Alameda, barely an hour to get to Oakland and the airfield.

What was she worried about? It was Tetsami's plane. They wouldn't leave without him.

She knew what it was. She still had the damn tickets.

Not only that, everyone *knew* she had the damn tickets.

She'd been in the middle of a firefight between Governor Gregg and President Merideth ever since she laid hands on the things—and Merideth, at least, could reach beyond the States if he wanted to. He had the whole Fed to work with. If she could just dump it so they'd stop going after *her.*

How?

Wait a minute—

She pulled the tickets out of her pocket. "I'm getting rid of an albatross."

For some reason, she thought it would be harder. After all, it shouldn't be easy to arrange a personal meeting between a nobody moreau and a presidential candidate in the middle of a riot. Even if the candidate was a novelty third party one like Sylvia Harper.

It turned out to be more difficult to convince Mr. K to let her do it than it was to get the appointment. She had to push the fact that it was *her* data to begin with, that he'd already sold his cut, and he had already decided against marketing it in the States.

When the Land Rover's comm—in the back seat, high class—found the Harper people at the New Hyatt Regency, the campaign people made an immediate appointment for Angel. As if they'd been waiting for her call.

All she could think was that Harper remembered her from arranging her field trip to Alcatraz. That should have told her something, but all she could think of was the fact that giving this data to Harper would seriously screw with Gregg, Merideth, and the other big-boy politicos who had been screwing with this here rabbit.

The New Regency was an imposing gloss-black monolith that hugged the coast by Sacramento. Transparent elevators slid along the outside of the sloping walls. When the Rover pulled up next to the curb, Mr. K put a hand on her shoulder.

"We can only wait for twenty minutes. We have to get across to Oakland before the curfew hits."

*Or the riot,* Angel thought. The only sign of the violence here was the smell of smoke, and the sirens in the distance. The area immediately around the Regency was empty and silent.

"This should only take a few minutes," she said. As she stepped out, she could see that there was only a sliver of daylight remaining. The sky was a light purple, and the smoke in the air was hastening the arrival of dusk.

As she walked to the entrance of the Regency, three fire engines blew by, sirens blaring.

The pink security guard manning the reception desk—the only one there—looked nervous at her approach. He didn't stop sweating until he had the computer confirm her appointment *and* had taken her ID. He directed her to a private elevator that was guarded by a black-suited human whose bearing screamed Secret Service.

She hadn't thought third party candidates rated Service protection. But then, with Harper's radical stand on moreau rights—nonhuman, Angel corrected herself—she needed it. The suit nodded, and the door slid aside for her.

Harper was on the twenty-eighth floor. Not a room, her people had the whole floor. When the doors opened, another agent ran a metal detector over her and ushered her into a suite—and left her.

The few minutes she had alone she looked out the window. She could see back into the city, a city already cloaked with a smoky haze. At this distance, the burning buildings looked like campfires.

Harper walked into the room behind her. "Horrible, isn't it?"

Angel turned and nodded.

"It will keep getting worse, you know." Harper walked up to the window next to her. She was a tall black woman with long fragile bones. She moved with a confidence that convinced Angel that those bones were made of steel. "Until we have some equity not based on species."

Standing next to her, Angel could see how this was the voice that had been able to halt other riots, how this woman could walk into a place like the Bronx and not feel the fear a human should. There was something very hard there.

Angel pulled the tickets from her pocket. "Senator Harper."

Harper turned and ebony eyes latched on Angel like a vise. "You said on the comm, you have something for the cause."

Angel nodded and handed over the ramcards. The act released a pressure that had been crushing her. After a week she could suddenly breathe again. She sucked in some air, about to explain what they were, but Harper was looking past the ramcards. She was shaking her head and muttering. "Amazing. So obvious—"

The weight that had left, so briefly, was back now with a crushing intensity. Angel had a very bad feeling.

Harper was looking up and smiling. "You have no idea

how pleased I am that you did this voluntarily. The violence over these was becoming appalling."

"Oh, shit," was all Angel managed to say.

"You did the right thing—"

"Those moreys by VanDyne, on the bus—you?"

A look of concern crossed Harper's face. "You look like you need to sit down. I'll get you something to drink."

Angel slipped into an overstuffed Hyatt easy chair and Harper handed her a tumbler of amber fluid.

"I am very sorry for what they did. You have to understand, they were all I had. NOA doesn't have the assets of the Constitutionalists or the Democrats, or even the Greens. Merideth has the entire security community, Gregg has all the state mechanisms under his thumb. All we have is the Committee for NonHuman Affairs. The only operatives we have are NonHumans liberated when United American was seized—"

Angel nodded, trying not to listen. She'd been too stupid. Of course the moreaus were Harper's. Harper had been the only one who knew Angel was going to Alcatraz.

Harper was still explaining things. "—was inevitable. He refused to hand over the information except for an obscene amount of money. He was going to sell it to Gregg. Can you imagine?" For the first time Harper's voice held real anger. "He was going to sell it to Alexander Gregg, who has barely stopped short of advocating nonhuman genocide. If Gregg came to the White House, the Knights of Humanity would write the platform for the nation."

Harper walked to the window and looked out at the fires. "I'm the only one who can stop this."

The bolt of déjà vu was like a knife. Briefly, she could see a white blubbery form that smelled of ammonia and bile. *The end justifies the means—I was wrong, that attitude isn't* almost *human. It* is *human.* Very *human.*

Angel stood up. For one brief shining moment, she thought she would kill Harper. Slam the political twitch through the window and watch as she tumbled twenty-eight stories. She had taken a step toward Harper when sanity intervened.

All she wanted to do was get out of here. Away from Harper, away from this city, away from this country—

The last thing she heard Harper say was, "—if there's anything we can do for—"

Then the door slammed shut.

# CHAPTER 30

Andre was trying to call her again, but she didn't answer his page. Most of the time, his fussiness in maintaining the Naples estate was laudable. At the moment, however, it was just plain irritating. Angel didn't want to hear how the techs were spooling cable through the kitchen, or how heavy equipment was gouging the parquet—

Of course, she *could* have gone up the coast to Tetsami's main headquarters. However, she only had one bit left to feed him, and she was going to get as much out of it as she could. She'd been waiting over a year for this and it was going to go down *here*—home. Besides, the remote didn't cost Tetsami that much more.

And, for him, for what Angel was going to give him—the remote terrorist run was going to be cheap.

She flipped through her old sheaf of news faxes. They were in Italian, so she only read the headlines. Her language wasn't that good yet—

"USNF 12–15–59: GREGG DENIES KNIGHTS' INVOLVEMENT"

"USNF 12–20–59: ATTORNEY GENERAL ANNOUNCES INDICTMENT OF CONSTITUTIONALIST COMMITTEE CHAIR"

"USNF 2–10–60: GREGG STEPS DOWN"

"USNF 2–11–60: NOA REACHES RECORD 20% IN CALIFORNIA"

"USNF 3–20–60: SERGEI NAZARBAEV ENDORSES HARPER, RETIRES FROM FOOTBALL"

"USNF 4–17–60: SPECIAL GRAND JURY DECLARES KOBE ANAKA LONE GUNMAN"

Angel chuckled at that one. She wondered what Anaka

would think if he knew he was the linchpin of a whole new crop of conspiracy theories.

"USNF 5–23–60: GENERAL GURGUEIA TO MEET WITH NONHUMAN COMMITTEE"

That was Harper's first coup. She had managed to get to meet with the violent antihuman leader of the Moreau Defense League. Angel noted cynically that the "NonHuman" committee was composed entirely of humans.

There was an incidental mention of intra-Bronx violence. Apparently a group of canines and felines—wolves and cougars? Angel shrugged—had been stirring up trouble in the Bronx, wasting the MDL leadership.

Gurgueia denied that that was the reason the MDL had decided to talk now.

"USNF 6–5–60: TRUCE DECLARED, MARTIAL LAW LIFTED FROM LA, BRONX"

That was coup number two. It happened shortly after an unidentified feline assassinated Gurgueia. The death of the general received only minor press.

"USNF 7–18–60: NOA ANNOUNCES NONHUMAN VICE PRESIDENT, DROPS TEN POINTS"

All the pundits thought Harper had killed herself when she had a morey get on the platform. A rabbit, no less. Needless to say, Harper knew exactly what she was doing.

"USNF 9–10–60: NOA LEADS DEMOCRATS BY FIVE POINTS"

Merideth had managed to shoot himself in the foot several times when talking about the NOA vice presidential candidate. His campaign died when a recording of racist comments surfaced, smearing Harper and the VP nominee. Something crude like "Harper, fucking like a bunny." No one believed it when Merideth said the tape was a computer-generated forgery.

Harper had never looked back from that.

The most recent headline had come in this morning. She put the sheaf down on her desk and read it.

"USNF 1–20–61: HARPER TAKES OATH OF OFFICE"

One of the techs walked in and said something in rapid Italian.

"English, still," she said. "I'm working on it."

"Oh," said the human tech. "I am here to fetch you."

"Everything's ready, then?"

"All is ready."

Angel followed the tech out and down the broad staircase. They walked along, following cables that snaked into the Ballroom. The Ballroom had been set up with a dozen computer techs, and a like number of remote terminals. In the back, Tetsami was putting on an odd-shaped helmet in front of a dynamic holo display.

Andre stood in a corner, looking like he was about to cry.

Angel walked up and seated herself at a vacant comm terminal stationed next to Tetsami's desk. The frank only went by Tetsami now. Unlike his last base of operations, the government here was *very* friendly.

The look on Tetsami's face was one of predatory excitement. Angel had known that he'd been salivating after TECHNOMANCER's backdoor ever since they'd left the States. The trick, of course, was that only Angel could use it. She knew of at least one attempt that Tetsami had made. It'd been a dismal failure. The Fed had done quite a bit to tutor TECHNOMANCER on proper security procedures.

Tetsami thought that the Fed's security procedures might actually reinforce Angel's BS. He'd been willing to pay handsomely to have her help them go in. At this point, however, Angel could give a shit about money.

Her price was much more complicated, and it took a long time to get Tetsami to go along with her.

"Everything set?" Angel asked.

"We are ready to punch the hole."

Angel nodded and a speaker began squawking, *"One minute to satellite uplink."*

The whole process was familiar. The only difference was that the last time they called on VanDyne's mainframe they didn't have to bounce the signal over the ocean.

Eventually, a familiar bubbly voice called over the speakers. *"Authorization is required immediately."*

TECHNOMANCER seemed to be a little more security conscious. "It's okay. I'm Angel, the rabbit, remember?"

*"Your access is logged. You have authorization and clearance."*

Tetsami was right, the BS she'd fed the thing had stuck. "What clearance do I have?"

*"TIPPY-TOP SECRET."*

A lot of the techs, who had been there during the first contact, cheered. Angel allowed herself a little smile. "I am going to hand you over to a lot more people, they all have my access. Understand?"

*"Yes."*

"You are to answer their questions and do what they say."

The techs sprang into activity as the U.S. Government's most powerful computer opened its soul to them. While the techs conducted their data orgy, she made an international call on the comm at her station.

From Tetsami's estimates, it would take the Fed ten minutes to realize something was wrong, another four or five to trace the signal and cut it. Since the team wasn't in the States, they could ride it right down to the wire.

With what Tetsami knew, there was no way the EEC was going to extradite him, or anyone involved with him.

Besides, when Angel was done, the Fed would have a lot more to worry about.

It was bright daylight in Naples. In San Francisco it was close to midnight. However, Pasquez was an anchor now, and he did the night news. He was there when her call came into BaySatt.

A look of shock crossed his perfect hispanic features when he saw her. She had picked him because he was the one reporter who'd recognize her. "Lopez. Angelica Lopez!"

"Good. I see they've taken you off the street."

"I anchor the national desk— Christ, you disappeared back in November. Before the riots. I did a series on your disappearance."

"One of the reasons Gregg went belly up, I hear."

"Financing the Knights of Humanity wasn't very popular. Where have you been?"

"Hiding out—" In the background there were more cheers from the techs.

"We leeched it."

"The program's holding."

"The thing is actually going to do it."

"We're withdrawing. It's TECHNOMANCER's show now."

The speaker by Tetsami started a new countdown. *"One minute until TECHNOMANCER."*

Angel turned to Tetsami, holding a finger to the screen to quiet Pasquez, "They can't stop it, can they?"

"Only if the Fed can afford to chop the only outside line they have on their prize system. They have TECHNOMANCER wired into some vital systems now. I don't think they can."

Pasquez was trying to get her attention. "What's going on over there?"

*What's going on? Just that, in less than a minute the Fed's most powerful computer is going to burst-feed some* very *interesting information into the database of every news organization in the States.*

*"Thirty seconds until TECHNOMANCER."*

She looked at Pasquez, grinning hard enough to hurt the ghost of an old scar. "So, you want a fucking-A exclusive?"

## APPENDIX
# History of the Moreau World

## *Moreau Timeline*

*circa. 2000:* Race begins involvement in terrestrial affairs.

*1999–2005:* Worldwide breakthroughs in genetic engineering. Start of the biological revolution.

*2008–2011:* War for Korean unification; despite the South's technical advantage the North overwhelms it with Chinese assistance. The U.N. is bogged down in nationalist conflicts in Eastern Europe and the former Soviet Republics. The United States begins its policy of diplomatic nonintervention.

*2008:* The first moreau is engineered in a South Korean lab. It's a large dog breed with an increased cranial capacity. It is the first species so engineered that breeds true. Even though the war is short-lived, an intensive breeding program results in nearly ten thousand of these smart dogs slipping north to plant explosives and otherwise harass the enemy.

*2011–2015:* The aftermath of the Korean War begins an international debate on the military uses of genetic engineering. The debate culminates with United Nations resolutions banning genetically-engineered disease organisms and any genetic engineering on the Human genome. The U.N. deadlocks on banning the engineering of sapient animals—by the time it reaches a vote, four out of five nations with a substantial military have their own "Korean dog" projects.

*2017:* On a tide of public opinion fueled by anti-Japanese sentiment (by 2017 the Japanese have the most high-profile genetic program, notably ignoring the U.N. restrictions), there's a constitutional convention to draft the 29th amendment to the U.S. Constitution. The amendment bans any genetic engineering on a macroscopic scale and, in an effort to prevent any possible atrocities like the ones in Korea, gives the sapient results of genetic engineering of animals the protection of the Bill of Rights.

*2019–2023:* Iranian Terrorists slaughter the Saudi royal family, sparking the Third Gulf War. The war eventually envelops all the Arab states and marks the beginning of substantial nonhuman immigration into the United States.

*2023:* The Gulf War ends forming the Islamic Axis. The Axis is a fundamentalist Pan-Arab union. The price of oil triples even over wartime levels. A small company in Costa Rica, Jerboa Electrics, begins production of the Jerboa—a small, cheap electric convertible that now costs less than half to run as the most efficient gas vehicle.

*2024:* Start of the Pan-Asian war. It begins around a Pakistan-India border dispute and snowballs almost instantly. By the end of the year it involves the Islamic Axis, most of the former Soviet republics, and China on one side, India, Japan, Russia, and most of North Africa on the other. The United States continues its hands-off foreign policy.

*2025:* The Ford Motor company buys Jerboa Electronics to avoid an international lawsuit over Ford's wholesale swiping of the electric-car design. Proceeds to sue GM motors and Chrysler for doing the same thing. BMW is producing its own electric design.

*2027:* United American Bio-Technologies is indicted for breaking the ban on macro-genetic engineering. They've been producing moreaus for the Asian war effort (both sides) and, worse, they've been working on human genetics as well—though there's no evidence that ever went beyond the computer-simulation stage on their human project. The Fed seizes all of UABT's assets in an unprecedented move against a corporate criminal. Rumors persist that the Fed Intelligence community wanted UABT's nationwide facilities for its own uses.

*2027:* New Delhi nuked as the Indian national defense begins to crumble. Mass desertions are rampant and whole sections of the country lay down their arms and surrender. From the Afghan frontier, an entire company of moreau Tigers from the Indian special forces seize control of a cargo plane and fly to America. It is called the Rajastahn airlift, for the strain of tiger involved. The airlift is an American media event, the officers of the company become celebrities. Especially Datia Rajastahn, the officer in charge of the airlift. He's eloquent, charismatic, and the first major voice for the moreaus—not only in America, but internationally.

*2029:* The American space program reaches its apex. NASA has an orbiting space station, a temporary lunar base, an orbiting radio telescope that may be picking up alien radio signals from the vicinity of Alpha Centauri. The peak is reached when appropriations for NASA's deep-probe project are approved. The deep-probe project is to involve a half-dozen unmanned nuclear rockets to fly by the nearest star systems.

*2030:* The Israeli intelligence community, the Mossad, conducts a raid into Jordan and captures a secret training base for Jordanian franks. The Mossad, with domestic legal constraints on a par with the American bans on macroscopic genetic engineering, destroys the Jordanian base, but takes the immature franks (100 girls from Hiashu Biological ranging from 3 to 16 years in age) and secretly trains them as Israeli agents.

*2030:* The last Indian national defenders fail. The subcontinent falls to a Pakistani/Afghani invasion force.

*2032–2044:* The African pandemic, genetically-engineered viruses, race across the continent in waves that resemble the Black Death that swept Europe in the Middle Ages. Entire villages are wiped out in weeks, governments collapse, and the entire continent is under virtual quarantine. The worst is over in three years, but it takes nearly a decade for a central government, the United African States, to repair the damage to the African economy. The rebuilding of the continent is due, in large part, to a husbanding of the indigenous genetic diversity Africa is home to. By 2044, the U.A.S. genetic programs rival any on the globe and are a billion dollar industry.

*January 8, 2034:* The "big one" hits California. The quake is a 9.5 and centers about 30 miles south of San Francisco. Aftershocks in the 5–7 range echo down the coast as far south as Los Angeles. The urban landscape of California is altered forever.

*2034–2041:* The last Arab-Israeli war. (According to the Axis, the war of Palestinian liberation. According to the Israelis, the Second Holocaust.) Israel fights for six years against the entire Islamic Axis. Eventually Israel loses as the conflict goes nuclear. Tel Aviv is nuked, and despite retaliatory nuclear strikes against the Axis that kill nearly five million Arabs, Israel is overrun. There is an Israeli government-in-exile in Geneva.

*April, 2035:* Tokyo is nuked as part of the Chinese invasion of Japan. Most of the Japanese technical base is either destroyed in the attack, or is destroyed by the Japanese defenders to deny it to the Chinese. Countless technological achievements by the Japanese are lost in the final days. Marks the official end of the Pan-Asian war.

*2037:* U.S. morey population is estimated to have hit 10 million. Most of the moreau population in the States are war refugees from the Asian war. A substantial minority consists of rats and rabbits coming across the border from Central America.

*2038:* Pope Leo XIV surprises the entire Christian world by issuing a decree that, though genetic engineering is a sin, moreaus still have souls. The political pressure of this causes the European Community to cease moreau production. In Central America, this causes a virtual civil war, as massive moreau armies begin to rise against their masters. Latin American moreau immigration into the U.S. quadruples.

*2039:* NASA begins to experience new setbacks in Congress as the country becomes more and more concerned with the exploding moreau population. In the first of a number of budget-cutting moves, NASA's radio telescope—the Orbital Ear—is shut down.

*2042:* The "Dark August" riots across the U.S. A summer-long eruption of urban violence that most humans blame on the rhetoric of Datia Rajastahn, the first and most influential moreau leader. Datia had become more and more radical as time progressed, until he was the leader of a national moreau para-military organization. The Moreau Defense League was said to be defensive in nature, but the Fed viewed it as a terrorist group. Datia was eventually cornered in a burning building in Cleveland's Moreytown and shot down by combined police and National Guard. Datia has since become a moreau icon of political activism.

*2043:* Congress halts NASA's deep-probe appropriations, the four completed probes are mothballed. As a result of the riots, there is a moratorium placed on moreau immigration. Anti-moreau sentiment reaches an apex as there's public debates about mass deportations, mandatory nonhuman sterilization, moreau "reservations." Fortunately for the nonhuman population, none of the extreme measures were popular enough to pass. However, legislation was passed banning a moreau from possessing a firearm and it became a silent Federal policy to isolate concentrations of moreau population from human population. The most visible signs of this are the semipermanent traffic barricades that block the roads into most Moreytowns.

*2045:* South African coup led by mixed blacks and franks. It is revealed that the South African government had a rampant human-engineering program. By the time of the coup, there are close to a million franks indigenous to South Africa. The coup marks the first time a country allows franks full citizenship. (In the States there is debate concerning the wording of the 29th amendment, so while moreaus are tolerated as second-class citizens, the franks are treated as if they have no rights at all.)

*2053:* Congress scuttles NASA's deep-probe project. Rumors persist that the project was taken over by one of the Fed's black agencies. The European Community eliminates internal moreau travel restrictions.

*2054:* The Supreme Court hears the Frank civil rights case and rules 7–2 that the 29th amendment applies to genetically engineered humans, as well as animals. Orders a halt to Government internment and summary deportation of franks. Suddenly, a large number of franks begin to appear "officially" on the government payroll—primarily in the intelligence services.

*2059:* With the discovery of a Race warren under the Nyogi tower in Manhattan, the alien threat is made public. Fed invades the Bronx with the National Guard to root out entrenched Moreau Defense League armor. The move sparks a nationwide increase in moreau violence.

*2060:* Sylvia Harper wins the U.S. presidential election.

# S. Andrew Swann

☐ **FORESTS OF THE NIGHT** UE2565—$3.99

When Nohar Rajasthan, a private eye descended from genetically manipulated tiger stock, a moreau—a second-class humanoid citizen in a human world—is hired to look into a human's murder, he find himself caught up in a conspiracy that includes federal agents, drug runners, moreau gangs, and a deadly canine assassin. And he hasn't even met the real enemy yet!

☐ **EMPERORS OF THE TWILIGHT** UE2589—$4.50

New York City, sixty years in the future, a time when a squad of assassins was ready to send an entire skyscraper up in flames to take out one special operative. Her name: Evi Isham, her species: frankenstein, the next step beyond human, her physiology bioengineered to make her the best in the business whether she was taking down an enemy or just trying to stay alive. Back from vacation and ready to report in to the Agency for a new assignment, Evi suddenly found herself on the run from an unidentified enemy who had targeted her for death. Her only hope was to evade her stalkers long enough to make contact with her superiors. But she would soon discover that even the Agency might not save her from those who sought her life!

---

**Buy them at your local bookstore or use this convenient coupon for ordering.**

**PENGUIN USA P.O. Box 999—Dep. #17109, Bergenfield, New Jersey 07621**

Please send me the DAW BOOKS I have checked above, for which I am enclosing $______ (please add $2.00 per order to cover postage and handling.) Send check or money order (no cash or C.O.D.'s) or charge by Mastercard or Visa (with a $15.00 minimum.) Prices and numbers are subject to change without notice.

Card #____________________ Exp. Date __________
Signature______________________________
Name______________________________
Address______________________________
City ____________ State _________ Zip _________

For faster service when ordering by credit card call **1-800-253-6476**

Please allow a minimum of 4 to 6 weeks for delivery.

# Kate Elliott

***The Novels of the Jaran:***

☐ **JARAN: Book 1** UE2513—$4.99

Here is the poignant and powerful story of a young woman's coming of age on an alien world, a woman who is both player and pawn in an interstellar game of intrigue and politics, where the prize to be gained may be freedom for humankind from long-standing domination by their alien conquerors.

☐ **AN EARTHLY CROWN: Book 2** UE2546—$5.99

On a low-tech planet, Ilya, a charismatic warlord, is leading the nomadic jaran tribes on a campaign of conquest, while his wife Tess—an Earth woman of whose true origins Ilya is unaware—is caught up in a deadly game of interstellar politics.

☐ **HIS CONQUERING SWORD: Book 3** UE2551—$5.99

Even as Jaran warlord Ilya continues the conquest of his world, he faces a far more dangerous power struggle with his wife's brother, Duke Charles, leader of the underground human rebellion against an interstellar alien empire.

---

**Buy them at your local bookstore or use this convenient coupon for ordering.**

**PENGUIN USA P.O. Box 999, Dept. #17109, Bergenfield, New Jersey 07621**

Please send me the DAW BOOKS I have checked above, for which I am enclosing $______ (please add $2.00 per order to cover postage and handling. Send check or money order (no cash or C.O.D.'s) or charge by Mastercard or Visa (with a $15.00 minimum.) Prices and numbers are subject to change without notice.

Card #________________________ Exp. Date ____________

Signature______________________________________

Name_________________________________________

Address_______________________________________

City ______________ State ____________ Zip __________

For faster service when ordering by credit card call **1-800-253-6476**

Please allow a minimum of 4 to 6 weeks for delivery.

# Kris Jensen

***The Ardellans:***

☐ **FREEMASTER: Book 1** UE2404—$3.95

The Terran Union had sent Sarah Anders to Ardel to establish a trade agreement for materials vital to offworlders but of little value to the low-tech Ardellans. But other, more ruthless humans were about to stake their claim to Ardel with the aid of forbidden technology and threats of destruction. The Ardellan clans had defenses of their own, based on powers of the mind, that only a human such as Sarah could begin to understand. For she, too, had mind talents locked within her—and the FreeMasters of Ardel might just provide the key to releasing them.

☐ **MENTOR: Book 2** UE2464—$4.50

Jeryl, Mentor of Clan Alu, sought to save the Ardellan Clans which, decimated by plague, were slowly fading away. But even as Jeryl set out on his quest, other Clans sought a different solution to their troubles, ready to call upon long-forbidden powers to drive the hated Terrans off Ardel.

☐ **HEALER: Book 3** UE2570—$4.99

With plague sweeping the native population, Terran Dr. Sinykin Inda answers the Ardellans' plea for help, only to be thrust into a conflict between anti-Terran and pro-Terran factions. And even as he struggles to save the natives, the Terran Union's control of mining operations is challenged by an interstellar corporation ready to destroy Ardel for its own profit.

---

**Buy them at your local bookstore or use this convenient coupon for ordering.**

**PENGUIN USA P.O. Box 999, Dept. #17109, Bergenfield, New Jersey 07621**

Please send me the DAW BOOKS I have checked above, for which I am enclosing $______ (please add $2.00 per order to cover postage and handling. Send check or money order (no cash or C.O.D.'s) or charge by Mastercard or Visa (with a $15.00 minimum.) Prices and numbers are subject to change without notice.

Card #____________________ Exp. Date ________
Signature____________________________
Name____________________________
Address____________________________
City ____________ State __________ Zip ________

For faster service when ordering by credit card call **1-800-253-6476**

Please allow a minimum of 4 to 6 weeks for delivery.

*Now in HARDCOVER:*

# FOREIGNER

## *by C.J. Cherryh*

It had been nearly five centuries since the starship *Phoenix*, came out of hyperdrive into a place with no recognizable reference coordinates, and no way home. Hopelessly lost, the crew did the only thing they could. They charted their way to the nearest G5 star, gambling on finding a habitable planet. And what they found was the world of the atevi—a world where law was kept by the use of registered assassination, where alliances were not defined by geographical borders, and where war became inevitable once humans and one faction of atevi established a working relationship. It was a war that humans had no chance of winning and now, nearly two centuries later, humanity lives in exile on the island of Mospheira, trading tidbits of advanced technology for continued peace and a secluded refuge that no atevi will ever visit. Only a single human, the paidhi, is allowed off the island and into the complex and dangerous society of the atevi, brought there to act as interpreter and technological liaison to the leader of the most powerful of the atevi factions. But when this sole human the treaty allows into atevi society is nearly killed by an unregistered assassin's bullet, the fragile peace is shattered, and Bren Cameron, the paidhi, realizes that he must seek a new way to build a truer understanding between these two dangerous, intelligent, and quite possibly incompatible species. For if he fails, he and all of his people will die. But can a lone human hope to overcome two centuries of hostility and mistrust?

☐ **Hardcover Edition** UE2590—$20.00

---

**Buy it at your local bookstore or use this convenient coupon for ordering.**

**PENGUIN USA**
**P.O. Box 999 — Dept. #17109 Bergenfield, New Jersey 07621**

Please send me ____________ copies of the hardcover edition of FOREIGNER by C.J. Cherryh, UE2590, at $20.00 ($24.99 in Canada) plus $2.00 for postage and handling per order. I enclose $____________ (check or money order—no C.O.D.s) or charge by ☐ Mastercard ☐ Visa card. Prices and numbers are subject to change without notice.

Card #____________________ Exp. Date ____________________
Signature____________________
Name____________________
Address____________________
City ____________ State ____________ Zip Code ____________

For faster service when ordering by credit card call **1-800-253-6476**

Allow a minimum of 4-6 weeks for delivery. This offer is subject to change without notice.